The Junkie

John Hagen

Dedication

To my wife, Ileana, the love of my life.

Acknowledgement

During my forty years as a surgeon in a bustling city hospital, I've seen colleagues grapple with the emotional toll of long hours and life-or-death decisions, alongside personal challenges that tested their resilience. Often, the outward success of a surgeon masks a hidden battle with addiction, a secret buried deep within their psyche, unbeknownst to their patients and colleagues. While the characters in this novel are entirely fictional, and any resemblance to real people is purely coincidental, some struggles they face reflect the harsh realities of life.

I would like to thank my sailing and surgical colleague, Marco, for his insight into the officer's training program in the Canadian Armed Forces. He and his son Matthew accompanied me on a memorable trip this past winter from the British Virgin Islands to Samana, in the Dominican Republic on my sailboat.

My editor, Janet Gyenes, patiently reviewed the manuscript, correcting the many editorial issues. I am grateful for her wisdom and expert advice. Any mistakes in the novel are mine. I thank KDP publishers for their help with the book cover and publishing tasks.

Contents

Prologue

Bill's practised hand quickly found the soldier's appendix, making the procedure seem simple. The 36-inch screen showed the image of the inflamed organ, red and swollen, dominating its surface. No bigger than a thin pencil, the tiny five-mm laparoscope provided a flawlessly clear, magnified image of the mesentery and the rhythmic pulsing of the appendicular artery. The cautery hook hissed as Bill used it to dissect the mesentery, revealing the appendicular artery, which he carefully isolated.

Many of his colleagues would clamp the vessel with small clips, but Bill preferred to cauterize it with the hook because it was faster. Using an endoloop, he encircled the base of the appendix, then placed another loop further up, effectively isolating the infected portion. After cleanly dividing the appendix, he placed it into a plastic specimen bag and removed the organ with an umbilical incision. Steri-Strip tapes, like tiny white bridges, closed the incision. The entire operation took less than 10 minutes.

"You've got to be kidding, doctor!" said Debbie, the scrub nurse and surgical assistant. "That was lightning-fast! Fastest appendectomy I've ever seen." She looked up at him. "What's the rush, doctor?" her voice was laced with amusement. "Are you scheduled to tee off at a specific time?"

"Ha ha," Bill replied, a mischievous glint in his eye. "In this barren desert, the only hint of green comes from the mould on our sandwiches. Iraq couldn't be farther away from the rolling green hills of a golf course. It's been..." he said, pausing for a moment's thought. "... six long months since I've had the chance to play."

After the soldier regained consciousness, Debbie and the anesthesiologist carefully moved the man to the recovery room, making sure he was comfortable. Bill remained in the operating room. The sterile smell of disinfectant clung to the air as he dictated the operative note and wrote the post-operative orders. He glanced around, his heart pounding with anticipation. The hallway was silent. Empty. The operating room was quiet too, save for the faint hum of the ventilation system. He stood alone. Bill heard the clatter of metal instruments and the muffled voices of the nurses from the orthopedic room, knowing the cleaners were busy and wouldn't be available for another 10 minutes. The orthopedic surgeon in the adjacent operating room had just finished carefully securing a metal plate to a soldier's fractured tibia. It was a reminder of the previous night's excessive drinking that had led to the injury.

The drug safe, a metal box humming from its "silent" security system, held the anesthetics. The grey colour marked its presence only in contrast to the blue of the nearby ventilator. Bill quickly punched in the code. His fingers fumbled slightly as he heard a deep mechanical click interrupt the silence. The door popped open. Bill's eyes darted back and forth, taking in every detail of the empty room as he once again confirmed he was alone.

The pharmacist had clearly labelled the drugs. Each bottle sported a bright legible sticker. The colour-coding on succinyl choline, fentanyl, morphine, and Demerol made it easy to distinguish between them. Bill knew enough not to take any of the narcotics, as that would alert the MPs to launch an investigation. What he searched for was propofol. Uncounted and unobserved, the massive, clear glass ampules, full of white liquid, rested as if forgotten in the well-stocked drug cabinet. He carefully placed two of the large ampules in the pockets of his scrubs, feeling their weight against his leg. Bill closed the safe door, noting the distinctive click. The sterile white of the operating room faded behind him as he stepped out and entered the recovery room, where the soft hum of medical equipment filled the air. Debbie was giving the report to Valerie, the recovery room nurse.

"Everything okay?" asked Bill.

"Yes," said Valerie. "I just gave him a little morphine for the pain, but now he is resting comfortably."

"I'll just wander back to my barracks then, and catch up on my emails," Bill said.

He walked out of the makeshift air-conditioned hospital. The heat hit him like a wall of fire. The bright sun was so intense that he had to squint. His eyes stung from the glare. Bill slipped on his wraparound Oakley sunglasses, blocking out the harsh rays, and hoped the world would fade into a muted hum. It was 40°C in the desert. The heat radiating from the sand baked everything in sight. The swelter was unbearable, intensified by the relentless wind that seemed to carry the sun's heat right to his skin. Every day, the monotonous routine of the desert repeated itself, leaving no room for excitement.

"This place is a shithole," he muttered under his breath, speaking to no one but the stifling air. "The only thing that gets me through is what's in my pocket." He felt the smooth glass of the vials against his fingers as he patted the pockets of his scrubs, double-checking they were still there.

By the time he got to his barracks, sweat was pouring down his face, even though it had only been a short walk. The blast of cold air from the air conditioner, running at full speed, hit him as he opened the door, a welcome relief from the heat. Since Bill was the only civilian surgeon on the base, he was given his own room by the base commander. It afforded him the privacy to indulge in his addictions. The only beverage he drank was ice-cold Coke, and his small fridge was always stocked with cans, the condensation dripping down the sides. Bill sucked back eight cans every single day without fail. It was an obsession for him and a condition he gave to the commanding officer of his deployment to this godforsaken land.

He pried open the fridge and pulled out a Coke, ritualistically noticing the can's cool metal against his palm. Bill drained half in a single, thirsty gulp, the fizz tickling his nose, before he had to stop for a moment to breathe. "That's better," he almost whispered. Not that anyone was around to hear him.

The base Wi-Fi let him stream endless movies on Netflix, but the lack of anything else to do made him bored quickly. The drugs were the only thing that could momentarily dull the gnawing monotony, providing a fleeting escape. In the US, he easily got cocaine from his friend Jimmy at the Coyote Ugly Bar, and sometimes he would sneak narcotics from the hospital. He knew the pharmacist at his local hospital in Little Rock, Arkansas, suspected it was him who'd been pilfering the drugs. But he needed more concrete evidence before taking action. That was one reason Bill agreed to be deployed to Iraq as a civilian surgeon: to avoid suspension and the inevitable legal action.

Six months feels like multiple life sentences when you're longing for the sights, sounds, and smells of the real world. The $500,000 he was saving for the year, enough to set him up forever, would vanish in a haze of gambling and drugs within a few short months once he left this place. He had made a commitment to stay for the full year, so he was going to make the best of it, no matter what.

Bill sighed deeply, a heavy weight settling on his chest. A deeper, more profound sadness washed over him than his usual daily gloom. Pushing himself up from his cot, then carefully kneeling down beside it, his gaze focused on the small, metal safe hidden beneath the metal frame. He opened the safe, punching in his day and month of birth: zero-nine-zero-eight. Bill carefully placed a single ampule of propofol inside. Then he quickly grabbed a 50cc syringe, its needle already attached and gleaming with a 20-gauge tip. A sharp snap of the ampule breaking echoed in the room as he filled the syringe with the white liquid.

A sickening thought flashed through his mind: the memory of Michael Jackson's death, caused by Dr. Conrad Murray, overdosing him with propofol. The typical anesthetic dose ranged from 100 to 200 milligrams, but Bill had previously taken up to 50 mg and still regained consciousness. Today, he decided he deserved to treat himself to that dosage. He would leave the needle in his vein so when he awoke, he could pump another dose of propofol and its hypnotic magic. This would ensure that the vivid erotic dreams he craved wouldn't fade until the reveries were over.

Bill lay on the bed and placed a rubber tourniquet around his left arm. A prominent bulge appeared in the antecubital vein at the elbow. He carefully inserted the 20-gauge yellow angiocath and connected it to the 50cc syringe. With a practiced hand, he secured the angiocath in place with clear plastic tape to make sure it wouldn't budge when the medication kicked in. He injected half of the white liquid into the vein. Immediately, he felt intense burning as the drug travelled along the vein. With a sigh of relief, he eased onto the pillow. The weight of his head sunk into the soft down.

Then he pulled off the tourniquet. In just 20 seconds, he could sense a growing feeling of arousal. The last vision he had was of Debbie straddling him, completely naked. A smile stretched across her face, and she opened her mouth, as if a word was about to escape. Her green eyes, flecked with mischief, darted around the room, leaving a trail of provocative glances in their wake. As his hypothalamus released a cocktail of dopamine, serotonin, and oxytocin, his nerves buzzed with anticipation and ecstasy. He felt the familiar thrill of excitement course through his body.

And then there was nothing but a deep, impenetrable blackness.

Chapter 1

The 51-foot sailboat, driven by the northwest wind, sliced through the waves, the spray creating a salty mist. The rhythmic rocking of the vessel, the smell of the salt air, and the sound of the waves crashing against the hull filled Jack MacKay with exhilaration, pure joy. Jack squinted at the chart plotter, trying to make sense of the swirling lines and numbers. He was the only one in the boat's cockpit; the other two on board were in their bunks, catching up on their sleep. The measured speed over the ground (SOG) was an astonishing 15 knots!

Jack smiled. The boat could comfortably sail at nine knots in the strong winds of the North Atlantic, but coupled with the five-knot Gulf Stream current, and the surfing action from the enormous waves, its speed was the highest he'd ever seen. The absence of the moon allowed the stars to shine with unhindered brilliance, transforming the night sky into a mesmerizing display of twinkling lights. Evenings like this, quiet and peaceful, filled Jack with a sense of calm he rarely felt during the hectic days of his surgery career, when the constant rush of patients and procedures left him questioning the meaning of it all.

The steady hum of the autohelm filled the air as the boat sliced through the waves, charting a southeasterly course towards Antigua. With a weather window finally opening, the trio had left Hampton, Virginia, 36 hours earlier. A cold front had just swept through the North Atlantic, leaving behind a crisp, invigorating chill. Relying on this powerful low-pressure system that would propel them on their journey to the Caribbean island, they glided effortlessly across the Gulf Stream's warm waters. Jack had estimated it would take them about 10 days to get to Antigua.

"You need to cross the Gulf Stream when the winds are in a northwest or westerly direction," explained Chris Perkins, the maritime meteorologist, during the Zoom meeting. "If you try to cross when the winds are from the northeast, you'll encounter a dangerous combination. The five-knot Gulf Stream flowing against the wind creates monstrous, crashing waves that could easily destroy your boat. It looks like October 31 will be a good time to leave."

Hurricane season was still in full swing in October, but come November, the danger of being hit by such a weather system had significantly faded. Chris, however, had pointed out a developing tropical depression in the Gulf of Mexico, a swirling mass of clouds that was heading towards Florida and the Bahamas. Although he'd explained that the storm had an 80 per cent chance of becoming a category-one hurricane, he reassured them that the boats heading southeast towards the Caribbean were unlikely to be affected.

But even though AI models had made weather prediction vastly more accurate over the past decade, Jack felt a lingering uncertainty. Mother Nature, with her capricious whims, could always throw a curveball. The ocean's unpredictable nature was what made sailing so thrilling, and he relished the challenge of battling its powerful forces. The rush of adrenaline, the feel of the wind whipping through his hair, the spray of salt water on his face. It all made him feel truly alive as he relied on his honed senses and sailing skills to navigate the choppy seas.

"How's it going?" asked a female voice.

The unexpected question breaking the silence of the night made Jack jump. He quickly recognized Katherine's voice. She was another adventurer sharing their journey.

"This is an amazing night," he replied. "You can feel the warmth of the Gulf Stream radiating off the water, like a gentle hug. It was so hot I had to take off my foul weather gear."

"Look at all those stars," said Katherine in a dreamy voice. "You never see anything like this at home, do you?"

Jack glanced up at the heavens, his gaze lost in the vastness of the sky, as it had been dozens of times since he'd started his three-hour shift. As they gazed up, the starlight painted fantastical images in their minds, leaving them speechless. The Big Dipper and the North Star were on their port stern, and the three stars of Orion's belt were directly overhead, casting a faint, silvery glow. Coming from a surgical environment where every second was accounted for, it filled Jack with great pleasure to have the time to appreciate the beauty of nature.

"It's 4 a.m., so your shift is over," said Katherine, "and it's my turn at the helm. Any boat traffic?"

"The only one on our chart plotter in the last hour was that enormous oil tanker, and it's gone now. I have two reefs in the mainsail. The winds range from 22 to 26 knots, blowing steadily from the broad reach. The boat seems to handle the winds nicely, partly because of the extra push from the Gulf Stream. Be sure to monitor the autohelm closely, as it can unexpectedly fail, forcing you to manually re-engage it. It often gives you a warning, a high-pitched beep, before it happens."

"Huh," replied Katherine. "Anything else?"

"I'll stay in the cockpit with you and pass out on the starboard bench in case you need anything."

Jack carefully unclipped his tether, releasing the metal clasp with a satisfying *click*, allowing Katherine to slide into the helm's seat. She clipped her tether so she could move between the two chart plotters, one in front of each of the twin steering wheels. One monitor showed a map pinpointing the location of any ships within 20 miles, while the other constantly displayed real-time data about wind conditions and the boat's speed and course.

"Thanks; I appreciate that," replied Katherine. "I'm new at this and still a little nervous out here on the big ocean. How is it you remain so calm?"

"You know, I think the love of sailing is passed down through generations," Jack said, a hint of wistful nostalgia in his voice. "My father was a Scot. He tells the story of Vikings coming to Scotland in the 10th century to rape and pillage. Vikings had no fear of the water, even though most did not know how to swim. They loved the ocean and would sail on open boats for weeks at a time before arriving at the land they wished to conquer. I believe I have Viking ancestry in my blood," he said, watching Katherine. "The gentle swaying of the boat and the sound of the water lapping against the hull have always calmed me, never frightened me. However, somewhere along the way, I seemed to have lost the inclination towards rape and plundering... at least after my teenage years."

"Ha ha," laughed Katherine. "I certainly hope so, for my sake!"

Jack curled up on the cockpit bench and fell into a deep sleep. Within a few minutes, the rhythmic rocking of the boat, combined with the gentle lapping of water against the hull, lulled him into a deep sleep. Despite rarely experiencing seasickness, he would always eat sparingly during the first 24 hours of any ocean voyage, making sure to drink enough fluids to avoid dehydration.

After a full day on the water, he finally found his sea legs, the queasiness in his stomach replaced by a growing appetite.

With a sudden, jarring jolt, the boat changed course, abruptly pulling him out of his sleep. He had only just closed his eyes when Katherine's voice, filled with urgency, pierced the quiet.

"Jack, the autohelm's quit on me, and I'm having trouble keeping the boat on course."

He sat up. The sailboat, now headed directly into the wind, was bucking and rolling, its mainsail and jib flapping wildly in the strong breeze. The waves crashed against the boat, sending it violently back and forth, the sound of the water filling the air. Jack walked to the helm, the salty air whipping at his face. He saw Katherine's eyes darting around nervously. She seemed anxious, as if she expected danger at any moment.

"Don't worry," Jack said, looking directly into her eyes. "The exact same thing happened to me when the autohelm went out, leaving me to steer manually. In this oppressive blackness, the instruments feel slow and unreliable, making it difficult to get a fix on the right direction."

He spun the wheel to starboard. A wave surged forward, pushing the boat just enough to give it some direction, allowing the sails to catch the wind and begin moving eastward. Then, Jack pointed the bow towards the southeast. "I usually find a star to aim for in the southeast, then set the autohelm." He pressed the autohelm engage button. "I'll fine tune the heading when we pick up a bit of speed."

"You seem so calm," said Katherine. "I'm not sure what I would have done if you weren't here. I felt so disorientated."

"Katherine, you are an excellent sailor. You would have figured it out; I'm not worried about you. Sailing at night on the gigantic waves is a different experience than on Lake Ontario. It just takes a little time to get used to it."

Katherine just shook her head, still seemingly a little rattled by the autohelm's failure.

"I'll check the weather on the PredictWind app," said Jack. "Be right back. I love sleeping in the cockpit at night, anyway. If you need me, I'm right here."

Jack untethered himself and ambled to the main salon, the soft creak of the ship's floorboards under his feet a familiar sound. He sat at the table, flipped open the laptop, the screen illuminating the room with a soft white light. The computer connected to the Wi-Fi signal from the Starlink dish, which was mounted on the back of the boat. With a few clicks, he had the most recent weather models and predictions at his fingertips. The hurricane churning in the Gulf of Mexico, a swirling mass of fury, had a name: Sandy.

The path of the hurricane had changed. All the models now predicted the hurricane would pass within 100 miles of Bermuda in a few days, bringing 40-knot winds and enormous seas that would pound the island with crashing waves. His email pinged, a sharp, electronic sound cutting through the silence. The message was from Chris Perkins.

I suggest that all boats travelling to Antigua make a stop in Bermuda within the next 48 hours to wait for the sea conditions and strong winds to calm. Slower boats, those unlikely to reach Bermuda in the next 48 hours, should turn back and seek shelter in Charleston. Wait for the next weather window before resuming your journey.

Jack frowned at the news, his brow furrowed in concern. The boat was fast, but even with its speed, it would be a close race to reach their destination within the tight 48-hour deadline. Jack climbed back into the cockpit.

"I fine tuned the autohelm, and we are back on course to Antigua, 1,200 miles away," said Katherine, now smiling and clearly proud of herself.

"Good navigating," said Jack. "I've got a weather update from Chris Perkins. The hurricane is barrelling towards us, and while he predicts it will bypass us, we'll still get pummelled by howling winds and monstrous waves. Chris thinks we should head to Bermuda if we can make it there in 48 hours. He advised the slower boats to return to Charleston until the weather calms down, unless the conditions improve. Any thoughts on what our next move should be?"

A crease appeared on Katherine's forehead as she crinkled her brow in thought. Her long ponytail flowed down her back, and with a quick twist and tuck, she tied it into a neat bun at the back of her head. Jack noticed she chewed on her lower lip, a habit she had when she was deep in thought. "We have a fast boat." Katherine glanced at the map and placed the cursor on Bermuda. "We have 350 miles to go, so I think we will make it," she said decisively. "My vote would be to head to Bermuda."

"I agree with you," said Jack. "I'm going to wake up Bill to see what he thinks."

Jack knocked at the third crew member's door and longtime friend. "Hey, Bill?" he shouted. "Can I come in?"

A grunt from inside was the response, so Jack opened the door. Bill was curled up on the starboard edge of the bunk to take advantage of the heel of the boat. He was lying against the cushions and still seemed asleep.

"Bill," said Jack sharply. "Wake up. I need to discuss something with you."

Bill suddenly sat up and softly bumped his head on the roof of the cabin. "Is everything okay?" he asked, heaving his large frame forward in the cramped space.

"We need to look at the weather app and decide if we should stop for a few days in Bermuda. Let me show you."

Bill, still warm and cozy in his bunk, begrudgingly crawled out. He sat beside Jack. The two of them pored over the weather prediction and the projected path of Hurricane Sandy. "I agree," he said. "We should take our chances with Bermuda. I think we'll make it in time. Besides, I have always wanted to visit St. George's. They just opened a new casino at St. Regis Hotel there. We should check it out when we arrive!"

For a fleeting moment, Jack's eyes met Bill's as he turned his head slightly. Jack found his friend's excitement about going to Bermuda strange, particularly the mention of casinos, given Bill's past problems with gambling. Jack shook his head, wondering if it would be safer to just take their chances with Hurricane Sandy.

Chapter 2

Bill and Jack had been best friends since childhood, growing up together in the small farming community of Brantford, Ontario, located an hour and a half west of Toronto. When they both got accepted to medical school at the University of Toronto, sharing an apartment was the logical next step, allowing them to navigate the challenges of their demanding studies together. Four years later, they plunged headfirst into the rigorous demands of general surgical residency. Their bond as best friends remained unbroken.

Bill was a burly man with a robust appetite for high-calorie foods. He chugged Coke like it was water, emptying case after case. His insatiable appetite had led to a noticeable potbelly, but it didn't seem to discourage women from finding him attractive. Often, Jack would get home after a brutal weekend on call and find a different woman than the one that had been there with Bill the night before. She could be sipping coffee, with the steam curling up from the mug in the kitchen, or she might have wrapped a towel around herself, fresh from the shower. Bill, with a mischievous glint in his eye and a wicked grin spread across his face, would always wink at Jack as he lumbered by to his own room. Jack often pondered what qualities in Bill had attracted women so much. He suspected his infectious laughter and ability to brighten any room were what made him so irresistible. For them, he was the epitome of comfort and safety, a big teddy bear they could always snuggle up to.

"When I grow up, I want to be just like you... skinny," Bill said to Jack one night. The scent of dinner lingered in the air as they sat around the kitchen table. It was a rare night off from their demanding jobs at the hospital. A delicious aroma of spices filled the kitchen as Bill finished cooking the stuffed red peppers that were packed with hamburger. They were absolutely divine, thanks to the copious amount of brown sugar and sour cream sauce drizzled over the top, creating a sweet and tangy symphony of flavours. Jack, his stomach full, could only manage one, but Bill was on his third.

"Us skinny guys don't seem to have the same luck as you when it comes to getting laid," replied Jack. "Besides, I'm perpetually exhausted from the long hours. I don't know how you find the time or the energy after you convince a woman to come home with you."

That was the first time Bill produced a plastic packet of white powder. "When I combine this with an amphetamine, I can endure any demanding on-call shift for a full day without issues." Bill held up the cocaine for Jack to see.

Jack felt a chill run through him. "You can't be serious," he whispered. "If you get caught with that stuff, they'll kick you out of the surgery program."

"Chill out. Don't be so conservative. Everyone does cocaine. It's harmless if used right. Besides, it's the recreational drug of choice now. Taking it is like stepping into a different world, full of relaxation and tranquility, without even having to pack a bag. Here, try some." Bill laid out a line of the white powder and handed Jack a small straw.

"Bill, you are familiar with the insidious nature of cocaine addiction. Our medical school professors relentlessly drilled that concept into us. This is not okay, and you're just fooling yourself by thinking otherwise." He lowered his voice, taking a serious tone with his friend. "Maybe it would be helpful to have a conversation with someone from the addiction clinic. What do you think? They guarantee anonymity for any of us residents who go down the cocaine path. You know it will eventually catch up with you and destroy your life."

Bill leaned over, pinched one nostril shut, and shoved the straw that Jack had refused into the other nostril. In less than three seconds, the white powder dissipated into his mucous membranes, getting absorbed into the blood circulation, leaving no trace behind. His eyes glazed over, the pupils expanding rapidly, and the whites of his eyes turning a frightening shade of red. The corners of his mouth twitched upwards, forming a menacing grin that sent chills down Jack's spine. A strangled croak was all that came out when Bill tried to speak to Jack. He stood up, turned around, and walked to his room. The soft thud of his footsteps echoed in the quiet apartment. He slammed the door shut. The sound reverberated through the empty house.

Jack's heart pounded in his chest as he stared in shock. He thought he knew Bill, but he knew nothing about him using cocaine. Jack felt a responsibility, a weight of obligation that wouldn't let him simply walk away. Bill was his best friend. The thought of watching him self-destruct was unbearable. Jack knew he couldn't live with himself if he didn't try to stop him.

Jack had witnessed the devastating impact of cocaine addiction on his patients. During his cardiology rotation in medical school, he admitted a 30-year-old patient suffering a massive heart attack, triggered by cocaine use. The man's heart was so weak that he became a "cardiac cripple," unable to walk more than a few steps without gasping for air. He was on the cardiac transplant list. Because of his history of cocaine use, the transplant team hesitated to give him a new heart, despite the dire need for the life-saving procedure. As they discussed the patient's case, the transplant surgery fellow had given Jack a look of weary cynicism and said, "Once a cocaine addict, always a cocaine addict."

After a sleepless night, the exhaustion weighed heavily on him as he pondered his next move. The enormity of the situation washed over him. He realized he was in over his head. If he ignored what he had witnessed, he would be enabling the addictive behaviour. In medical school, he learned that addiction wasn't a matter of willpower, but a complex disease with biological and psychological roots. Just like any illness, treatment was essential.

A cure was not possible, but once Bill acknowledged he had a problem, abstinence would prevent the damage the addiction would cause.

The other factor was the denial on Bill's part that would inevitably happen if Jack confronted him again. Studies in neurophysiology revealed that addicts had a deficiency in dopamine receptors. Dopamine, a neurotransmitter that floods the brain with a sense of reward, was the key to feeling satisfaction and contentment. Addicts often describe the feeling of using their drug of choice—be it alcohol, cocaine, or narcotics—as a sense of normalcy, achieved through an intense dopamine surge that temporarily eases their cravings and anxieties. It was the feeling of returning to normal that drove the addiction, not the desire to get high.

Jack made an appointment to speak with his program director, Normie Gallinger, for the next day.

*****

The following afternoon, Jack walked the bright hallways to the office of Normie Gallinger, the general surgery program director and chair of surgery for the University of Toronto. Her door was open. He wordlessly slipped inside and sat down in the chair in front of her desk.

"Hi, Jack," she said, sitting back in her chair and letting out a sigh as if bored. "How are things going?"

Jack suddenly felt uncomfortable, a cold prickle running down his spine. His palms were sweaty and now sticky, dangling uselessly at his sides at the awkwardness of talking to her. *Please, please, Normie, don't ask me to shake your hand.* He pressed his right hand against his left to prevent it from trembling. His mouth opened, but the words seemed to stick in his throat like a dry lump. The conflict in his heart was a raging storm, caught between his loyalty to his friend and his obligation to discuss Bill's problem with the higher authority.

A patient's complaint had necessitated his previous meeting with Normie, which had taken place some time ago. A young woman in her early twenties experienced complications following bowel surgery. She had to be hospitalized for more than a month. Jack felt a deep sympathy for her, understanding the profound suffering she had endured since the onset of Crohn's disease at the young age of 15. Even after undergoing seven surgical operations, she continued to experience persistent health complications that required repeated hospitalizations. In his naivete, Jack was completely unaware of the profound emotional impact he was having on the young woman. Following her discharge, she used the hospital's contact information to phone him, extending an invitation for dinner at her place.

Accepting the invitation would have been a clear breach of professional standards. The invitation quite startled Jack. He politely declined. When addressing her allegations to the program director in a written complaint, she detailed how Jack's excessive kindness to her during her hospitalization had given her false hope. He led her to believe that he had romantic intentions. A lengthy and furious scolding from Normie ensued. It focused on the importance of maintaining boundaries and the fact that he should have exercised better judgment in this situation. Once again, he felt like he was in the hot seat.

"Jack," said Normie, looking annoyed. "Just come out with it. You look nervous."

Jack took a deep breath. "This is difficult for me. I... I... I have a friend," he stammered. He had been working diligently to overcome a persistent problem with stuttering that had plagued him since childhood. His speech impediment was especially noticeable when he was being less than truthful or when he was hesitant about discussing a particular subject, betraying his uncertainty and discomfort. "Who I... I... I think has a problem. I... I... I want to help him before he gets himself into trouble."

Normie fixed her gaze on Jack. A question filled her eyes. She finally broke the silence. "You wouldn't happen to be talking about your roommate, Bill, would you?" Jack nodded his head in silent acknowledgment. "You want to discuss his drug use with me?" Jack nodded once more in agreement, his eyes now bulging in surprise.

Normie continued. "We are well aware of this. The routine hair sample analysis yielded a positive result, confirming our suspicions. Bill willingly handed it over. We told him it was that or a mandatory visit to the alcohol and drug program we have set up for residents with suspected substance abuse. He was acting strangely on the surgical ward last month. His erratic movements and mumbled words drew everyone's attention. His restless energy and wandering concentration raised concerns, leading to a urine test that confirmed our suspicions."

"Oh my God," cried Jack, no longer stuttering now that he realized his friend was in big trouble. "Are you going to kick him out of the program? We need to help him! Tell me what I can do to help. Please don't kick him out. He's going through a rough time right now." Jack's voice trembled as he pleaded.

"Look," said Normie, "you were incredibly brave to come here and tell me this. It's clear you care about your friend. Our experience with similar situations gives us the confidence to handle this. We'll make sure he receives the support he needs. Just be a reliable and supportive friend, ready to lend an ear whenever he needs you." She leaned forward, placing her elbows on the desk. "Let's keep our conversation between us. I plan to speak with him within the next few days, likely by the end of the week or sooner. We know what we are doing."

Jack thanked her and made his way home. Thirty minutes after his meeting with the program director, he entered the apartment, still feeling anxious about what would happen next. The stillness of the empty living room confirmed a fear he didn't even know he had.

Bill was gone.

*****

Time seemed to crawl by, and it took three full months before Jack saw Bill again. Exhausted from his busy shift tending to sick patients, he pushed open the door to his apartment one day. The familiar smell of Bill's cooking greeted him. A rich, spicy aroma, the heady mix of peppers, onions, and savoury herbs hung heavy in the air, announcing his famous stuffed red peppers.

Bill sat at the kitchen table, his back to Jack, sipping a cup of tea. Seemingly lost in thought, the sound of the door opening jolted him out of it, and he stood up as Jack entered the kitchen. Bill approached Jack, a smile spreading across his face, and pulled his friend into a comforting hug.

"Thanks for being there for me," was all he said.

Chapter 3

"I was hoping it would be alright if I listened to music through my earphones while working on this," Bill asked tentatively. Bent over his laptop, he intently concentrated on the task assigned to him moments before, his focus unwavering. The assignment was to find a solution if the ailerons failed on the tail of the jet, which stabilize the aircraft in a roll. He needed to develop an algorithm that would give the pilots a 95 per cent chance of surviving.

Gary, the chief instructor at CFB Cold Lake, Alberta, let a smile spread across his face. "Of course. Is that your secret? The earphones?" he asked.

With a confused frown, Bill glanced up at his instructor, the silence heavy with unspoken questions before he spoke. "I'm.... I'm sorry. I don't understand." In a quick mental assessment, Bill noted that Gary still had the identical ballpoint pen, the one Bill had lent him only yesterday, securely positioned in his Air Force shirt's upper right-hand pocket. Bill's self-designed pen, a marvel of miniature engineering, would transmit crystal-clear audio and video to his smartphone app.

"At first, we harboured some reservations regarding your qualifications and suitability to participate in the Canadian Air Force's Basic Officer training program. As a favour to Normie Gallinger, chair of surgery at the University of Toronto, and a former Canadian Air Force pilot, we agreed to assist with your recovery from substance misuse. Your aptitude for jet piloting has been undeniably remarkable, surpassing anything we've ever witnessed. The flight simulator's capabilities are so advanced that even our most experienced pilots, those who have dedicated their entire careers to our company, can't match your performance. You joined us just 10 weeks ago, and, well, frankly... we have experienced no one like you, someone who can learn so quickly. Keep up the great work."

With that, Gary quietly left the room, the soft click of the closing door barely audible above Bill's focused typing.

With a determined expression, Bill hunched over his laptop, the one he had built himself. His fingers flew across the keyboard as he completed the assignment in a mere 30 seconds. Except for the sharp click-clack of keys and his controlled breathing, a heavy silence hung in the air. His task was to design a life-saving algorithm for pilots—a procedure with a 95 per cent chance of pilot survival. They were to follow a series of steps in the extremely improbable event their jet lost its tail aileron, to prevent the jet from crashing. The solution came to him in a flash, the thought process completed within the first 15 seconds. In the next 15 seconds, he rapidly considered a flurry of similar alternative solutions, each with a comparable end result. The computer whirred and clicked for the next two minutes, diligently plotting solutions on a chart and generating a detailed dialogue of explanations for all the possible solutions.

While the computer hummed and screens flashed by, Bill pulled out his cell phone. He tapped the icon of his custom-designed app. The vibrant colours were a stark contrast to the muted tones of his workspace. The video and audio functions installed in the pen Gary had borrowed from him yesterday were working perfectly. General Richards, the base commander, appeared on Bill's cell phone screen, his expression grim and serious.

A steady stream of Gary's words washed over Bill, a dull roar in the background. "The pilot survival algorithms task I assigned him will keep him busy for the rest of the week. Commander, I've encountered nothing remotely similar in my years of service. The sheer scale of it is unprecedented. His mind works with the speed and precision of a powerful computer, processing information rapidly and efficiently. The flight simulator presented the scenario, and in under a second, he was analyzing the data. With incredible speed, he assimilated the data, and a second later, the solution was in effect! While the other pilots frantically flipped through their manuals, struggling to keep up, he effortlessly recalled every step *from memory*."

Bill watched on his smart phone as the commander, looking perplexed, sat back and scratched his head. His fingers tugged at his short, bristly hair. He seemed lost in thought, a faint smile playing on his lips as if he were remembering something pleasant.

"You know, many of these young guys strut around with a swagger and cocky confidence. Some can beat the simulators with ease, but the real thing? The pressure leaves them frozen, their breath trapped in their throats, unable to move. The true test of their skills comes when they're airborne, facing a life-or-death emergency, requiring split-second decisions under immense pressure. It demands a rapid response in a high-stress environment. What about taking him up in the air? Ensure that the test flight includes elements that will cause him suffering. Do the usual stuff, turn off the fuel just after takeoff, send him into a graveyard spiral at 15,000 feet, fake a fire on the engine, that sort of thing. He'll be shitting himself." The commander let out a chuckle. "That would be a humiliating truth, instantly reducing his arrogance."

A loud, boisterous laugh from Gary reached Bill's ears. "You are right," he said, his voice a low rumble. "I often witness that as well. These kids, digital warriors with lightning-fast reflexes in virtual worlds, stumble when faced with real-world challenges. I enjoy taking them down a notch. It's something I love to do."

"Put on a real live air show performance around 11 a.m. tomorrow," the base commander instructed, his voice sharp and demanding. "I expect something memorable. The rest of the officers will be on hand, lined up on the tarmac to oversee the performance. Maybe they'll all learn a thing or two about flying a jet."

Bill observed the base commander's eyes return to the many documents on his desk, a clear sign that the meeting had concluded. As he listened intently, he heard the distinct sound of a chair scraping against the unforgiving hardness of the floor, simultaneously observing on his cell phone screen a door swinging inward. Bill switched off his cell phone, then carefully placed it back in his pocket. He proceeded back to his laptop and powered it up, revealing the screen's contents, a perfect algorithmic solution to the problem they had tasked him with. Fifteen seconds later, the door to his room opened and Gary walked in.

Without looking up, Bill said, "This is really tough," shaking his head. "It might take me a while to find a solution."

Gary smiled knowingly, fully aware that he'd assigned an extremely difficult and challenging problem that would require a great deal of effort to solve. "I can give you until the end of the week, but that is it," he said in an authoritative tone. "In the interim, the base commander has requested that I take you aloft in an aircraft to rehearse several flight manoeuvres. We're keen to witness firsthand how effectively you can apply your skills and knowledge in scenarios that accurately reflect real-flight conditions and demands. Please don't feel any anxiety or apprehension. Everything will be alright. If you find yourself in a tough spot and can't handle it on your own, I'll be there to help you get through it. Considering your skills and abilities, I have nominated you for the prestigious officer training program's highest distinction. Among the 600 officers currently in training, your performance has been exemplary, placing you at the top of your class. However, your performance tomorrow will be a significant factor in determining the overall outcome."

*****

By 11 a.m., the sun was already high in the sky. Gary and Bill stood before the powerful CT-155 Hawk single-engine fighter jet, its sleek body gleaming under the sun-baked tarmac. The smell of jet fuel was heavy in the warm air. It was a two-seater, a training version.

"I'll take charge of orchestrating the events, and if it's needed, I'll take action. I'll sit right behind you," Gary promised, a reassuring hand resting on Bill's shoulder. "Otherwise, you will have to take charge of the situation. Best of luck to you!" After Bill's thorough preflight inspection, they shook hands and climbed aboard.

With a final confirmation from the control tower, the plane taxied onto the runway. The hum of the engines was a steady beat against the morning calm. Bill revved the engine, a powerful roar that vibrated through the ground, then pushed the throttle forward. He gracefully took off. As he expected, the low fuel light went off, a small, satisfying *click* punctuating the quiet hum of the engine after takeoff, and the faint scent of oil and metal filled the air. Bill's hands moved quickly, a blur of motion as he completed the standard checks. With the indicator's light blinking and the tower's confirmation echoing in his headset, he landed smoothly. A triumphant feeling washed over him as he passed the first test.

The next incident happened at 15,000 feet. Again, Bill was expecting it. The aircraft spun into a graveyard spiral with alarming speed. As Gary took over the controls, the aircraft's movements became increasingly erratic and beyond his ability to manage. The G-forces intensified. With the spin and speed accelerating, Bill felt a rising nausea building within him. He could see the earth below him revolving faster and faster as gravity pulled them closer to the ground. Although Bill attempted to use the controls, he discovered Gary had not yet returned them to him. He was aware of the inevitability of a wait and accepted that he would simply have to be patient. Making another attempt 10 seconds later, he realized he now had control of the spinning jet. It dawned on him that likely Gary would take charge in about 30 seconds, a critical time frame he couldn't ignore.

To heighten the tension and make Gary feel the pressure, too, Bill chose to delay his action, waiting a deliberate 20 seconds before finally making his move. As he decreased engine power to idle, he carefully centered the ailerons. He countered the spin by applying the opposite rudder. Then, with a decisive push forward on the yoke, the jet accelerated faster toward the ground, which was no longer spinning. When the opportune moment arrived, he expertly levelled the jet, a smooth manoeuvre executed in conjunction with a decisive increase in throttle. They were at 2,000 feet when the plane roared over the air base.

From the prior conversation he had overheard with the base commander, Bill knew that the upcoming last scenario would involve a realistic simulation of an engine fire. Not only would this exercise be incredibly tedious and dull, but it also annoyed him to no end that Gary had so clearly underestimated the full extent of his capabilities. Upon reaching their cruising altitude, Bill carefully leaned over the cockpit controls and pretended to adjust the pitch. With Gary's gaze averted, he quickly inserted a specially prepared microchip into the control panel. This action would ultimately teach Gary a valuable lesson about his abilities.

Thirty seconds later, through his headphones, he heard Gary's urgent voice. "Something is definitely wrong. I'm unable to assume control of the aircraft. I believe some type of electrical failure has occurred, which may require professional attention.

Bill, given that I can't act as a backup, are you still confident in your ability to land independently?"

"No problem," replied Bill. "Are you okay if I do one more gentle exercise? I'm getting a feel for this jet, so I would like to try one last manoeuvre before we land."

Gary chuckled and said, "So far, you have performed marvellously. Go ahead, but remember, I won't be able to bail you out if there is a problem."

Bill's voice crackled over the radio as he informed the control tower he'd be performing another flyby before landing, assuring them there was no cause for alarm. They agreed. Bill turned the jet, the hum of the engine a steady thrum, and headed it back towards the airfield. When he was directly overhead, the jet screamed as it entered another graveyard spiral, its deafening roar amplified by the increasing speed and proximity to the ground.

"Pull out of it!" yelled Gary. "You are too close to the ground! You are going to crash!"

With increasing speed, the jet propelled itself forward, causing the ground below to appear as though it were spinning and rushing towards the aircraft at an alarming rate. Into the earphones, Gary unleashed a scream so bloodcurdling and terrifying that it could make the dead rise from their graves. Seconds later, the pungent scent of feces and urine filled the jet's cockpit, making it hard for Bill to breathe. At the very moment before the plane crashed, Bill, exhibiting extraordinary skill, recovered from the dangerous spiral manoeuvre. Then he immediately flew directly towards the large group of officer trainees who were observing from the tarmac.

The jet, now flying upside down, had its glass-covered cockpit mere inches from the asphalt below. With the upside-down jet hurtling towards the trainee officers at 300 mph, Bill could only watch as the trainees desperately sought shelter, hoping to avoid being splattered by the jet. When the runway ended, Bill yanked the jet skyward, executing a graceful right-side-up rotation at approximately 2,000 feet, a breathtaking feat of aviation skill. Having gotten the clearance for landing from the tower, he carefully guided his plane toward the hangar and successfully parked it inside.

Bill spun his head to look at the seat located directly behind him. Although Gary had lost consciousness, his breathing remained steady. His head drooped, hanging heavily to the right side. Something knocked his mask off, leaving his face exposed. From the corner of his mouth, a viscous stream of vomit and drool dripped down his chin and onto his clothes. A pool of liquid stool and urine soaked his Air Force pants, the ones he so proudly paraded around in before the flight.

Chapter 4

The wind roared through the sails, a constant, powerful force driving the Hanse 508 sailboat forward. With two reefs in the mainsail and the jib taut, the boat sailed with grace. It cut through the waves. The sound of the wind whistling through the rigging was a constant companion. They were on a beam reach as they desperately tried to outrun the approaching hurricane. The three of them took turns standing watch, alternating three-hour shifts at the helm, scanning the horizon for other ships, and constantly adjusting the sails to catch the ever-shifting wind.

"I think we are going to make it in time," said Katherine. "The only drawback is we will enter St. George's harbour in the middle of the night. I calculate we will get there at 11 p.m. How do you feel about entering an unfamiliar harbour at night? Should we wait until daylight?"

Jack checked his phone, a frown crossing his face. "The weather app says 40 knot winds at dawn. We need to move now if we don't want to fight the winds," he said. "Shallow reefs surround the island, and we might get blown onto them and shipwrecked. I think we should risk it and try to reach the safe harbour tonight, even though it's dark. The red and green navigation buoys mark the entrance. All we need to do is follow them."

Squinting at the PredictWind app on his phone, Bill said, "Sure, they're saying 40 knots, but the gusts could hit 55 knots... That's going to be rough! Forecasters expect the waves to swell to fifteen feet tonight. By morning, they predict the waves will crest at a daunting twenty feet. The storm and the rising waves crashing against the harbour walls would make entering a risky endeavour. I say we put our navigation skills to the test and get ourselves safely into harbour tonight."

They glanced at each other, their eyes searching for confirmation in the other's gaze, a silent plea for validation as they nodded in agreement.

As the sun dipped below the horizon at 5 p.m., casting the sky in shades of orange and purple, they could see the twinkling lights of Bermuda emerging on the horizon. "We need to stay at least a mile offshore," said Jack. "Those white lights on our starboard mark the edge of the reef."

Gusts up to 35 knots built in the wind. The waves, now towering and close together, slammed into the boat with powerful, rhythmic blows, the impact shaking the vessel. The sails billowed in the wind as the boat careened along at 9.5 knots, surfing down the waves.

"Let's put a third reef in the main," shouted Jack above the roar of the wind. "We are getting overpowered!"

With a practised hand, Katherine lowered the main halyard, while Bill carefully tensioned the third reefing line. The boat's tilt lessened as the pressure on the mainsail reduced. The sails lost their fullness and only half of the mainsail remaining taut. As the boat settled into a smoother ride, the autohelm hummed contentedly, and the groaning and complaining from below the deck finally subsided.

"We just passed Mill light, a key landmark marking the harbour entrance," said Katherine. "Should we take down the sails and motor through the town cut into the harbour?"

Jack and Bill agreed.

"Turn the boat into the wind, and I'll furl the jib!" shouted Jack, his hands already reaching for the sail. With a rumble and a sputter, Katherine brought the engine to life, then carefully nudged the boat forward, just enough to keep the bow pointed into the wind. The power winch whirred and hummed as Jack carefully furled the jib and secured it to the forestay. The boat bounced violently up and down on the waves, the spray from the crests showering the deck with salty water.

"Let's take the mainsail down!" shouted Jack, his voice carried away by the wind. A powerful gust whipped the main sail, creating a cacophony of snapping and flapping that echoed across the water. Jack knew it would be difficult for the others to hear him. He leaned over and shouted into Bill's ear. "Release the main halyard!"

The mainsail started to come down, but then it suddenly stopped, as if something was holding it back. A tense silence filled the air as the boat lurched slightly. The three of them stared at the mainsail as it whipped and snapped in the wind, the sound growing louder and more insistent with each gust.

The wind lashed at their faces, carrying Jack's words as he shouted, "One of us must go up the mast and see if we can pull the rest of the sail down by hand."

"That's madness!" roared Bill, his voice barely audible over the howling wind.

"I'll be the one to do it since I'm the most familiar with the boat," replied Jack calmly. He talked directly into Bill's ear so he could hear above the sounds of the storm. "I'll take the walkie-talkie, just in case we need to communicate. Hopefully, you'll hear me."

"The waves are crashing against the side of the boat," shouted Bill. "And you're going to be washed overboard if you're not careful. I say we try to sail into the harbour."

"The winds are getting too strong," Jack countered. "And we could lose control if we don't get the sail down. We might end up on the reef. I've done this before in rough weather. To prevent myself from going overboard, I'll clip myself into the jacklines. Hold on to the walkie-talkie tight—I'll be giving you instructions through it. Katherine might need some help keeping us in the wind, especially if the gusts pick up."

The rhythmic slap of the waves against the boat was a constant reminder of Jack's precarious situation as he clipped his harness onto the jacklines that ran along the side of the boat. The boat tossed and turned so violently that Jack had to crawl on his hands and knees to avoid being thrown overboard. He scrambled up the first two rungs on the side of the mast, gripping the base with one hand as he shouted into the walkie-talkie. "I'm climbing up the mast now. Let me know if you see a wave that might break on me."

Jack clipped the walkie-talkie onto his PFD. The boat rocked violently as he climbed up the third rung on the mast. He timed his movements perfectly with the swaying motion. He saw a tight twist in the mainsail halyard as it entered the mast. It prevented the mainsail from coming down. It made a slight snapping sound. Untwisting it was easy. The rest of the mainsail fell cleanly into the sail cover, safely away from the wind.

Just as Jack began his climb back to the deck, the walkie-talkie came to life. A sharp, urgent "Watch out!" crackled through the radio. Jack's heart pounded in his chest as he watched the enormous wave, a wall of white water, about to crash down on their boat. He lunged onto the deck, the salty spray of the ocean stinging his face, and snatched the jib sheet line. Its tautness was a testament to the wind's force. With a desperate grip, Jack wrapped his wrist around the rough, worn jib sheet line. He hoped it would be enough to keep him from being swept off the boat.

The tower of moving water slammed into Jack, sending him flying backwards. It crashed over him, tearing his life jacket away and sending searing pain up his wrist as he was tossed and tumbled into the water. Pressure in his ears built, his lungs were filling with water. A terrifying thought that he might accidentally inhale more water overwhelmed him. The ferocious torrent of the wave thrashed his body. It pummelled him. It spun his legs wildly and uncontrollably in the relentless surge of water. On the verge of surrendering to the overwhelming pressure, he suddenly felt the warmth of air against his face. The sensation triggered an instinctive gasp, a desperate inhalation of life-giving oxygen that expelled the seawater still clinging to his lungs.

The jib sheet line bit into Jack's skin. His wrist burned as he hung over the side of the boat. He reached for the lifeline with his free hand. Gripping it tightly, he pulled himself back onto the slippery deck. He rolled on his back and took a deep breath. His mangled wrist throbbed agonizingly. Jack was worried he might have fractured it. No sooner had the thought come to mind, Jack felt someone tugging at his ankles, pulling him back towards the cockpit. His weakness kept him from moving on his own. Bill's hand clamped onto his shirt, pulling him abruptly onto the hard cockpit bench.

Bill's eyes were darting around. He was hyperventilating. "We thought we lost you!" he choked out over the wind. "Are you hurt?"

Jack shook his head. "Maybe my wrist," he whispered.

"Stay here," shouted Bill. "Katherine and I'll navigate into the harbour."

The engine roared to life, reaching a deafening 2,500 rpm, as Jack felt the boat lurch and turn sharply downwind. The wave had left him battered and bruised, his wrist aching. He lay on the cockpit bench, afraid to move, dreading the possibility of a broken bone. It throbbed with the beating of his rapid pulse. Each wave slammed against the boat, making it shudder and bounce. A flashing red buoy on starboard and a flashing green light on port that he could see out of the corner of his eye were clear indicators they were safely navigating the channel. Having been tossed about by the waves, the boat finally entered the calm waters of St. George's Harbour. The land mass provided a barrier against the rough seas.

Jack sat up, wincing as he rubbed his sore wrist. The rope had worn through his skin, leaving a raw, painful patch, but when he rubbed the exposed bone, it didn't seem fractured. The rocking of the boat subsided. He gingerly rose to his feet. He felt the unsteady deck beneath him. They were safe.

"I think I'm okay," he said to Katherine, his voice strained. Her hands gripped the steering wheel so tightly that her knuckles were white. Her eyes flicked around, searching for anything that might threaten their safety. Jack reached over and gave her a warm hug, his arms wrapping tightly around her. "You did a great job steering the boat into the harbour, navigating through the choppy waves with ease." He gently kissed her forehead as she trembled, her body shaking like a leaf caught in a strong wind.

Katherine's mouth turned downward and her eyes moistened. Her face crumpled, and a torrent of tears erupted as her emotions overwhelmed her.

Chapter 5

Bill's hands trembled slightly as he gripped the microphone, his voice a little shaky as he began his presentation to the audience of over 500 surgeons. The talk was on the use of powerful magnets to create an anastomosis, a groundbreaking alternative to traditional laparoscopic surgery techniques. This eliminated the need for incisions during the surgery. Surgeons positioned the magnets by inserting them into the body using endoscopy, either through the mouth or the anus. After a year of painstaking work with his mentor, the renowned Dr. Marcel Garner, Bill had successfully used magnets to create an anastomosis in 20 patients. Prior testing of the device on pigs showed it to be safe enough for human trials, meeting all safety standards. Only a handful of minor complications arose, easily overcome as their experience with the procedure progressed.

From the front seat of the lecture hall, Jack watched as the crowd erupted into a thunderous applause. The sound was like a wave crashing against the walls after Bill finished his presentation. Jack shook his head, a wry smile playing on his lips as he recalled how perilously close Bill had come to ruining his career with his cocaine addiction years ago. His friend had remained sober and was still actively taking part in his group meetings, which gave him hope and support for his ongoing recovery. Jack's heart swelled with pride as he watched Bill, illuminated by the surgical spotlight, receiving the well-deserved recognition.

They had both achieved their goal of becoming surgeons, completing five years of demanding training, and now felt ready to take on the world. To further his expertise in thoracic surgery, Bill had to spend an additional year learning the intricacies of this complex field. The University of Toronto selected Jack for the highly competitive Minimally Invasive Surgery Fellowship. With a year of training left in the program, he was already attracting interest from employers eager to hire him once he was fully skilled in laparoscopy and robotic surgery.

Jack watched anxiously as the surgeons, their faces tense and serious, gathered around Bill, peppered him with questions. Bill glanced over at Jack with a satisfied nod and smiled at him. Jack pantomimed he was going back to the room and would meet up with him later. They were staying at The Paris, a lavish hotel in Las Vegas, complete with a replica of the Eiffel Tower. Over 3,000 delegates attended the meeting, eager to hear about the latest advancements in surgical technology. The conference hall buzzed with energy. The bright lights and excitement of Las Vegas drew medical conference attendees, providing them with a spacious venue to gather by day and the dazzling allure of shows and casinos to keep them entertained at night.

Jack opted to have a nap, as the late afternoon heat lulled him into a state of drowsiness. Attending medical meetings as a surgery resident offered a rare opportunity for him to catch up on much-needed sleep, a precious commodity during his gruelling hours. For the past five years, he was used to getting only about four hours of sleep each night. Sometimes he would work through the night with no rest at all, and then he would be expected to perform surgery the next day. He savoured the afternoon nap, sinking into the soft mattress and feeling the weight of the world slip away.

The clock struck 6 p.m., rousing him from his sleep. A quick shower and he was heading down to the lobby, eager to meet the representatives from the surgical staple company who were taking him and the other residents out for dinner. Jack expected to see Bill. But he suspected his friend's new stardom as a leading surgical scientist had him tucked away in a plush, high-end restaurant, surrounded by eager venture capitalists hoping to get a piece of his revolutionary technology. Jack knew how much Bill loved food, so he wasn't worried about him missing out on the free dinner.

"Anyone seen Bill?" Jack asked the other residents when they arrived at the restaurant after a short walk.

"You know Bill," said Jill, a fellow Toronto resident, her voice laced with a hint of amusement. "He's probably buttering up the bigwigs at some investment firm, hoping they'll throw millions his way."

Aromas of sizzling steak and melted butter filled the air as they gathered around a long table. Indulging in filet mignon with creamy bearnaise sauce and fluffy garlic-mashed potatoes, a lavish meal was a rare delight for the residents. The red wine, an expensive Chianti, filled the glass with its deep ruby colour. After the delicious meal, Jack felt a wave of exhaustion wash over him. He couldn't wait to get back to his room and fall into bed.

*****

Rays of morning sunlight streamed through a crack in the hotel room blinds. Jack woke up and stretched. It surprised him to see Bill's bed still perfectly made up. That Bill didn't return last night wasn't unusual. It likely meant he was getting laid. With the Las Vegas sun rising, Jack quickly put on his running gear and headed out the door for his usual 10 kilometres before the heat became unbearable. He ran down the city's main strip to the airport and back, the crisp morning air of the desert biting at his lungs, bringing a smile to his face. Jack had worked up a sweat by the time he returned to the hotel, his clothes clinging to his skin, but he felt invigorated after the workout.

The bright lights and the constant whirring of slot machines were almost blinding as Jack pushed through the throng of people, even at that early hour in the morning. He dodged gamblers and dealers alike on his way to the elevators. He noticed a man sitting at one table, surrounded by a small fortune of gambling chips. Jack stopped in his tracks, his eyes widening at the sight before him. The large man had rolled up the cuffs of his dress shirt. His loosely hanging suit jacket, draped over the chair, contained a partially rolled-up tie in the pocket. The dress pants, having slid down from the potbelly, revealed the all-too-familiar sight of a peeking butt crack. Jack reached over and touched his shoulder.

"Bill?" he asked. "You're bouncing off the walls and your pupils are dilated—you haven't slept a wink, have you? What are you doing? You could be trading one addiction for another."

Bill looked up from his pile of chips, a smile lighting up his face at the sight of his friend, then quickly returned his attention to the table. "Hit me," he said to the dealer, his eyes fixed on the cards in his hand. The dealer flipped over a card. "I'll stay," Bill said, his voice firm as he looked at the seven of spades that lay before him.

Jack said, his voice tinged with disbelief, "Don't tell me you were here all night? I thought you were getting laid. And that's why you didn't get back to the room."

With a flourish, the dealer flipped over his cards, revealing his hand for all to see. He had the king of hearts and the five of clubs. With a flick of his wrist, he turned over another card. The crisp snap clearly cut through the noisy room. The 10 of clubs.

"Busted," Bill yelled, a triumphant grin spreading across his face as the dealer slid the pile of poker chips across the table.

"I'm taking a break," Bill said to the dealer, who seemed relieved. "I need a caffeine hit," he said to Jack. "Let's go."

The aroma of coffee and bacon wafted through the air as they sat at the hotel's breakfast restaurant. The server finished taking their order. Jack turned to Bill and whispered, "Do you think this is really a good idea? Similar to the grip of drug addiction, gambling can ensnare people in its relentless cycle. Taking risks activates the same reward pathway in the brain, leading to the release of dopamine, as do other activities that provide pleasure. Bill, you know that—it's all the same with addiction."

Bill looked at his friend. "You worry too much. How much do you think I made last night?"

Jack shrugged. "I'll tell you then," said Bill. "I have over $100,000 in chips! I have a system. You could work for a year and a half as a resident and never see this kind of cash." Jack stared at Bill incredulously. "I didn't tell you this," Bill continued. "You could say I'm a Vegas aficionado. I've been here at least once every two months for the past year." His voice was a whirlwind of urgency, each word a breathless gasp that threatened to outrun his thoughts. "The total amount in my bank account exceeds half a mil!"

A wave of shock washed over Jack, leaving him breathless. He could hear the frantic tone in Bill's voice, and he knew his friend was in trouble again. It was hard to believe that the casinos, with their reputation for meticulously guarding their wealth, would let one person walk away with such a massive fortune; the air was thick with disbelief. They would know he was cheating them. The evidence was clear, and it felt like a punch to the gut. The cracks in Bill's world were growing wider, and he could see the inevitable collapse looming on the horizon.

"This is crazy," whispered Jack, his voice barely a breath in the stillness. "Bill, you are in trouble again. You need to talk about this with your addiction advisors. You are going to crash again. Please. Stop this madness."

The server brought the coffee and the food Bill had ordered. A large cheese and mushroom omelette with toast and strawberry jam. He began eating with the same vigour with which he had been talking and demolished the food within a few minutes. After he dabbed the crumbs from his face with the napkin, he said, "I need to get back. I'm on a winning streak!"

Jack watched as Bill, his face flushed with excitement, got up from the table and headed back to the blackjack tables. The familiar weight of despondency settled upon him, just like it had all those years ago when Bill had gone to rehab for three months. This time he didn't know where to turn, or how he could help his friend. Bill was so convinced he was on to a good thing. Jack knew he could not convince him otherwise.

Jack sighed. *Sometimes a person needs to hit rock bottom themselves before they realize they are there.*

Chapter 6

Jack woke to the motion of the sailboat nestled in the sheltered harbour of St. George's, swaying gently as the strong winds churned up small waves. He could feel the rhythmic pull of the anchor, a constant tug and release as it caught the gusts. The boat's interior was hushed and peaceful, a stark difference from the cacophony of high-pitched whines the wind created as it whipped through the rigging outside. The nasty weather promised by the forecast had arrived. He hopped out of the bed and got dressed. Katherine was sitting at the table in the main salon. She was glued to her phone, oblivious to her surroundings as she delved into the vastness of the internet.

"I'm looking for things to do in Bermuda," she said absentmindedly. "You want coffee? The Nespresso machine is working."

Jack made himself a cup and sat beside Katherine. "Are you okay?" he asked. "After what happened last night?"

"More to the point," she said sharply. "Are *you* okay? You are the one who almost died. It's one of the few times I have ever heard of where if you had kept yourself attached to your life vest, the search and rescue team would still be looking for your body. The system supposedly designed to save your life failed... yet you lived." Her voice continued to rise in a feverish pitch. "This is powerful evidence that you... you actually have horseshoes up your ass." Her dark eyes flashed with anger and a tinge of confusion as she glared at Jack. "What's wrong with you? How can you remain so calm?"

Despite her raised voice, Jack could hear a flicker of vulnerability in her words, sensing she was still shaken and not truly mad at him. Jack chuckled. "You can plan all you want, but life has a way of throwing curveballs. You never know what's around the corner. As I explained to you, I have never been afraid of the water. A bit of skin is missing from my wrist, but that's nothing compared to my desire to be back on the ocean when the weather improves."

Katherine scrunched up the paper towel she was using as a napkin and threw it at him. "You asshole. You scared me half to death. I don't understand you." She shook her head in disbelief at Jack's nonchalance.

"Sometimes things work out," Jack said wistfully. "Last night was one of them. I know you were terrified and overwhelmed by my brush with death, but you managed to stay calm and focused on getting us to safety in that moment of crisis. Your skilful manoeuvring brought us into the harbour's calm waters. You showed remarkable strength and courage. I asked you to come on this trip because I knew I could rely on you."

Katherine stared at Jack and shook her head. "Your dad was supposed to sail this boat to Antigua with you as part of his retirement strategy. The only reason he didn't come was because he had a heart attack. If he would have been on the boat last night, he would have had another one watching you practise your man-overboard drill."

"You're right," said Jack, laughing at the way she characterized the event. "But he will meet us down there in the Caribbean when he has recovered. I'll try to behave for the rest of the trip. In the meantime, what do you think we should do while we are here? Bill wants to check out the new casino. I have no interest in that—and neither should he, given his past history with casinos."

She cocked an eyebrow at his comment, but swiftly changed the subject. "We need to check in with customs and immigration, then I want to wander this historic town, St. George's. It looks lovely."

"What's this I'm hearing about checking out the town?" said Bill sleepily. He rubbed his eyes as he exited his cabin.

"We need to clear customs first," said Katherine. "Jack says you want to see the new casino at St. Regis."

"Yeah," said Bill. "Do you want to come? Just like last night, you could play the role of Lady Luck."

"You would never catch me in one of those places," said Katherine.

Jack piped up. "Bill, given what happened in Las Vegas, do you think that is a good idea?"

Bill took his time to answer. He made himself a cup of Nespresso and sat beside Katherine, across from Jack. He spoke slowly, as if choosing his words carefully. "That was a few years ago now. Water under the bridge. Besides, no one knows me here. We'll be gone in a few days anyway, once the weather clears."

Jack shook his head in disbelief. A scoff escaped his lips. Bill, seemingly unable to learn from his mistakes, was going to return to the gambling table, even though his poor decisions had cost him dearly. The memory of Las Vegas, with its bright lights and flashing neon signs, flooded Jack's mind. He couldn't endure a repeat of what had happened.

The last morning of the meeting dawned at the Paris hotel, when Jack woke up to Bill's untouched bed. It was a stark contrast to the rest of the room, with clothes and papers carelessly spread throughout. He shook his head. *Thank God this is our last day here before we catch the red eye back to Toronto*, he thought as he got dressed in his running gear.

The run to the airport and back was particularly invigorating, knowing it would be his last run in the desert. Given the stress Bill had caused him with his gambling, Jack hoped it would be his last visit to Sin city. He had his hand on the door of the hotel lobby, ready to step inside, when his phone pinged, a notification indicating an incoming message. It was from Bill.

"Meet me at the back of the hotel near the dumpsters. Hurry! Please!"

Jack's heart sank. *What now?* Jack looked down the street and found a paved alley that led to the rear of the hotel. He saw the blue dumpsters at the end. Making slow, deliberate steps, Jack moved towards them. Despite the urgent nature of Bill's message, an eerie quiet pervaded the air, adding to the tension. Then he spotted something moving.

Sitting on the pavement between two dumpsters was Bill. His face, swollen and bruised. Jack got closer, then stopped in his tracks. Blood was running from Bill's nose, which was bent to the right.

Bill looked up at Jack, his finger silently pressed to his lips, signalling for him to stay quiet.

Jack went to his friend, leaned over him, and whispered, "What the fuck?"

"The security team wants to kill me," he whispered back. "They think I'm cheating the system. They want to know how I have made so much money off them. We need to get to the airport.

The cameras in the hotel will alert them if I try to get to the room. Grab your stuff in the room and meet me here with a cab in five minutes. Hurry! We need to get the first flight out of here!"

Jack spun around, a frantic energy propelling him to the room, where he snatched his bag and laptop. A thought rushed through his head. Bill's bruised and bloody face, a gruesome sight, might frighten the cab driver away. He went into the washroom, feeling the comfort of the cool tile on his warm skin as he selected a couple of fluffy facecloths. He dampened the starched white terry towels with cool water and placed them carefully into a plastic bag he retrieved from the ice bucket. At least now he could clean Bill's face, removing the blood and grime. With a quick glance at his watch, Jack noted the time, a nervous flutter in his chest. He'd better pick up the pace; every second counts.

Exiting the hotel, he sprinted toward the yellow cabs lined up in front of the hotel, their horns beeping rhythmically in the humid air. Guiding the driver to the back of the hotel, past overflowing dumpsters and the pungent smell of rotting garbage, he instructed the driver to stop between the two blue bins. Bill quickly slipped into the back seat. With a grimace, Jack wiped the blood from Bill's face, the damp cloth clinging to the drying crimson. With a sigh, Bill let himself fall against the backrest.

Just as they approached the airport, Bill lifted his blood-stained shirt and showed Jack the blood dripping out.

Jack dabbed at the blood with the wet cloth. "Holy shit. They shot you!"

Bill shrugged, wincing at the dabbing of the cloth as it brushed the open wound. He whispered, "Yeah, I got shot."

Jack glanced at the wound, a slow but steady stream of blood flowing out. "We need to take you to the hospital! Now!"

Jack turned his attention to the driver and was about to give him instructions when Bill whispered, "If we go to the hospital, they will be waiting for me. They will kill us. Both of us. You need to get us home. It's only a flesh wound. I'll be okay. You'll see."

The taxi driver, unaware of Bill's injury, pulled up at the curb at Harry Reid International Airport's departure platform. Jack remained seated, not knowing what the best option was. *If the bullet wound was a serious injury and Bill died on the flight, I would be complicit with his death. If I insist on taking Bill to the hospital and we both get killed as soon as we arrive...*

"We need to go," hissed Bill. "If the bullet wound was a serious injury, I would be dead by now."

Having weighed all the options, Jack made his final decision. As he exited the taxi in a hurry, he caught sight of a wheelchair left unattended on the curb and immediately seized it. Jack carefully helped Bill into the wheelchair, the leather refreshingly cool against his hands, a brief reprieve from the oppressive heat, despite the car's AC. He paid the driver. Then, to cover the bleeding from his abdomen, Jack frantically pulled out his bright yellow raincoat, blood pooling on its slick surface, a contrast to it spreading and soaking into his shirt.

"Wear this," he whispered in Bill's ear as he carefully draped the garment over his shoulders, concealing the crimson stain. With a grunt, he pushed Bill's wheelchair toward the busy Air Canada counter, the sounds of announcements and chatter washing over them. With only 45 minutes until a direct flight to Toronto departed, they raced to catch the plane. The boarding announcement was loud in their ears as Jack wheeled the big bleeding man with urgency.

Arriving in Toronto five hours later, Bill's pain had intensified, particularly upon landing. His face contorted in agony as the jarring impact of the wheels hitting the ground shook their seats. Jack could almost feel waves of pain that rifled through his friend. Leaning over, Jack took Bill's pulse. He was surprised to find it was 128 beats per minute. He reached out and gently touched Bill's abdomen, his fingers tracing the contours of his midsection. The slightest contact triggered a wince of agony as pain surged through Bill's face. The diffuse tenderness made his abdomen rigid. There was no doubt in Jack's mind the bullet had penetrated his intestine. The injury resulted in a leak of intestinal contents that spread throughout his abdomen.

Even before the plane had arrived at the terminal, Jack was on the phone to his surgical mentor, Larry Klapman. "Bill's with me," he said to the surgeon. "He got shot in the abdomen in Las Vegas. At first, we thought he might have dodged major damage, but now he has peritonitis. I think he needs an urgent operation. Can you meet me in the emergency room? We should be there in 30 minutes."

Within two hours, Bill was lying on the operating table.

"The CT scan shows a lot of fluid around the liver and in the pelvis," said Larry as he viewed the images on the computer in the operating room with Jack.

Jack replied, "Looks like the bullet is lodged in the psoas muscle on the right, but there does not appear to be any damage to the kidney or ureter."

"What's your plan for the operation, then?" asked Larry.

"We should put in the laparoscope and assess the damage..." he said. "We could see whether we can fix the problem that way and then decide if we need to do a laparotomy."

"You know that most surgeons would proceed with a laparotomy rather than waste time with a laparoscopy," Larry said matter-of-factly. "His life is in danger, and it might be more likely to miss an injury if we don't open him up."

"Yeah," replied Jack. "I know the stats. But few surgeons have your skills and judgment with laparoscopy. I would trust our combined abilities to make the right decisions, and my vote would be to start with the laparoscope."

"I agree with you," said Larry. "I wanted to be sure about how you felt."

Larry and Jack scrubbed at the sink, the smell of antiseptic filling the room. The circulating nurse scrubbed Bill's abdomen with chlorhexidine, the gentle sound of the scrub brush against his skin breaking the silence of the operating room. She then draped him with the sterile towels. A "time out", while the entire operating staff stopped what they were doing to take part, ensured they were operating on the correct patient and performing the correct operation.

Using a scalpel, Jack made a precise incision around the umbilicus and inflated the abdomen with five litres of carbon dioxide, creating a pocket of space for him to work. He inserted the laparoscope and started the video. Then he inserted the three remaining ports, each measuring five millimetres in diameter. Through the port on the left side, the suction cannula swiftly extracted 1.5 litres of bile-stained fluid. Starting with the small bowel closest to the cecum, and running the bowel using the atraumatic graspers, Jack identified the injury in the terminal ileum. The bullet had penetrated the front wall and exited through the mesentery and into the psoas muscle.

"I think the safest option is to resect this damaged bowel rather than try to repair it," said Jack. Larry simply nodded in affirmation.

Jack used the laparoscopic stapler to divide the small intestine distal and proximal to the injury. He divided the mesentery containing the blood supply to the damaged intestine with the ultrasonic scalpel. Next, he completed the anastomosis with the stapler and sutured the defect in the small intestine where he had stapled the bowel together. After examining the rest of the abdomen for any other injuries and washing out the abdominal cavity with three litres of warmed normal saline solution, he placed the damaged intestine into a plastic specimen bag and removed it through the umbilical port. He finished the entire operation in less than 30 minutes.

Bill's recovery from the surgery was swift. After a few days, he returned to their apartment to continue healing. He went back to work a week later, his face remaining composed and his demeanour unchanged, as if nothing had happened. The incident remained a silent understanding between Bill and Jack, never spoken of again until today in St. George's.

"Don't expect me to fix you up if they shoot you on site when you visit Bermuda's casino," said Jack, his thoughts returning to the present.

Bill's smile was knowing as he said, "You can't help yourself, Jack." His booming laughter filled the room, like a dark humour stemming from his morbid thoughts. "I can always count on you to come to my rescue."

Chapter 7

Katherine and Jack sat in the restaurant overlooking the harbour and Ordnance Island, the scent of fresh seafood hanging in the air. The remnants of their lunch at the White Horse Pub and Restaurant sat forgotten as they sipped their Heinekens, warming their hands over the fire crackling and popping beside them. The wind howled outside, making it impossible to appreciate the charm of the historic village. It was simply too miserable to venture out.

"So, what is with you and Bill?" asked Katherine after Jack explained to her what had happened in Las Vegas. "Why do you continue to bail him out of trouble?"

Jack took a sip of his beer, the cool liquid contrasting with the heat of the fire that had warmed his face and hands. The bar was almost completely empty, save for them and the bartender who was polishing glasses at the end of the counter. "We go back to a long way. Bill has always held a special place in my heart. His father, a truck driver who often sought solace in alcohol, was a distant figure in his life. Although they had revoked his driver's license, he continued operating his truck, which ultimately led to a six-month jail sentence. Bill's father couldn't stand the constant reminder of what he had lost, so he moved away, leaving behind the memories and the place that held his sorrow. He vanished from Bill's life."

Jack took another swig of beer. "It seemed like Bill lived at my house. He was there so often. He was a wild spirit. Always up for a good time. Never afraid to take risks. I remember one time we'd spent hours crafting cardboard wings, dreaming of flight, and then, with a running leap, launch ourselves off the edge of the garage, hoping for a moment of weightless freedom. Although we never actually flew, we laughed so much that day that it felt like we were soaring. He was almost like a brother to me. In fact, my parents partly funded his university education. His mother, Ruby, had to juggle two jobs to keep food on the table and couldn't spare the money for his fancy schooling. Bill is highly intelligent and extraordinarily skilled in surgery. Unfortunately, he struggles with addiction problems. I have a feeling that he inherited those genes from his father."

"He's all charm and smiles," Katherine said, "but he's definitely a womanizer. In Hampton, while we waited for a weather window for this trip, I watched as he zeroed in on a solitary sailor woman sipping margaritas at the bar. The sun was setting as you and I made our way back to the boat, leaving him behind. He never made it to his cabin that night."

"That's Bill for you," said Jack. "He attracts women like honey attracts bears. I think they see him as a big, loveable teddy. It has always mystified me how he does it."

Katherine laughed. "You seem disappointed in yourself." She took a drink of her Heineken as she crinkled her brow in thought. "It's too miserable to go on a tour of Gibb's Lighthouse, like we planned. Why don't we pay him a visit at St. Regis Casino to see how he is doing?"

Jack laughed at the suggestion. "I do *not* want to encourage him. And I'm deliberately choosing to stay uninformed about his gambling activities. Let's just sit here and enjoy the warmth of the fire, breathing in the smoky aroma, and watching the flames dance."

"Jack, come on. Don't be so dull! Let's have some fun," she urged, her eyes sparkling with mischief. "We'll savour the last drops of our beers here before hopping into a cab and heading to the hotel. I'll buy you a beer at the bar in the famous St. Regis lobby, right there."

"Oh, I don't know. I think we are heading for disappointment by going there."

With their beers drained, Katherine pushed back her chair and stood up. Her fingers tightened around Jack's hand, pulling him towards her with unexpected strength. "You... my fearless captain, are coming with me," she whispered, her breath warm on his cheek as she kissed him playfully. With Jack in tow, she headed for the door.

Jack felt the adrenaline pumping through his veins as he recognized something had changed between them. The warmth of her kiss lingered on his cheek, a tingling sensation that made him smile. His thoughts seemed to be tangled, and he felt himself becoming increasingly confused. Her provocative demeanour, coupled with the lingering memory of that brief physical encounter just seconds ago, kindled a growing attraction within him. He knew Katherine was involved with someone in Toronto, so he hadn't expected this to happen on the trip. Her fingers nestled comfortably into his, and he felt a rush of warmth spread through his body. He was totally captivated by her in that moment and would have gone anywhere she asked.

"To the St. Regis Casino," she said to the cab driver. She turned to Jack, who was still holding her hand. "It's a five-minute drive."

The stucco hotel, with its pristine white façade, stood prominently overlooking the stunning pink sandy beach. While the wind continued to blow with powerful gusts, the hotel's location behind the land mass provided some shelter. Having paid the driver $10, Jack hopped out of the cab with Katherine, and together they made their way to the casino. Upon entering the facility, it was as if they had stepped into a different world, a world filled with glittering lights, the sounds of slot machines, and the anticipation of winning big. The atmosphere was bustling and lively, with the sounds of ringing bells and people moving around the tables contributing to the vibrant energy of the place. Every slot machine in the casino seemed to be occupied, creating a buzzing atmosphere of excitement.

"I don't think we'll find him," shouted Jack. Jack saw Katherine glance around the room. "Let's leave," he said hopefully.

Giving him a shove, Katherine said in a playful tone, "There he is, silly!" With a quick gesture, she pointed to a blackjack table. Gamblers occupied all six seats at the semicircular table that faced the dealer. Bill's position was in the centre of the pack, surrounded by the others. An enormous pile of chips, so large it resembled a small hill, was in front of him. Four scantily clad women gathered around Bill, their excited chatter and bouncing bodies creating a vibrant atmosphere as they watched him gamble. A loud cheer erupted from the crowd as the dealer, with a flourish of his hand, slid another stack of chips towards Bill, adding to his already impressive pile. *Oh no,* Jack thought to himself. *Not again.*

He surveyed the scene, hoping to warn Katherine, but she had already barged through the gaggle of women surrounding Bill. She touched his shoulder, then whispered something into his ear and pointed to the spot where Jack was standing. Bill briefly interrupted his concentration on the blackjack table to wave at Jack, then returned his attention to the game. Wanting Katherine to approach him, Jack waved his arm in her direction. With a gentle nod and a bright smile, Katherine came back.

"This is what you warned me about, isn't it?" said Katherine.

"Don't forget you owe me a beer," said Jack. "Let's go to the lobby bar." This time, he grabbed her hand, and she followed him into the quiet of the hotel.

"What's the best beer you have on tap here?" he asked the server who approached after they sat down. The server opened her mouth to speak, and Jack interrupted her. "Never mind. Surprise us. We'll have two glasses of your finest."

The lobby bar was serene, with just a few scattered patrons, since most of the hotel guests were drawn to the flashing lights and the buzz of the casino. A soft piano melody, tinged with a hint of melancholy, drifted from the overhead speakers. The clinking of glasses from behind the bar, almost musical in its regularity, was the only sound that broke the silence as Jack stole a glance at Katherine.

"This will not end well for Bill," Jack said, a grim expression on his face. "He had a mountain of chips piled in front of him, probably worth at least $20,000, and he'd only been playing for a few hours. If past experience is any prediction of what is coming next, the casino will offer him a free room as long as he continues to play. They know it will encourage others to take bigger risks with their money, leading to increased profits for the casino."

Concern spread across Katherine's face as she gazed at Jack. Her brows furrowed, and she bit her lip, her eyes narrowed in concentration. "When is it they will decide to shoot him?" she said without irony.

"They will probably just deport him," said Jack, a hint of bitterness in his tone. "The gun-free policy in Bermuda makes shooting him less likely. As the only hotel in Bermuda with a casino, St. Regis would suffer an enormous loss if they were to lose their license because of violence. The imminent risk we face is my prediction that Bill will want us to leave without him once the weather clears up in the next day or two. We need to plan for that. What do you think we should do if he tells us that?"

"You were right, Jack. He's absolutely obsessed with gambling," said Katherine, her voice laced with worry. "I felt that when I talked to him. He's got a chance to make a fortune at the gambling tables and I can't see him choosing six days of rough travel in the unpredictable Atlantic Ocean over that. How does he pull it off? With winning all those chips."

"I'm not sure. I think he counts the cards. He has a photographic memory."

"But they shuffle the cards and use four decks to prevent that from happening. How is it possible for him to win so much so quickly?"

"That's one of Bill's remarkable gifts. His intelligence is evident in his quick wit and ability to process information rapidly. He makes it so the odds are in favour of him rather than the house. On balance, he will win more than he loses. They watch him through the cameras for clues, but they will never figure out how he does it. Eventually, they will get fed up with the drain of cash and ban him from the casino."

"If he wants to stay here, then maybe you and I should sail the rest of the way ourselves," Katherine suggested. "I'm fine with that. As soon as we get to the trade winds, which are about a few hundred miles south from here, the sailing will be smooth and easy. With so many couples proving that sailing together is possible, I'm confident we can make it work too."

A shiver ran down Jack's spine, and he felt his heart skip a beat when she mentioned the word "couples." The air crackled with tension as he realized, in less than an hour, his relationship with Katherine had taken a sharp turn. A wave of helplessness washed over him as he grappled with the realization that he might not have the willpower to resist this provocative but sensitive woman. He realized it had been a long time since he had felt this way about someone; the way Katherine made his stomach do flips and his body tingle.

"Jack? Are you okay?" asked Katherine. Her face crumpled with confusion, her eyes darting around as if she feared Jack's disapproval of her plan.

Shaken out of his thoughts, Jack lied, "Sorry, Katherine. I was thinking about Bill." Then he smiled and saw Katherine's face light up. "There is nothing more in the world that I would like to do than spend six days alone on a boat with you."

Katherine leaned over the table, her touch gentle as she cupped his face in her hands. She pulled herself over to him, their eyes meeting, and kissed him softly on the lips. She separated his lips with her tongue and slipped it into his mouth, savouring the intimate moment.

Jack no longer had any uncertainties about what would happen next with Katherine.

Chapter 8

The wind was from the northwest, blowing at 15 knots, providing a perfect point of sail for heading south. Despite the lingering swells from Hurricane Sandy, the boat sliced through the water at a steady 8.5 knots. With a full mainsail billowing in the gentle breeze, they also deployed the massive Code Zero sail to maximize their speed. They were 200 miles south of Bermuda, just the two of them, as expected.

After leaving the St. Regis's casino in a taxi, Katherine and Jack motored the dinghy back to their anchored sailboat. Waves crashed over them, driven by the wind, leaving them soaked to the bone when they finally reached it. Despite the unexpected drenching from every enormous wave, they found themselves laughing uncontrollably. It wasn't as if the freezing cold salty water amused them, but more like they accepted the situation and laughed it off because they couldn't do anything to stop it. Their teeth chattered and their bodies trembled as they stepped into the sailboat's frigid interior.

"Why don't you have a hot shower to warm up?" suggested Jack.

Katherine wasted no time in removing her wet clothes, leaving them in a heap on the floor of the main salon as she stood naked. Drawing close to Jack, she wrapped her arms around him in a tight embrace. Her voice was husky, almost a purr, as she whispered, "Why don't you join me? Our long trip requires us to be mindful of our water usage... We need to make sure it lasts."

That was how it started. Jack spent the next two days with Katherine on the boat, anchored in the harbour, waiting for a weather window to head south. They filled the mornings with the soft murmurs of their whispered conversations and the warmth of their entwined bodies. They had provisioned enough food for 15 days for the three of them when they left Hampton, so they did not need to venture off the boat. Both Katherine and Jack were excellent cooks and took turns trying to impress each other with their culinary skills. The water maker replenished their water supply. They were completely self sufficient in their love nest and were happy just to spend the time together.

A text from Bill came in. "I've decided to stay here for a while." Jack read the message out loud to Katherine. "I hope you can manage without me."

"No worries," Jack typed back. "We were expecting you would want to stay. Call me when you need bailing out. I'll rush back to rescue you in the boat in, say... one to two weeks, but it could be in a month..."

"Don't you worry about me," was Bill's reply. "I always seem to land on my feet..."

The weather forecast showed a two-day break in the stormy weather, the perfect window for them to make their move. The skies were bright blue, the wind barely a whisper, as Katherine and Jack set off from Bermuda. They had to motor sail because the winds were light. By the afternoon of the first day, a crisp 15-knot breeze filled their sails, sending the boat skimming across the waves.

"This is heaven," said Katherine, lying naked on the foredeck in the bright sun. Jack rubbed the sun block into her back as she lay on the cushions. "The way I feel now, I could keep sailing forever. We could cross the Panama Canal and head for the South Pacific." Katherine sighed. "But we need to get back to our lives in Toronto, don't we?"

Jack thought about his surgical practice, the long hours, and the constant pressure to perform perfectly. The heavy call schedule at work made it nearly impossible for him to get three weeks off to sail to the Caribbean, as his colleagues had to shoulder an extra workload to cover for his absence. His last girlfriend, tired of his relentless work schedule, left him for a wealthy investment broker who oversaw a portfolio of $400 million. Over a year had passed since they'd broken up, and the ache of her absence still lingered within him. Glancing over at Katherine, he felt his life had turned around; the ache had disappeared.

Jack first met Katherine last summer when she sailed with him and six others on the weekly club races on Lake Ontario. She had mentioned she lived with her boyfriend, but Jack knew little more about her relationship. It was just a comment she made when they were drinking beer in the cockpit of the boat after a Wednesday night race.

"I can't race this Saturday," she had said. For Jack, that was a tremendous disappointment because she was the foredeck person and managed the spinnaker, the massive sail they used for downwind sailing. No one else on board could do it as well as she could. Although she was slender and delicate, she was incredibly swift. Her dependability and her infrequent mistakes made her a valuable asset. She rarely missed a race.

"Yikes," replied Jack. "Not sure we could manage this without you, Katherine. No one else can fly the spinnaker."

"My boyfriend has a final baseball game, and I said I would go." She smiled at Jack. "Let me see if I can get out of it. I would rather be sailing, anyway."

Katherine turned up for the Saturday race and never mentioned her boyfriend again. In fact, he knew little about her personal life. When it came time to choose the crew for the southern trip, Bill was an obvious choice, and after him, she was the next one he picked. Katherine didn't hesitate; she eagerly agreed to go.

"What about your work?" he asked her. "Could you get time off?"

"I'm self-employed," she replied. "I do psychotherapy as a family physician and haven't taken a holiday in more than a year. It is not a problem for me to take three weeks off from my patients."

That was as much as Jack knew about her until two days ago. He didn't want to venture into a conversation about "the boyfriend." Instead of interfering, he chose to let events take their course. Yet, if the bliss of this romance faded once they were back home... well, he didn't want to think about that right now. He desperately hoped she wouldn't bring it up, either.

"What's on your mind?" she asked, bringing him back to reality.

"I can't help but feel so lucky to be here on this boat with you, surrounded by nothing but the vastness of the water. I'm happy to live in the moment. This isn't something either of us can do with our busy schedules back home, so let's not think about it." With a soft smile, Jack leaned over and kissed her softly on the lips, her taste lingering long after he pulled away. Katherine gently caressed his chest with her warm fingertips. A feeling of arousal washed over Jack.

The sun's warmth softened on their skin. A gentle breeze whispered through Katherine's hair. The rhythmic rocking of the sailboat lulled them into a state of blissful contentment, making the moment a perfect one.

Chapter 9

Six days after leaving Bermuda, they arrived in Antigua at 3 a.m. The bright red and green navigation buoys guided them through Falmouth Harbour, helping them to avoid the dangerous reefs. They found a calm spot to anchor in 15 feet of water near the Cat Club. Aside from one stormy night with 30-knot squalls, the rest of the trip was uneventful, a pleasant journey with calm seas and clear skies. They divided the three-hour watches. While Katherine took her turn, Jack usually slept in the cockpit, prepared to spring into action if she needed him.

The early season meant few boats had arrived, making the anchorage near the Cat Club ideal. Although the darkness enveloped the harbour, all the anchored boats had their masthead lights switched on. Still, the boats were hard to spot on the water, so Katherine grabbed a powerful flashlight and went to the bow, guiding Jack with the walkie-talkie.

"I think this is a good spot," she instructed. "Head into the wind, and I'll drop the anchor."

Jack steered as directed and disengaged the engine. The boat's progress halted, and he could hear the anchor being dropped into the water. A whining sound emanated from the motor as it worked hard to rotate the windlass. Katherine let out 80 feet of chain. With the boat's Yanmar 86 hp engine humming at 1,500 rpm, and the engine in reverse, the boat churned backward as Jack carefully set the anchor in the soft, muddy bottom. They crawled into the cozy master cabin, exhausted from their journey, and fell asleep in each other's arms.

*****

The bright sunlight streaming through the hatch felt warm on Jack's face, rousing him from sleep at 9 a.m. He slipped out of bed, careful not to disturb Katherine's sleep, and tiptoed into the galley. The whirring of the generator filled the quiet air as he brewed his Nespresso. The rich scent of freshly brewed coffee must have woken Katherine up. Wrapping her arms around his midriff as he leaned over for his coffee, she whispered, "Welcome to Antigua, darling," her breath warm against his ear. Her lips brushed softly against his neck, a gentle kiss that sent shivers down his spine.

Jack passed the coffee cup to Katherine. "This is for you," he said. "I'll make another. Let's sit in the warm sun on the deck. I'll call Nelson's Dockyard and see when they are ready for us."

Jack grabbed the handheld VHF radio as they sat on the cushions of the foredeck and switched it on. Pressing the transmit button, he said, "Nelson's dockyard, Nelson's dockyard, Nelson's dockyard, this is sailing vessel *Ileana* on channel 68."

"*Ileana*, this is Nelson's Dockyard. Go to channel 11."

Jack changed the channel and said, "This is *Ileana* on channel 11. We have reservations. When should we come over?"

Jack's question hung in the air, unanswered. He was about to ask again when the radio suddenly buzzed to life, its static-ridden voice announcing, "Come over by 10 a.m."

"Will do. This is *Ileana* signing off," he finished.

Jack fired up the engine and started moving the boat forward. "A little more to starboard," came Katherine's voice over the walkie-talkie. She had positioned herself on the bow and was peering over the edge at the anchor chain. "Okay, anchor coming up." She pressed the button on the chain counter and the windlass creaked into motion, raising the anchor. It slid into the cradle with a resounding clunk.

They motored out of Falmouth Harbour, past the Pillars of Hercules, into English Harbour and onto Nelson's Dockyard. The harbour master skillfully guided them in, instructing them to drop their anchor three boat lengths before reversing into the stone dock, Mediterranean style.

"Throw me your stern lines," a familiar voice called out. Jack turned around, speechless. Bill was standing on the mooring wall, a wide grin on his face. "Don't be shy! Throw me your lines and welcome to Nelson's Dockyard."

"Bill!" Jack's voice echoed across the deck, a raw scream of disbelief, as he launched the rope towards his friend, who caught it with ease and secured it to the cleats with a snap. "Don't tell me you're already in trouble!" Jack exclaimed, his voice trembling slightly as he recovered from the shock of seeing him. "Hop on board while I take care of the paperwork at customs. I'll make you a coffee when I come back."

As Jack emerged from the customs office and returned to the boat, he found Bill deep in conversation with Katherine in the cockpit, their voices hushed and their expressions serious. With a furrowed brow, Katherine listened to Bill, concern written on her face. Both looked up when the sound of Jack's shoes on the swim platform interrupted their concentration.

"You'd better repeat to Jack what you just told me," said Katherine.

Jack felt his chest constrict, and the sudden, erratic thump of his heart against his ribs served as a harsh reminder of his returning anxiety. "Not sure if I want to hear about it." A nervous laugh escaped his lips. Jack noticed Bill's blank expression, a clear sign that something was amiss. "Alright, let's hear it," he sighed.

Bill reached for his cup of coffee and took a sip. "You are right about me being in trouble again," he said. "I'm staying at the Admiral's Inn, which is right there." He pointed to a stone building a few hundred feet away. Jack glanced at the stately hotel, which seemed quite small but elegant.

"I'm here with a woman I met at the casino, Simone," Bill continued. "My success clearly fascinated her, and she pushed me to keep winning big. After the casino shut down the first night at 3 a.m., she came back to the room with me. I honestly had no idea at the time, but her husband is a part owner of the company. We had spent the next few days in heavenly bliss before she dropped that bombshell on me."

Bill shook his head as if he was having difficulty believing this himself.

"She told me he was a mafia boss, and he pushed her around from time to time, sometimes slapping her. He had flown to Miami, but she wanted me to take as much cash as I could from the casino to get back at him before he returned. To make her getaway, she needed some money and asked if I could give her a portion of my winnings. I gave her $100,000."

"Bill, your usual modus operandi would have her miles away from you at this point in the relationship," said Jack. "What's different this time?"

"Yesterday morning, she received a text message from the manager of the casino, telling her that her life was in danger and she should hide." He stopped and took a deep breath. "The manager also said her husband wanted to kill me, too. I suggested we come here and told Simone that you'd know what to do. So we caught a flight to Atlanta and then a direct flight here last night."

Jack's eyes widened in shock. "Are you serious? Why in the world would I have any idea what to do?"

Bill smiled. "You have a history of coming to my aid whenever I'm in a difficult situation. Come. Meet Simone in person. Perhaps after meeting her, inspiration will strike. She's just over there." Bill waved to the hotel.

Jack shook his head. He glanced at Katherine. "What do you think?"

Katherine's gaze shifted from Bill's face to Jack's. "Jack, what Bill said is spot on; there's no way to stop yourself. You'll always bail out your friend. How about you go over and introduce yourself to her? Once you're done with that, come back and we can discuss the possibilities."

With a hint of reluctance, Jack got to his feet and joined Bill, who was already on the way to the Admiral's Inn. Squinting in the bright sun, he pulled out his Ray-Bans and slipped them on, then hurried after his friend. The dockyard was bustling with many sailors lingering around. Although it still was early morning, some were savouring the warmth of their coffee, while other sailors were enjoying the refreshing taste of rum punch. As Bill and Jack passed by, he caught snippets of murmured sailing phrases.

Upon entering Admiral's Inn, they ascended the creaky stairs to the door of the corner room, offering a picturesque view of Nelson's Dockyard and Jack's sailboat. Using his keycard, Bill opened the door with a soft click.

"Hi, honey..." Bill said.

Jack's heart skipped a beat when he saw what had interrupted Bill's sentence. Lying on the bed was a woman, her nightie covered in blood, with her throat slit.

Chapter 10

"Let's get the fuck out of here!" Bill shouted as he headed to the door to exit the room.

Everything had happened so quickly, but Bill's initial reaction was predictable. Having lived with Bill most of his life, Jack knew how he would respond. Although highly intelligent, too often he was impulsive.

"Wait!" yelled Jack. "Let's think this through." With a heavy sigh, Jack sat down on a chair at the small wooden desk, his eyes scanning the scene of carnage. He watched Bill's eyes darting around the room with a panicked expression on his face. Jack's thoughts were clear enough to know what needed to be done.

"Don't touch anything," Jack commanded. "I'm going to call 9-1-1. We need to call the police."

"That's crazy!" shouted Bill. "They'll think I did it." He headed for the door again.

"Imagine the police's reaction when they discover the man who paid for the room with his credit card had just been spotted running away. The situation will be worse for us. Plus, there are cameras everywhere in this hotel, so if they see you bolting out of here, they'll still assume you're guilty."

Bill looked defeated. He sat on the large suitcase resting on the luggage rack with a confused expression, as if to say Jack needed to come up with a better plan.

The shrill of sirens filled the quiet of the morning. Within five minutes, the ambulance and police had arrived. The authorities immediately ushered Jack and Bill into separate police cars and drove them to the main precinct in the capital city of St. Johns.

*****

Five hours later, they were still at the police station, the fluorescent lights buzzing overhead, the air thick with tension and the stench of stale coffee. Although they allowed Jack a bathroom break and brought him a bottle of water, he was hungry, having not eaten since the night before. Two different detectives had interviewed him, and then left him alone with his thoughts. Finally, one detective returned and said, "You can go now."

"That's it?" asked Jack. "You are not going to tell me what happened? I've been here for five hours. I need some answers!" Jack's voice was loud, and he even surprised himself. He knew he had to control his emotions with the police. "Sorry to yell," he mumbled. "I'm a little rattled by what I saw in the hotel room."

"That's understandable," said the detective. "We are still investigating, so I don't want you to leave Antigua for the next few days. We may have more questions. And I do not have any answers to share with you yet."

He led Jack to the precinct's main reception. Katherine was sitting in a chair. Seeing Jack, she leapt up and embraced him.

"Thank God you are okay," she cried. Tears streamed down her cheeks. "They told me what you found in the hotel room. So awful!" She sobbed and buried her head into Jack's shoulders.

After a minute, Jack whispered, "I need to find out what they've done with Bill. Sit here while I try to find out." Jack led her back to the chair and went to the reception desk.

The blank look from the officer at the desk suggested they were still interviewing him. "Do I need to get him a lawyer?" he asked.

After a long moment of silence, the officer looked up from what he was doing and said, "Look, I don't know what is going to happen to your friend. More questions than answers right now. That's usual at the beginning of an investigation. My advice? Go back to your boat. We'll be in contact. I'll have someone drive you." The officer reached under the desk. "Don't forget these," he said, and passed Jack his cell phone, wallet, and passport. "Thanks for cooperating with us."

Jack and Katherine were both lost in thought on the drive back to the boat, their silence heavy with unspoken words. They exchanged a knowing glance and agreed to keep quiet about the incident until the police were out of earshot. With a grateful nod to the officer for the lift back to the dockyard, they headed back to their boat, the sound of the lapping waves ringing in their ears, no longer peaceful but almost foreboding. Darkness had enveloped the boat. They flicked on the cockpit lights as they entered from the stern. Jack descended the stairs to the main salon and went to the fridge. Cool air rushed out as he opened the door. He grabbed two Heinekens and popped off the caps with a satisfying clink, then offered Katherine a bottle. She immediately took a big gulp. Then they settled into the cockpit cushions, debriefing about their experience.

"The police came to the boat and told me to get in the cruiser," said Katherine woefully. "I was so worried about you and that something awful had happened. They wouldn't tell me anything. I had to wait until I got to the precinct." Katherine dabbed at her cheek with a trembling hand, brushing away a single tear.

Jack recounted the scenario at the hotel and Bill's knee jerk reaction. "At the precinct, they kept me for a long time. I tried asking them what was going on, but they wouldn't offer any information. The officer's response to my question about whether Bill should get a lawyer was a chilling silence, the kind that makes your blood run cold. I hope he's okay."

"They want us to wait here for the next few days in case they have more questions," said Katherine. "What if it takes longer? Our flight back to Toronto is in four days."

"Let's plan on returning to Toronto when we are scheduled," said Jack. "Maybe in a few days, we can move the boat to Jolly Harbour on the west side of the island. The marina is way larger there, with a dock that will make it much easier for my dad to board and disembark his boat when he arrives next month. In the meantime, we've gotta eat. I'll get started on making dinner. We have some fresh tuna in the freezer, which I can thaw. I'll sear each side for 90 seconds, just like last time, creating that beautiful crust you love. We can add a squeeze of lemon and some sprigs of fresh dill for a bright, tangy flavour.

"I'll make some fluffy rice. That will go perfectly with the fish," said Katherine.

"Mmm. My stomach is growling so loudly, I'm sure the neighbours can hear it."

"I wasn't even hungry until you mentioned the fresh tuna. Sounds just what we need right now."

The tuna steaks sat in a Ziplock bag, thawing in the cool water. Once the rice was almost finished cooking, the tuna was ready to be added to the hot frying pan of melted butter. Three minutes ticked by, and then it was time to eat. They'd lit candles in the cockpit, where they felt the boat swaying slightly, the cool, salty air from the harbour mingling with the aroma of grilled fish. As they sipped the chilled pinot grigio, its refreshing taste and aroma heightened the enjoyment of their perfect dinner, a well-deserved moment of normality after the day's shattering events.

After dinner, Katherine rested her head on Jack's shoulder as they sat on the cockpit bench. Shadows from the candlelight flickered against the awning as she looked skyward. "Look at the stars," she sighed. "Even though today was a nightmare, I wouldn't want to be anywhere else in the world but here with you by my side. Is it possible for us to extend our stay here beyond four days? The past week in Bermuda with you, with its swaying palm trees, and the gentle rhythm of the waves, followed by six days at sea, with the salty air and the endless horizon... I could go on and on... It's been magical."

A wide grin spread across Jack's face. Such a surreal and wonderful past week made him finally grasp the meaning of "I thought I had died and gone to heaven." The contrast was glaring. The terrifying near-death experience during the storm near Bermuda, followed by the overwhelming happiness he found in Katherine's arms. He continued to avoid the subject of the boyfriend, preferring the comfortable silence they shared to the disappointment that lurked behind the word. He would rather continue down this blind, delusional path of perfect happiness.

"Can we keep that option open and see what develops over the next few days?" Jack asked. "Bill, no doubt, will throw a wrench into any plans we try to make, anyway. I don't want this time with you to end, either. It has been a very special."

Katherine leaned over and kissed him softly, her lips lingering on his. Jack's heart raced with familiar excitement, lost in the moment as the kiss stretched on. The candle flame danced and flickered, fighting against a sudden gust of warm wind that swept over their naked skin, snuffing out its light in a puff of smoke. Complete darkness enveloped them. The plastic dishes crashed onto the cockpit floor with a loud bang as Katherine clambered on top of Jack, but they barely noticed. The day's tension in the precinct, with its harsh lights and echoing voices, only served to heighten their attraction. After satisfying their hunger, they lay naked on the soft cushions of the cockpit bench, intertwined in a loving embrace. Exhaustion overcame them, and they both drifted off to sleep within minutes.

Sounds emanating from the swim platform jolted Jack awake. He instantly knew someone was there. He snatched the high-powered flashlight and, with a blinding flash, illuminated the intruder, at the same time startling Katherine awake.

"Don't shoot!" the voice cried out, its words trailing off into a raucous laugh that seemed to mock the fear it had instilled.

It was Bill.

Chapter 11

"They kept asking me the same questions," said Bill. "They wanted to know how I could win so much at the casino and why I would give Simone $100,000. When I explained I didn't know myself and that it was a spur-of-the-moment thing, they looked at me suspiciously."

Jack just shook his head and glanced at his watch. It was 3 a.m. The three of them were in the main salon, sitting around the table.

"Why did they let you go?" asked Katherine.

"They said they found some skin underneath Simone's nails and did a rapid DNA test. They did a buccal swab for my DNA as well. Turns out that skin belonged to someone black and obviously didn't match my DNA," explained Bill. "The only DNA match they identified from me was from the vaginal swab, a fact I had forewarned them about. Hotel surveillance footage revealed a muscular man of African descent entering the hotel 26 minutes before you and I did. The last image captured by the cameras showed him walking toward my and Simone's room before disappearing from view. They showed me the video and asked if I had ever seen him before and if I knew him."

"Huh," said Jack. "Did they think you might have hired him or something?"

"Well," replied Bill, "they let me go, so I don't think so." He pulled out his cell phone. "They demanded I show them all my recent communications, from calls to text messages and even emails, right there on my phone. The detectives logged onto my Google timeline, scrutinizing it for inconsistencies, and demanded an explanation. You, too, must have been subject to their 'investigation,'" he said, using air quotes. "Or should I say invasion of privacy? The detectives told me that when you mentioned visiting customs, they discovered you hadn't stopped by the room."

"You'd think they'd need a warrant to do that," said Katherine, her voice tinged with disbelief. "Antigua seems to make their own rules and do as they please."

Jack sighed. "It's late," he said. "Let's get some sleep. We'll be able to think more clearly about this tomorrow when we've had some rest."

*****

Mere hours later, Jack could smell the familiar rich aroma of Nespresso. That would mean that Bill was already up. He quickly got dressed and quietly left Katherine softly snoring. Sure enough, when he entered the galley, Bill was sitting at the table eating a bowl of cornflakes.

When he glanced up at Jack, his expression was one of curious confusion. His eyes were wide and his brow slightly furrowed. It startled Jack.

"So how did the emotionally insecure Jack end up with a gorgeous dish like Katherine?" he blurted out. "I recall something about her having a boyfriend?"

"Er, I..." stumbled Jack.

"I'm just giving you a hard time," Bill said, laughing. "I'm glad you hooked up with her. She is a lovely person."

Eager to get back to a more comfortable subject, Jack said, "What do you think we should do now?"

Bill's expression became more serious. "I think I'm next on the list to have my throat slit. I slept with the speargun loaded by my side last night."

"Are you out of your mind?" exclaimed Jack. "They say never load that thing out of the water. It could cause serious injuries! You are lucky you didn't skewer yourself."

"What's all the racket?" asked Katherine. She was standing at the door of the cabin wearing her nightie, rubbing her eyes briefly before she glanced at the two of them.

Jack felt a shiver run down his spine as he stared at her silhouette. The sunlight streamed through the cabin window, illuminated her face, framed by her ruffled hair, and highlighted her perfect figure. She looked like a goddess, stepping out of a dream. Her beauty held Jack's gaze captive, leaving him speechless and momentarily entranced.

"Jack is one lucky fella." Bill laughed, shaking his head. "Look at him drooling. He's all tongue-tied, just staring at you with his mouth agape. I knew I couldn't leave you two alone."

"Fuck off." Katherine laughed. "You're the lucky one having us save your ass." She crinkled her brow in thought. "We need to figure out what we are going to do."

The three of them sat at the table, a thick silence hanging in the air, each lost in their own thoughts. Finally, Katherine spoke first, her voice a welcome interruption to the quiet. "Let's leave for Jolly Harbour this morning. This place gives me the creeps now, after all that has happened. The detectives didn't explicitly prohibit movement, but their words were clear: stay put in Antigua. They can track us anyway if they want to find us."

"I need to get off the island," said Bill. "This guy is going to hunt me down like he did to Simone. It's just a question of time. I'm putting you all at risk by being in the same place as you. I need to get out of here quickly."

Jack thought about what Bill was saying. "I vote we head to St. Martin," said Jack, his eyes sparkling with anticipation. "I have to agree with Bill. If we don't act soon, that assassin is going to track us down before the day is out. I'll take care of customs so we can get on with our trip."

*****

The sound of the waves crashing against the hull of his boat was a welcome change for Jack, as he headed out of English Harbour and into the open sea, letting out a sigh of relief. As soon as the boat was free of land, he steered into the wind, the salty air filling his lungs as Katherine and Bill raised the mainsail. The wind was from the east, pushing them on their westward journey. They had to motor for the first 10 miles, battling the current, until they cleared the reefs and could finally set a course northwest toward St. Martin.

The wind filled the sails. Jack felt the boat come alive. It sliced through the water, the sound of the waves and the rhythmic creak of the rigging washing away the troubles of the past 24 hours. As the sun glinted off the waves and the seagulls called out from above, Jack could feel the day suddenly became brighter.

"It's amazing how the peace and beauty of being out on the ocean seem to make all our troubles disappear," Katherine whispered into Jack's ear as she leaned into his side while he steered. It's like she'd read his mind. They stood together, and a hush fell over them as they both absorbed the peaceful silence and serene beauty of the ocean. Jack's arm rested on Katherine's shoulder as they watched, in quiet awe, the relentless surge of the waves.

Bill emerged from the companionway and slumped onto the cockpit cushions, abruptly interrupting the moment and jolting Jack back to reality. "I've always been aware that a day would arrive when I'd have to disappear," Bill remarked, his tone hinting at the inevitability of his decision. "Wasn't sure if my struggle would be because of some chick, my love for playing cards, or me just pissing someone off. Life is meant for living. And I'm not ready to die yet." Bill was looking at his cell phone and scrolling. He stopped at a page and looked up at Katherine and Jack.

"The Las Vegas incident... That served as a catalyst for me to develop a plan for *this* scenario," he continued. "I have a new identity lined up. Doubt they'll find me. The St. Regis casino handed over $1 million to me, so they will have another reason to be after me as well."

Jack's jaw dropped. He looked at Bill in stunned silence. Bill seemed to always have a new scheme brewing, a back-up plan, a side project. His life was a constant dance of possibilities. Jack's life had a clear and easy path, unlike Bill's, which was filled with twists and turns. Once he collected his thoughts, Jack sighed and said, "Okay, Bill. Let's hear it."

"I'm moving to Little Rock, Arkansas!"

"What? Honestly, Bill—" Jack exclaimed.

"They tried to recruit me once I had finished my training. A definite 'maybe' was what I told them when they offered me a job in thoracic surgery a few years ago. I just got off the phone with them now and said I'm coming. With my American green card already approved, I can start work next month."

Jack continued his shocked stare at Bill. "You are a never-ending source of surprise for me," he said, shaking his head. "You clearly haven't thought this through. You can't just disappear and expect no one will find you. Just changing locations and thinking your past will not catch up to you is crazy."

Bill smiled. "Jack, you know I'm a survivor. It is what makes life worth living for me. If I drift into a routine of boredom with a lack of stimulation, that is when I feel pressure to slip back into my addictive behaviours. If I lived your life. Ha! I'd be dead by now. Trust me, friend. This is the right thing for me—right now."

Jack laughed a loud, raucous laugh. "I would take my boring life over your constant drive for unhealthy excitement any day." Jack felt his face soften as he said, "You know I'll help you, Bill. What do you want me to do?"

Bill told him.

Chapter 12

When they arrived in St. Martin, an impenetrable darkness shrouded Marigot Bay. The faint glow of the stars illuminated the water. The twinkling lights on shore reflecting off the sea illuminated the anchored boats, making it easier to find a suitable spot to anchor. Katherine walked to the bow of and over the walkie-talkie, instructed Jack to manoeuvre the boat while she released 80 feet of anchor chain, sending the anchor plummeting down into the 15-foot-deep water.

Bill had offered to make dinner that night. "My WORLD-FAMOUS stuffed PEPPERS!" he said, his voice thick as the aroma of savoury spices filled the galley. "I'll make six of them... I figure both of you will only eat one, which means the rest will be for me. Since I suspect this may be our last meal together for a while, let's savour every bite and make it unforgettable."

The meal was spectacular. The aroma of the roasted meats and spices filled the air, accompanied by a symphony of flavours that danced on their tongues. They uncorked a bottle of Chianti, the aroma rich and inviting. Then it was time to discuss how to help Bill start his new chapter in his life. The morning would bring the necessary, though tedious, process of checking in with customs, a bureaucratic hurdle, before their journey could truly begin. Bill had booked a flight to New York City at 2 p.m. the following afternoon. He was excited about the trip ahead.

With heavy eyelids and weary sighs, they tumbled into bed after midnight, the boat settling into a quiet stillness around them. A soft thud, barely audible, somehow woke Jack from a deep slumber. It was a muffled *thwack*, the distinctive sound of an inflatable dinghy bumping against the boat's hull. Jack glanced at his watch, its face gleaming 2 a.m. in the dim light. With a worried sigh, Jack untangled himself from Katherine, the sheets clinging to his legs as he quietly slipped on his shorts. He heard the soft thud of footsteps above him on the boat deck. Someone had come aboard.

A dull, red glow emanated from the electrical panel, the sole light source in the main salon, casting long, distorted shadows and humming faintly. Jack held his breath as he scanned the area, his hands instinctively clenching, hoping to spot something he could use to defend himself. The only thing on the counter was the empty Chianti bottle, its faint scent of wine still lingering. *This will have to do.* Jack had left the companionway open last night, letting in a cool breeze that carried the sea's salty scent.

He stood at the companionway, the Chianti bottle poised above his head, the cool glass slick against his skin, ready to defend the main salon from the intruder climbing the stairs. Though partially hidden in the shadows, the element of surprise would be his greatest weapon. As the intruder made his way down the steps, Jack saw a worn leather sandal on a man's left foot, the sole scuffed and dusty. With a start, he saw a head emerge from the shadows, dark eyes gleaming, his skin the colour of rich earth.

The man looked right at Jack, who made his move. The glint of the glass bottle in the dim light reflected menacingly as he swung it. Jack missed. The intruder knocked the bottle from his hand. It crashed to the floor with a loud bang, sending shards of glass scattering.

A brutal punch connected with Jack's jaw, sending him sprawling backward onto the polished floor of the main salon. The impact of his weight was a distinct thud in the sudden silence. With a quick, violent movement, the man leaped into the main salon and onto Jack's chest. Jack saw the glint of a knife in his right hand. He wriggled, but the man's firm grip held him fast, the pressure tightening with each attempt to escape. Jack was trapped in a vise-like scissors grip. A cruel smile twisted the intruder's lips, the corners of his mouth tugging upward into a chilling expression. He raised the knife. The steel reflected in the cabin's red light. Jack knew he intended to plunge it into his neck and braced himself. Suddenly, a scream escaped the man's lips, and the knife clattered to the floor.

Jack saw the man clutching his abdomen, his face pale and drawn. A metal spear, cold and sharp, was protruding from his belly. He grasped it with a trembling hand. The man got to his feet, his breath caught in his throat. With disbelief written on his face, he slowly turned around. Bill stood behind him, facing the intruder. He held the empty speargun heavily in his hands, ready to use the barrel as a club. A faint metallic tang of the blood clinging to the shaft hung in the air. With a sudden burst of speed, the man turned and ran up the narrow companionway stairs, each step reverberating in the quiet space.

With a sharp tug, the line attaching the spear to the gun went taut, yanking the weapon from Bill's hands. As Jack watched, the shaft disappeared up the companionway, still connected to the spear in the man's abdomen. The metallic clang echoed as it banged against the stairs, then vanished into the darkness of the cockpit. A loud splash, like a small whale breaching, resounded from the port side of the boat, followed by the metallic clang of the speargun hitting the fibreglass hull before it too went over the side of the boat. Jack heard another splash, this one softer as the attached barrel of the gun flew into the water.

Jack briefly glanced at Bill, his eyes reflecting the urgent anticipation before they both raced toward the cockpit. He focused the bright beam from the flashlight as it cut through the water's inky blackness, revealing shimmering reflections. The man was thirty feet out, desperately pulling himself toward the dinghy, his grip slipping on the slick inflatable rubber tubing. It was obvious the spear, embedded deep in his abdomen, made it impossible for him to climb aboard. He groaned in pain, churning up the water as he floundered. The dinghy, tossed gently by the waves, continued its slow drift toward the shore.

An ominous dark fin, slicing through the water with a disturbing silence, appeared, heading towards the bleeding man. A flurry of other sharks arrived, their movements causing a maelstrom of churning water. A bloodcurdling scream sliced through the quiet morning, a chilling alarm across the still bay. Silence followed, interrupted by the frantic, thrashing sound of the water. Sixty seconds later, an unnerving quiet filled the air, thick and heavy like a blanket. The empty dinghy quietly drifted towards the shore. Jack and Bill stared, mouths agape, imagining the gruesome scene that must have unfolded underwater.

Katherine had joined them by now. Jack, still shaking from the experience, clung to her. "We had an intruder," he explained when he could get the words out. "Bill shot him with the speargun and he jumped into the water. The blood must have attracted the sharks."

"I heard him scream," said Katherine.

Bill continued to search the waters for signs of the man. Except for the occasional ripple from a gentle breeze, the water lay still, a mirror to the sky above. No sign of the man remained.

"What should we do now?" asked Bill, nervously chewing on his lip.

Jack looked out over the water. "I'm not sure," he said. "We have a slip reserved at the marina. We should probably wait until morning to decide if going to the police is the best course of action, after we have had some time to think this through. Since we lack the legal documentation to be in this country, our access to the shore is prohibited until the customs authorities have processed our entry."

Jack thought for a second. "Any chance he was the same man you saw in the video at the police station?"

"Hard to be sure, but I think so," said Bill, still looking at the water and the beam from the flashlight. "I wonder if he was on his own."

The three of them stood around in stunned silence as they thought about that possibility. "I have an idea," said Katherine. "St. Barts is 20 miles away. We could be there in three hours. No one knows we are here. We should turn off the automatic identification system, so we remain invisible. Bill could take a commuter flight to St. Martin in the morning and catch his flight to New York City in the afternoon."

Bill and Jack, with no hesitation or delay, immediately agreed. Having started the engine, Jack watched as Katherine expertly raised the anchor. Within a mere 10 minutes of their decision to depart, they were already speeding across the open ocean. The autohelm diligently steered their course toward the idyllic shores of St. Barts. The chart plotter had them arriving just as the sun was rising.

Chapter 13

Unsure of what to do next now that Bill was gone, Katherine and Jack sat together on the cushioned bench in the cockpit, slowly sipping their ice-cold beers. As the sun prepared to dip below the horizon within the next 60 minutes, the breathtaking azure waters of the Caribbean Sea enveloped them on all sides. They gazed toward the west. The faintest whisper of wind brushed their skin, a gentle caress barely felt. Good fortune had made their arrival in the picturesque Anse de Colombier bay in St. Barts even more pleasant when they found an available mooring ball. Despite there being at least 20 other boats either anchored or secured to mooring balls, the beach's lack of road access contributed to a sense of seclusion and safety.

"What do you think happened to the intruder?" asked Katherine.

"The most likely explanation is that he didn't survive," Jack said grimly, his voice barely a whisper, "but you can never tell with these things. The beach wasn't far, a few hundred yards at most, and I thought he might attempt to swim. Local and national news remain strangely quiet. Because shark attacks are so infrequent, they usually generate global news coverage and widespread interest. If he had died, there would be some evidence, an arm or foot would wash on shore."

"Assuming he survived," Katherine mused, "how would he account for that spear embedded in his stomach? The sight alone would be gruesome."

A low, warm chuckle rumbled in Jack's chest. "I warned Bill about that speargun. On the information package, printed in bold red letters, is a warning against loading the gun on land. They described abdominal injuries as being a risk when trying to load the spear into the heavy rubber sling, which could cause death."

"So maybe he's still alive," Katherine sighed. "At least we can be certain he won't come after us. The silence is a welcome relief after his menacing presence. Knowing that allows for a slight easing of tension. I can relax a bit now."

A pensive stillness settled over Katherine as she paused, her mind adrift in a sea of thoughts. Jack studied her, his eyes lingering on the details of her face. He worried about how the trauma of Simone's death and the brutal boat attack would affect her in the coming days. The vivid images, the sounds of screams, the lingering smells of blood and fear.

As a surgeon, he had witnessed terrible complications like infections and organ failure following surgery, leaving him with a profound sense of responsibility and feelings of helplessness. Often, the weight of his responsibilities from a terrible surgical outcome would settle on his chest, making sleep elusive and his nights restless. However, to cope with the devastating event, many surgeons compartmentalized their emotions, a common coping mechanism involving the detachment of feelings from the experience. The surgeon, freed from the paralyzing fear, was able to concentrate on the next patient, making the life-saving decisions that were necessary, with confidence and steady hands. He desperately hoped Katherine possessed the same uncanny ability with the last attack. He'd witnessed firsthand this skill with her during the storm sailing near Bermuda.

Jack saw Katherine's lips curve upward, her eyes twinkling as a smile blossomed across her features. "Do you think Bill made it to New York City?" she asked, anxiously twisting a lock of her hair as if trying to make herself think of something else.

Jack glanced at his watch. "He's going to land in about an hour, and then on to Little Rock by about 10 p.m. He promised to text us when he arrives in Arkansas. We both know we have not seen the last of Bill."

"Although he has been a nuisance, I'm going to miss him," said Katherine. "He has a certain charm, and it's easy to understand how women want to reach out and help him. He is like a lost puppy, waiting to be picked him up and squeezed."

Jack thought about that for a moment and shook his head. "What do you think should we do? If it were up to me, I would rather spend the rest of the winter here with you. We could visit

Guadeloupe, Martinique, St. Lucia, and then head further south to Grenada. But... our flight back to Toronto leaves in three days."

Katherine sighed, "I suppose you're right. We should probably head on home. Any thoughts on where we should leave the boat for your dad?"

"We could go back to Antigua and leave the boat in Jolly Harbour. That would be the safest option. We could pull up our anchor in the morning and be there before the sun sets tomorrow night, although it would be nice to spend a few more days here." Jack glanced at the beauty surrounding him.

"Let's stay here for another day," suggested Katherine. "We can go snorkelling. I think it would be good to spend the day just hanging out and relaxing. We could leave for Jolly Harbour the day after tomorrow and still make our flight back to Toronto."

Day's end was approaching. The sun began its descent below the horizon, painting the sky with vibrant hues that shifted from pale orange to fiery red and finally settled into a breathtaking violet hue. They remained seated in thoughtful silence. Just as the sun disappeared, a fleeting green flash suddenly appeared. A second passed and in the blink of an eye, it had vanished. Jack and Katherine silently looked at one another, their gazes locked.

"I don't believe it!" Katherine finally exclaimed. "We just saw the green flash! You know what that means, don't you?"

Jack smiled. "It's said that once you've seen the green flash, you will never again go wrong in matters of the heart."

Gently, Katherine cupped Jack's head within her hands, her lips then softly pressing against his in a tender kiss. Overcome with emotion, she unexpectedly wept uncontrollably. "There is something I need to tell you." As she sobbed, tear after tear streamed down her face, each one a testament to the overwhelming emotion she felt. Katherine opened her mouth as if to speak, but she paused, seemingly reconsidering her words before they could leave her lips. With a gentle touch of his index finger, Jack carefully wiped away the tears that streamed down her face.

An unexpected surge of emotion, a feeling so intense that it caused Jack's heart to skip a beat, rushed over him. *I had a feeling that this was going to happen eventually, and unfortunately, my premonition came true. She is planning on discussing with me some details about the young man whom she describes as her boyfriend. I knew this was too good to be true.* A profound and overwhelming sense of hopelessness and despair washed over Jack, weighing heavily on his spirit. The depth and speed with which he fell for Katherine were unprecedented in his life. He was completely smitten. It was going to be incredibly difficult to recover from this. A major hurdle in his life. A constricting feeling, a tightness in his chest, made it difficult for Jack to breathe. He felt a sense of pressure and became overwhelmed with emotion, struggling to suppress the tears that welled up in his eyes and fighting back the urge to cry.

Taking a deep breath, Katherine slowly turned and gazed at Jack, her eyes meeting his. "I have never experienced such profound feelings for another person in my entire life. I could easily — and happily—spend the rest of my days with you. Seeing that amazing green flash, a rare and beautiful phenomenon, only solidified and deepened the emotions I've already felt so strongly for you. Jack, I worry things might be different when we go back. That's why I'd rather stay longer here with you. I don't want the magic to disappear."

With a renewed sense of confidence, Jack watched her face turn to his as his reservations faded into nothingness. An enormous sigh of relief escaped his lips, a wave of tension finally receding from his body. "I feel the same way about you," he whispered. "To be honest, and I must confess this, I was under the impression that your statement was going to include a comment about a boyfriend you left behind at home. I recall a previous conversation where you mentioned something about a boyfriend and attending his baseball game."

Katherine stared at Jack with an incredulous look, then smiled, shaking her head. "That was over six months ago!" She laughed. "When I told him I was going sailing with you that weekend instead of watching his stupid baseball game, he moved out. I haven't seen him since. In all honesty, we were always a poor match from the beginning, and it was probably inevitable that things wouldn't work out between us. The more time we spent together, the more it became clear that his focus was entirely on himself. Over the time we spent together, he showed less and less concern for me."

With a sigh of contentment, Katherine snuggled against Jack. Now that the sun had dipped below the horizon, the world became dark. The adrenaline rush of leaving St. Martin that morning had worn off hours ago, leaving only exhaustion. The quiet solitude, juxtaposed with the boisterous antics of earlier, settled around them like a comforting blanket. Overwhelmed by fatigue, their bodies ached, and their eyelids felt heavy. Katherine's fingers intertwined with Jack's, pulling him towards the master cabin, the low creak of the door a prelude to their arrival. They crawled into the cool sheets, sinking into a deep sleep within two minutes.

*****

The midday sun beat down as they finally emerged from the cabin, sweat beading on their foreheads. Another perfect day in paradise. The turquoise water sparkled. The breeze felt soft on their skin, the warm sun luxurious. They were ravenous, eating eggs Benedict, the rich yolks offset by lemony hollandaise. Glasses of bubbly Prosecco, with its delicate floral notes, completed the perfect brunch.

"Let's try our luck at snorkelling," suggested Katherine.

With a splash, they dove off the swim platform, the warm water enveloping them as they quickly donned their fins, masks, and snorkels. The vibrant coral reef, teeming with colourful fish, lay just 15 feet below the surface and about 50 metres from where the boat was anchored. As they snorkelled towards the reef, the clear blue water shimmered, its warmth a welcome sensation against Jack's skin swaddled inside a wetsuit.

A moray eel, its mottled skin glistening, poked its head from a crevice in the coral reef, its eyes fixed on Jack and Katherine. It was assessing them as potential prey. A puffer fish, round and spiky, floated by lazily, its movements slow and deliberate. In the blink of an eye, the moray eel shot from its coral crevice, its jaws snapping shut around the unsuspecting puffer fish: a flash of teeth and scales, then nothing but the disturbed water.

With a gasp, Jack recoiled from the eel. Its sudden, powerful movement sent shivers down his spine, a chilling reminder of the creature's predatory nature. A large turtle, its shell gleaming like polished jade, floated by the moray eel, seemingly unconcerned, a silent boast of its impenetrable armour. Jack glanced at Katherine. Her eyes were bulging, her face pale, having watched this underwater massacre play out in front of their eyes. When they ascended to the surface, the smell of seawater and something vaguely fishy hung in the air.

"Wow," exclaimed Katherine once they'd swum back to the boat. "That was the most amazing snorkelling adventure ever! That poor puffer fish was in the wrong place at the wrong time."

"Just like us with Bill," said Jack, laughing. "Speaking of our troublemaker friend, we've heard nothing from him. Last night, I attempted to call him but he didn't answer. I sent a WhatsApp message and an email, but still nothing. I hope he's okay."

Katherine wrinkled her brow. "Bill's a survivor. He's in survival mode now, so I predict we won't hear anything. I wouldn't worry."

Jack paused, a thoughtful expression on his face, considering the implications. "I have a feeling that Bill is in major trouble. Despite the warning signs, he's heading down the path less travelled, the wrong one. Any attempts to help him are useless. His fate is sealed. He holds a unique perspective on how to navigate life, shaped by his own experiences and values. I have a strong feeling that some shocking news about him is going to break soon, something that will send ripples through our lives."

Chapter 14

Bursting through the apartment door, Jack excitedly shouted to Katherine, "I heard from Bill!" his voice resonant with the thrill of the news.

With a startled expression, Katherine looked up from the kitchen stove, the clatter of pans momentarily silenced. "No way!" she replied, a disbelieving laugh escaping from her lips. "Tell me the tale behind it!"

Although it was 8 p.m. in Toronto, the sky still held the lingering light of a summer evening, painting the cityscape they could see through the apartment's floor-to-ceiling windows in soft hues of orange and pink. Even while cooking, they could watch the sunset and from every room in their apartment. The colours were amazing. It felt like a lifetime since they'd last seen Bill, though the calendar only marked six months. With the sailboat safely left at Jolly Harbour Marina for his father all those months ago, the warm Caribbean sun was a distant memory. Within a week of returning to Toronto, Katherine had moved in with Jack. The transition back into the routine of their lives was seamless, like a familiar song resuming after a brief pause. The comfort of habit quickly settled over them. Months flew by in a blur of activity and fleeting moments.

"Here, I'll show you." Jack's fingers fumbled with his phone. He opened WhatsApp, the screen illuminating his face in the bright kitchen light. A picture appeared of Bill, his hands on his hips, looking stern in his rumpled army fatigues. The stark statement below the picture simply read, "Off to Iraq," followed by a message: "I'll call you tonight."

Katherine seemed puzzled. "What happened to the dream job in Little Rock, Arkansas?"

Jack reread the cryptic message, a frown furrowing his brow as he shrugged his shoulders in confusion. "This is what it was like living with him for all those years. He'd disappear, then return with a wild grin, his clothes dusty and torn, spinning a fantastic yarn about his exploits. I really hope he calls us this time. It's been too long."

Katherine went back to her meal prep. Jack loved it when she cooked. Living as a couple, dinner time was when they had their most meaningful conversations. The aroma of garlic and herbs filled the air as Katherine and Jack sat down to a beautiful dish of fettuccine and oven-baked salmon, the fish's skin glistening. The dinner was delicious. As they reminisced about Bill, a half-finished bottle of chilled St. Margarite pinot grigio sat between them, its subtle fruity aroma mingling with the scent of old books and leather.

"It's weird that we never found out about what happened to that guy who attacked us. Do you think he could have made it to shore? Or did the sharks finish him off?"

"I've been searching the internet endlessly for a story about a shark attack in Marigot Bay—nothing!" Jack exclaimed, running a hand through his already messy hair. "No one could have survived a feeding frenzy like that. That scream—that desperate, agonizing sound. I'll never forget it." He shivered. "Then that thick, suffocating silence that descended. It felt like a scene out of a horror movie. I'm glad we hightailed it out of there."

"Me too." Katherine drained the rest of her wine.

"I expected a news report to find some trace of him, a piece of clothing or a personal belonging washed ashore. But nothing. No news items mentioned anything at all. The events seem unreal, as if we fabricated the whole thing in our imaginations."

"I didn't see him attack you," said Katherine. "But the knife he left behind was real. I threw it overboard so he couldn't grab it again."

Jack was putting away the last of the dinner plates in the dishwasher when his phone rang. A picture of Bill appeared for a video chat on WhatsApp. Jack's breath hitched. A flutter of anxiety took hold as he opened the phone, his heart quickening its pace.

"Bill!" screamed Jack. "I don't believe it! What the fuck? You disappear for six months and then send a cryptic message about going to Iraq."

A stony silence on the other end met his outburst. Jack continued, his voice softening. "Sorry; I missed you, man. Is everything okay? What's the story this time? Are you in trouble? Of course you are. Why else would you be going to the armpit of the world?" Jack realized he was babbling and stopped talking.

"Jack," replied Bill, smiling. "It's great to see you, too. I'll tell you my story, but first I gotta know something. What happened with you and that gorgeous dish, Katherine, after you came back? Did she go back with her boyfriend and dump you?"

"That gorgeous dish is standing right here beside him," said Katherine with a scowl on her face. "If *you* hadn't dumped us, *you* would have known this. Geez, Bill. Why didn't you call us?"

Jack watched Bill's hand move to his chin to scratch his beard, the familiar gesture preceding a torrent of words. "Honestly, I wasn't sure how much danger I was in... and I wanted to shield you from any potential fallout if someone was still hunting me." The air crackled with unspoken tension as he weighed Bill's words. "I caused you two enough grief in Antigua and St. Martin." Bill paused. "So Iraq—"

"Before you go further, I'm going to give you some unsolicited advice," said Jack. "Don't go there. The desert will bore you to death, and you'll have an awful experience."

Bill smiled. "Too late. I signed a one-year contract with the army to be the civilian army surgeon at the forward operating base of Abu Ghraib. My salary is $500,000 for the year. However, I'm stuck on base. They tell me that too many times surgeons in the past refuse to return after a leave, and they don't want to take any chances with me."

"They know you well," quipped Katherine.

"Little Rock VA Hospital was very good to me. I had a great salary with benefits, four weeks of holidays per year, reasonable hours, until..." Bill stopped speaking. "It wasn't my fault. The wife of the CEO had a thing for me. She and I went to Atlantic City together, and I lost a bit of the money I made in Bermuda. Maybe I lost my Midas touch with blackjack, or maybe she was just bad luck for me..." Bill looked down at his hands. "The CEO fired me when we returned. They can do that in the US, you know. Judges routinely throw out wrongful dismissal suits against powerful bosses from us lowly workers."

"Bill," said Jack, shaking his head. "You idiot. Why Iraq?"

"I'm without a job. Following the CEO's smear campaign on LinkedIn, I'm certain my job search will be fruitless. They were, essentially, my only option for employment. Nobody else will take a chance on me. I wanted to tell you I love you and not to worry about me. We can stay in touch with WhatsApp and email. I'll be there for 12 long months." Bill's voice caught in his throat, his eyes welling up slightly.

With a shared, unspoken tension, Jack and Katherine gazed at the phone's glowing screen, the silence punctuated only by their breaths. The sight of Bill, so visibly upset—his shoulders shaking, his breath hitching—was something Jack couldn't recall ever seeing. His go-to method for handling tough decisions was to dismiss them with a flick of the wrist, avoiding the tough conversations. Today was different. A knot formed in Jack's stomach. He knew this call was a farewell, perhaps their last.

"Bill, come back to Toronto," pleaded Jack. "You can do some emergency on call while you search for a job. I'll talk to our chief of surgery, Larry Klapman. He already knows you. We can work something out. You don't have to go."

Bill kept quiet for a few moments. "There are some things I haven't told you. I don't think I'll ever be able to come home. It would not be safe for me... or you if I returned. I'll be okay. I always land on my feet. We'll keep in touch."

"Whoa, Bill!" shouted Jack. "What haven't you been telling me? You can't just leave it like that. What the fuck is going on?"

"It's better you don't know," said Bill. "I'll let you know when things get sorted out. We'll have a laugh about it over some of my world famous stuffed red peppers." Bill smiled faintly. "Look, I have to go now. I just wanted to talk with you before I left. I love you, man."

Silence replaced the voice on the other end as the call ended abruptly. Katherine and Jack stared at each other.

"It was almost as if he was calling to say we'll never see each other again," said Katherine wistfully. "I hope he's okay."

A frown furrowed Jack's his brow as he considered the implications. Despite his accurate belief about his career options, Bill's resilience ensured he always landed on his feet, bouncing back from any setbacks. Yet there was a strange tenseness in his demeanour, a subtle shift in his usual easygoing nature. "This time, I think it's different," Jack said. "I don't think he is okay."

"Maybe a year in Iraq away from danger is what he needs most right now," said Katherine. "I saw a documentary about Abu Ghraib on the news. Layers of security fortify the forward operating base. It's the most secure facility globally. He will stay out of trouble. I think it's the best thing for him right now."

"Huh," said Jack. "Maybe you are right. No one can get to him there. One less thing we need to worry about with him for the next year."

Chapter 15

A crisp wind filled Jack's sails as he finished the Wednesday night club race. The crew roared with laughter and cheers, their voices loud as they crossed the finish line, having narrowly beaten *Bitter End* by a hair's breadth to win first place, their joyous shouts echoing across the water. It was their best race of the season yet.

The sudden ring of his phone sliced through the sounds of the waves and wind. He didn't recognize the number, but answered anyway.

"Jack, is that you?" It was a woman's voice, tinged with worry.

A cacophony of wind and sail filled the air, making conversation difficult. Yet he recognized the voice immediately. It was that distinctive, gravelly tone that he knew so well. Bill's mom.

"Ruby," replied Jack. "Is everything okay?"

The wind howled, and the sails creaked, making it hard for Jack to hear if there was silence on the other end, or if someone was trying to speak. "Ruby?" This time, a muffled, heartbreaking sob reached him through the phone line. Jack motioned to Katherine to take the helm, the sounds of the lake fading as he descended the companionway into the main salon's stillness.

"Ruby," asked Jack, "what's the matter?"

Ruby stopped sobbing long enough to gasp, "Bill's dead," her voice raw with grief, the unspoken details heavy in the air. "The army MPs who came to the house to deliver the news say he died in his sleep. Jack, they're returning in two hours. Can you come by the house and talk with them? I don't think I can manage..." Her voice faded, replaced by the soft sound of her weeping.

Jack, speechless with shock, finally managed to croak out a barely audible, "Ruby... I'm so sorry. Of course I'll be there."

*****

"Jack, no way a 32-year-old man dies in his sleep," said Katherine in the car on the way to Ruby's in Brantford. "The story must be much deeper than that."

"With Bill," replied Jack, his voice tight with frustration, "the true story may never make any sense. Even if we can discover what happened, the details will be too fragmented and unreliable."

The drive to Brantford took an hour and a half, passing fields of golden wheat and the occasional sleepy farmhouse. A pensive silence hung in the air between Jack and Katherine. His mind was a chaotic swirl of emotions: disbelief warring with profound sadness at the loss of his best friend, his heart heavy with grief and confusion. The pressure mounted as they approached the exit to Ruby's. A knot formed in his stomach as he anticipated the MPs' statements, his thoughts jumbled and unclear.

A government vehicle was in the driveway at Ruby's. Jack rang the doorbell, and Ruby flung open the door, red-eyed and tearful. "The MPs are already here," she said. "Can you speak with them?"

The moment Jack entered, two large, stern-looking army MPs straightened from their seats in the living room, a silent challenge in their eyes. Over their army fatigues, both wore MP armbands displayed prominently on their right biceps. Their crisp, clean uniforms bore the names Jose Cortes and Samuel Arnold, embroidered in dark lettering.

"We are so sorry for your loss," said Samuel.

Jack and Katherine sat down on the sofa. "Can you tell us what happened?" asked Jack.

Samuel glanced over at Jose before he spoke. "Here's what we know. When he didn't arrive to perform the hernia operation, the operating room staff made a call to his room. His unanswered phone set our emergency response in motion. We found him in his bed, the room undisturbed, no signs of a struggle. When we checked his vital signs, there was no pulse, no breathing, and his skin was cold. We summoned a medic, who confirmed our initial assessment, pronouncing him dead. Based on the body temperature charts, rigor mortis, and lividity, it appeared he had died approximately 12 hours before discovery."

Katherine had been observing the two MPs. "You are not telling us everything," she said pointedly. "A healthy 32-year-old man does not just die in his sleep. What else did you find?"

Samuel's eyes darted nervously to Jose. His silence spoke volumes. A palpable tension hung in the air. Jack immediately picked up on their hesitation, sensing a subtle shift in their body language. He heard the uncertainty in Samuel's voice, confirming Katherine's suspicions. "You need to tell us what you know," said Jack. "We are going to find out, eventually. You need to be honest with us. What did you find?"

Samuel gave a deep, shaky sigh. "The medical office instructed us to wait until they had finished the report before telling you... Jose and I were the ones who found him. Swear that you will keep this secret between us and never reveal its source." Samuel locked eyes with both Katherine and Jack, their faces full of worry. With a brief nod of understanding, they acknowledged each other.

"We found a needle in his left arm attached to an empty syringe," said Samuel. "We suspected he overdosed. There was an empty propofol vial and the needle cover nearby. The operating room staff corroborated our suspicions. They'd reported two vials of the anesthetic had gone missing from the room Bill had been operating in the day before."

Jack's heart skipped a beat. "There is no way he would have done that on purpose," he said. "As far as I know, he had been clean for the past few years..." He exhaled deeply. "... having replaced his drug addiction with gambling."

Samuel shook his head, his expression filled with sorrow. "The medical examiner recommended reaching out to his previous workplace to investigate the possibility of a history of drug addiction. We contacted the Little Rock VA hospital to inform them of his sudden and unexpected passing. Although they had been conducting an investigation into the missing fentanyl from the OR pharmacy, focusing their suspicions on him, they lacked sufficient evidence to definitively conclude that he was the perpetrator of the theft."

As Jack fell silent, the room's sounds seemed to grow louder, his quietness heavy with significance. Bill's relapse was a very real possibility. The high recidivism among drug users, marked by a cycle of relapse and drug theft, was a constant, grim reminder of substance abuse's devastating impact on lives. Yet something didn't add up. The sheer carelessness of Bill's actions, leading to his own demise, was something Jack found utterly impossible to accept. He was a thrill-seeker, always pushing his limits, yet his calculated risks made him seem almost supernatural.

Still, it made little sense to Jack. With his cunning mind, Bill was far too clever to orchestrate his own demise. A nagging feeling persisted—there had to be more to the story, more than just the surface details suggested.

*****

The air hung heavy with the scent of lilies and regret as Bill lay in repose at Thorpe Brothers Funeral Home. His face had almost an artificial look, with his eyes closed and a slight smile—or possibly a smirk—with the corners of his mouth turned up. To remember his love of Coca-Cola, someone had shoved a crumpled empty can into the front pocket of his army fatigues, a small, yet meaningful gesture of his love of life.

The US government had organized a full military funeral, complete with the crisp crackle of an American flag being folded, the mournful sound of bugles, and the sharp precision of salutes. Since Bill had died on the army base, they considered his death to be in the line of duty. A collective sob escaped Katherine, Jack, and Ruby as the casket descended, the metallic clang of the lowering straps. This new feeling of emptiness in their hearts flooded over them with sadness over their faces. Jack missed his lifelong friend's booming laughter, the way he always knew how to make him smile, the shared memories that felt distant now.

At Ruby's request, Jack was to give a short impromptu talk during the funeral while standing at a makeshift podium.

Because he hadn't prepared a speech, his comments were spontaneous. "Bill was my best friend," said Jack, choking back his tears. "Growing up together, we created lasting memories, our childhoods intertwined. He was like the brother that I had always wished for but never actually had. I have a secret to tell you, Ruby, that I've never shared before. Once, after being inspired by Mark Twain's *Huckleberry Finn*, we embarked on a memorable hike to the Grand River. The goal of our expedition was quite simple. We aimed to build a raft that would successfully carry us downstream on the river. The four empty water containers we were carrying each could hold twenty-five litres. You know—those familiar jugs for water coolers. Along with that, our meagre supplies consisted of 30 feet of rope, a few planks of wood, and a single paddle we had to share. Having ventured into the middle of the river, we found our raft disintegrating, forcing us into a desperate swim for survival. Yet the amount of laughter we shared that day was unprecedented, and our jokes about having cheated death only added to the joyous occasion."

Overwhelmed by grief, Jack paused, his shoulders shaking slightly, needing a moment for the intense wave of emotion to subside. "Bill was not so lucky this time." Jack paused again. "I miss him terribly." He cried, emotion taking over. Heavy sobs filled the otherwise quiet of the packed room. Others quietly wept at the sight of Jack breaking down. Katherine stood up, walked over to the podium, and hugged him. She guided him back to his seat. It was five minutes before Jack could compose himself.

Katherine whispered in his ear, "It's okay to cry, Jack. I miss him, too."

They were drinking tea and eating sandwiches in the funeral home hall when Jack's phone pinged, indicating he'd received a new email. He discreetly pulled out his phone to check the message.

"You are receiving this email because I have been murdered."

It was from Bill.

Chapter 16

"You can't expect me to believe he sent that email from beyond the grave," the police officer said, shaking her head in disbelief.

She raised a chipped mug, the scent of stale coffee and paperwork heavy in the air, and took a long sip. Fluorescent lights hummed overhead as Jack and Katherine sat in the sterile precinct of the Ontario Provincial Police in Brantford. Aside from the trio's quiet conversation, the building was almost eerily quiet, aside from the occasional clatter of a keyboard.

"Let's recap. You told me the MPs found him. He had a needle and syringe in his arm. They believed he died of an accidental overdose. This email has got to be a hoax," she muttered, a skeptical frown on her face. "How come it took five days for it to reach you after his passing?"

"Look," replied Jack. "You didn't know the guy. He was an exemplary doctor. He would never accidentally overdose. There's more to the story than what we are seeing."

The officer's dark eyes met Jack's. She took a less combative tone. "You're going through the grief phases and the first stage is disbelief." She paused and flashed a sympathetic smile. "We would need a lot more than an email to start an investigation into a potential murder. Besides, even if it was murder, it would have happened on a US military base. That's outside our jurisdiction. Have you contacted them? That would be the first step."

Jack mumbled his thanks, a frustrated sigh escaping his lips as he turned to leave. He and Katherine and Jack walked across the parking lot to his gleaming Tesla, the morning sun reflecting off its sleek surface. After spending three nights at the Brantford Holiday Inn, they were eager to drive back to their Toronto apartment. Even though he'd grown up in the Brantford, his childhood house now belonged to a new family. Full of fond memories, his parents recently sold the home, trading land for sea and starting their new life aboard their sailboat. Jack's parents, though heartbroken, heeded his suggestion to stay in their peaceful anchorage in Martin's Bay, Granada, rather than attend the sombre funeral.

"I can understand her reluctance to open an investigation," sighed Jack. "Knowing him like I do, with all his eccentricities and quirks, still makes this hard to believe."

"Honey," Katherine said, her voice flat with exhaustion, "we're emotionally drained. Perhaps a good night's sleep will help."

"Yeah, I feel like my mind is spinning. I can't think straight." Jack reached across the seat and squeezed Katherine's hand. "It's been a rough few days. Any thoughts on the next steps?"

"Nothing comes to mind. But it would not surprise me if you get another email with more information in a few days. Bill meticulously planned for every scenario, creating detailed contingency plans for any eventuality. Remember how he left us in St. Barts? A new identity as an American citizen, complete with a social security card and a new job offer letter in hand. That would have required meticulous planning, careful coordination, and countless hours of preparation. Maybe he'd organized things in case something happened to him."

"Sure sounds just like something Bill would do. Always planning and scheming, his active mind, formulating plots and counterplots."

*****

Jack was on call for the emergency room. The next few days were a whirlwind of activity, a blur of motion and fleeting moments. The emergency room doctor's urgent 6 a.m. call ripped him from sleep, and he spent the rest of the day immersed in the intense care of a patient suffering from perforated diverticulitis, the weight of responsibility heavy on his shoulders.

The 75-year-old woman was in a state of shock when he arrived at the hospital at 7 a.m., her eyes wide with fear and her hands trembling. To resuscitate her, he quickly administered 3 litres of Ringers lactate solution, the clear fluid rushing into the IV line while simultaneously inserting a central line and a Foley catheter. The anesthesiologist was then called to intubate and ventilate the patient before transferring her to the operating room.

After she was asleep and prepped for surgery in the OR, Jack carefully inserted a laparoscope through a small incision made in the umbilicus. There was a large quantity of pus within the abdominal cavity, so Jack washed out the abdomen, irrigating the affected area with five litres of normal saline. Jack readily identified a hole in the sigmoid colon resulting from a burst diverticulum, which was the obvious source of the infection he observed. In the middle of the surgery, he asked the nurse to make a call to his colleague and chief, Larry Klapman, to seek his expert opinion and advice as an intra-operative consultant. Larry arrived within minutes.

"Hi, Larry," said Jack. "This lady is unstable with a low blood pressure on vasopressors. I'm worried if I do a colon resection of the perforation and colostomy, she won't survive. I would rather just wash out the abdomen, patch the hole, leave drains, and get out. What do you think?"

As a senior surgeon, Larry carefully examined the laparoscopic image, which clearly showed the inflamed colon and the perforation. His eyes quickly flickered to the vital signs monitor, taking in the data displayed before shifting his gaze to Jack, his expression unreadable. "Considering all factors, that course of action would offer her the best chance of survival, making it the most sensible choice. I'll write a note agreeing with your management decision and overall approach."

By the time Jack finished the surgery and the staff transported the patient to the ICU, it was early afternoon. Jack went to his office, where he saw about 30 patients. It wasn't until 7 p.m. that he was finally prepared to head home. Jack made a stop in the ICU to check on the woman he'd operated on. Although the patient's vital signs had shown improvement, she remained dependent on vasopressors and mechanical ventilation to support her respiratory and circulatory functions. Feeling relieved that she was finally stabilized, he made his way to the hospital garage, to his Tesla, and hopped in. He drove home, the city lights a smear outside his window, his body heavy with exhaustion. The cheerful ringtone of his phone pierced the silence as he opened his apartment door, making him jump. *What now? Can't I just go home?* It was an unknown number. His pulse raced.

"Hello," answered Jack as he walked into the kitchen and sat at the counter in front of Katherine.

There was a moment of dead air before a woman's voice broke the silence. "Jack?"

"Yes," he said, raising his eyebrows as he glanced at Katherine. Jack didn't recognize the voice, but the woman sounded hesitant. "This is Jack. What's this about?"

"My name is Debbie. You don't know me. Is this a good time to talk? It has to do with Bill."

"Uhhhh. How do you know... Bill?"

"I worked with him in Iraq. I'm an OR nurse at the FOB Abu Ghraib."

Her voice was shaky, and Jack could tell she was crying. "It's okay, Debbie. Please go ahead."

"The day before they discovered Bill's body, I was in the operating room with him. It was so weird. He told me that if anything ever happened to him, to contact you. I just laughed it off. Bill and I used to joke about everything." She started sobbing. "He... he said you... you... would know what to do."

Jack was completely at a loss for words, unsure of what he should say in this awkward situation. Was this woman even telling the truth? Maybe she didn't even know Bill.

"Have we ever met?" asked Jack, trying to gauge how much information to share with her.

"No. Like I said, I don't know you, and no, we've never met," said Debbie. "I live in Buffalo. I'm actually flying back there for my two-week leave, which is why I called. I'm at the airport in Frankfurt, Germany, about to catch my connecting flight. Please, Jack. I really need to see you in person. I'm not comfortable discussing this over the phone."

"Discussing what?" said Jack, trying to mask his suspicion. Bill's involvement in drugs and gambling had already led to at least one death with the spear gun. He was worried about dragging Katherine deeper into more potential danger again, too.

"Please," Debbie said, pleading. "It's really important. Can we meet in person in two days? I can drive to Toronto or you could meet me in Buffalo. It's a one-hour drive."

Jack pondered this idea thoughtfully for a moment, considering all angles. If she was who she said she was, perhaps she could shed light on the events leading to Bill's demise, detailing the chilling circumstances.

"Let's meet halfway. Bill's hometown is in Brantford. How about at the Keg Restaurant, on Lynden Road, at 7:00 p.m. this coming Friday night? I plan on bringing my partner, Katherine, with me."

"I'll look forward to it," Debbie replied, her voice full of anticipation and excitement. "You were the subject of much of his conversation. He spoke about you extensively. And Jack..." she paused for a moment. "I don't think he overdosed."

"What do you mean?"

"I think someone killed him."

Chapter 17

Katherine and Jack left Toronto at 4 p.m., hoping to beat the Friday evening rush-hour traffic. Even with a smooth drive, the journey to Brantford took two hours, each kilometre ticking by slowly. They walked inside the Keg Restaurant at 6 p.m. The air was thick with the smells of grilling steak. They took seats at the bar and ordered two beers to wait for Debbie, who they expected at 7. The bartender slid the drinks across the counter, their foamy heads glistening.

"What do you think is up with this Debbie woman?" asked Katherine.

"Not sure," said Jack. "We spoke briefly. Our conversation barely took two minutes, but she gave the impression of being sincere and honest. Maybe she knows something the MPs didn't tell us."

"Well," Katherine said, her lower lip jutting out in a pout, "I hope she makes an appearance. When Bill wasn't with you, he associated with a rough crowd—the kind who looked like trouble and probably were. It wouldn't surprise me if she stood us up."

Jack fell silent, a poignant look in his eyes. "Bill, even with all his flaws, was the best friend I ever had. We shared cramped apartments, fuelled by coffee and ramen, throughout university and the long nights of surgical residency. I knew I could always count on him. His comforting presence was a reassuring anchor in the rare storms of my life."

Jack paused, the condensation clinging to his beer glass cold against his fingers, and took a long sip before continuing. "Once, during a hectic medical school day, I was instructed to check on a patient after class, a diabetic I was shadowing during my internal medicine rotation. I got into a lengthy discussion with a professor after his lecture and completely forgot about my visit to the ward. I later discovered Bill was on the ward just as my patient's laboured breathing and clammy skin indicated a serious turn for the worse. He meticulously documented everything, assuring my preceptor with a confident tone that the patient was stable based on my earlier assessment. He subtly deflected attention from my failure to see the patient, saving me from trouble. Later, he confessed, his eyes full of gratitude, that he felt he could never do enough to show his appreciation for everything I'd done for him. With a clap on the back, he said I could always count on him to help me out whenever he could. I remember how he told me, his voice thick with emotion, that he was indebted to me for life."

Katherine smiled and squeezed Jack's hand. "Very few of us ever get to have a friend like that. You two went through so much together. I know you miss him terribly—"

"What?" Jack turned and spotted a woman with a cascade of fiery red hair. She had a searching gaze and restless demeanour.

"That must be Debbie," Katherine concluded.

With a flourish, Jack caught her attention and waved her over. He marked her as in her late twenties and as she approached, he noticed a smattering of freckles across her nose, adding to her captivating appearance. Despite her pretty features, her anxious eyes revealing a whirlwind of worry behind her composed façade. The intricate lines of a sleeve tattoo snaked up her right arm, its colours a striking contrast against her pale skin.

"Jack?" she asked, her voice barely a whisper in the vast space.

"Yes—you must be Debbie," replied Jack. "This is Katherine, who I mentioned when we spoke. Can I get you something to drink?" With a quick wave of his hand, Jack signalled the server, who glided over in a flash.

"I could use a Bloody Mary," said Debbie as she sat across from them. "Thanks."

With the server gone, a hush fell, and Jack observed Debbie, noting the slight tremor in her voice and the way she fidgeted with her napkin. A frown tugged at the corners of her mouth, pulling her lips down, and her forehead creased with a deep wrinkle. As if in search of guidance, she stole a glance at her hands, unsure of what action to take. A tear formed in her eyes and rolled down her cheek. A deep sigh escaped her lips, the sound a physical manifestation of her genuine sorrow. Jack offered her a crisp, white napkin, and with a trembling hand, she wiped away the tear that traced a path down her cheek. "I miss him," she whispered between sobs, her voice filled with sorrow. "Bill didn't deserve to die."

"What do you think happened to him?" asked Jack.

"There is no way this was an accidental overdose," said Debbie. "He constantly talked about you. Once he said, should anything bad happen, you'd know exactly what to do."

Katherine responded, "They found him, you know, with a needle in his arm and an empty propofol container nearby. To all appearances, it would appear that it was self-administered."

The server returned and set down the Bloody Mary. Debbie, her hand trembling slightly, immediately pulled the glass toward her and took a sip through the red straw, the ice clinking softly against the glass.

Debbie looked down at her drink. "Bill was far too careful. There's no way he'd be that reckless." She paused, as if trying to decide how much to tell them. "Bill was definitely in his own world. He would use the propofol to enhance his sexual experience." She lowered her voice slightly. "The sensation from intravenous propofol often induces erotic dreams in some of us before we drift off. The memory of the dream lingers for days, intensifying the sexual desire long after its initial impact has faded."

Debbie paused for a moment, turning her eyes downward, then continued speaking. "We used propofol on each other, and the effect was nothing short of mind-blowing. The tingling sensation was electric. When Bill first suggested it, I hesitated, unsure if I wanted to try it. The unknown made me apprehensive. Bill convinced me the experience would be unforgettable, a truly unique adventure. His prediction turned out to be accurate."

Katherine's eyes met Jack's and the two exchange a knowing look. Debbie was really opening up, and neither of them would interrupt her in case she revealed any detail that might explain what had really happened.

"Bill's touch was gentle," Debbie said, almost wistfully, "as he found a vein and inserted the IV, a slight pressure against my skin. He would describe in explicit detail what he wanted to do to me to enhance our sexual encounters. The visual image would come to life 20 seconds after he injected the propofol. Ten minutes later, I would wake up with vivid images of Bill engaging in various activities with me. As he sat on the edge of the bed, the mattress sinking slightly beneath him, he waited for me to wake up. It was then I would attack him with such intense desire and passion, it was overwhelming." She paused and smiled at the memory, then took another sip of her Bloody Mary.

"Go on," Jack gently nudged.

"Other days, I'd be the one to administer Bill's injection, a nervous energy buzzing in me while I waited for him to regain consciousness. That's when he would engage in such passionate and vigorous lovemaking. I would be breathless for days just thinking about it."

Jack felt the shock of what she was saying. *It is all part of addiction behaviour, increasing the release of dopamine, oxytocin, and serotonin from the brain to compensate for the lack of dopamine receptors.*

"He was always on the computer," she continued, "sometimes for hours when we weren't having sex or operating. He said that was one reason he signed up to work in Iraq—he would have loads of extra time. I was suspicious of what he was up to. His hours-long computer sessions prompted me to ask: what held his attention? I admit, I fell head over heels for Bill and experienced intense emotions for him. But I also suspected that he frequented adult websites, chasing something else. I just... I just needed to know."

"When he was out tending to a patient, I seized the opportunity to snoop on his computer. He had what seemed like endless lines of complex computer code scrolling across his screen, a language I couldn't decipher. Driven by curiosity, I ended up scrolling through his Google timeline, noting the places he'd been and the times he'd been there. When in Little Rock, he'd frequently fly to Las Vegas. Like every two weeks. I did some research and found out he spent the weekend at the Mustang Ranch."

"Huh," said Jack, "I never would have figured Bill to be into horses."

Debbie looked at Jack incredulously. "The Mustang Ranch is the most famous brothel in Nevada." Debbie shook her head in exasperation and continued. "But then I got caught. By the time I'd heard his footsteps, he was already in the doorway and found me at his computer. Of course, he immediately questioned my actions. I told him I was curious why he spent all his time online. He didn't seem mad, but he scared me when he said, 'Don't ever do that again, or you'll be risking your life. Someone is trying to kill me.' Though the army's heavy presence in Iraq gave him a sense of security, a feeling of being surrounded by protection, I know Bill still felt threatened. When I asked him what was going on, he went completely silent, his jaw clenched tight in that way..."

"What do you think happened to him, then?" asked Jack.

"I think someone compromised security and made it look like he accidentally killed himself."

They sat quietly. "Who would do that then?" asked Katherine.

"I have no idea," said Debbie, shaking her head. "He kept a lot of information to himself."

"Do you have any ideas about how I can find out what happened?" asked Jack.

Debbie chewed on her straw, thinking for a few moments. "Well, I would check out the Mustang Ranch and see what that was about—maybe it *was* a horse ranch or something equally intriguing." She laughed at that thought. "I would also speak with his previous mentor, Dr. Marcel Garner. I remember seeing something on the computer about him, but it was all in French, so I couldn't understand what Bill had written."

Jack glanced at Katherine, then directed his attention back to Debbie. "I received an email from Bill five days after his death, saying that if I received it, it meant that he'd been murdered. Do you have any idea how he could have set that up?"

Debbie replied, "I don't, but that would be just like Bill to have this organized after his death."

As the last of their drinks disappeared, the lively chatter trailed off, replaced by the soft clinking of ice. "I guess I'll head back to Buffalo, then," said Debbie. "If you find something, can you let me know?"

Jack nodded. "Thanks for coming. We'll walk with you to the parking lot."

He and Katherine watched Debbie climb into her rusty, 15-year-old Toyota Corolla, the engine sputtering as she turned the key, and waved goodbye. They heard the engine rumble to life and the tires crunch on the gravel as she backed out of the space. A split-second later, a blast came from the car's engine, like a cannon going off, sending Jack and Katherine sprawling backward onto the hot pavement. A high-pitched ringing filled Jack's ears as he watched the car quickly consumed in a fiery blaze, the heat radiating towards him and Katherine. The inferno was so intense that it forced Jack back before he could attempt to reach the driver's side door. Another explosion rocked the area as the gas tank erupted in flames, ending any hope of saving Debbie.

Chapter 18

With a brisk nod, the same officer who had spoken to Jack and Katherine at the precinct days earlier took their formal statement.

"She told us she was a nurse at the army base in Iraq and wanted to talk about Bill," explained Jack, his voice almost too loud against the low background hum of the precinct. "She thought someone killed him, too."

"Did she mention who? Did she say she felt in danger?"

"No. Just that he was very careful and that he would not have accidentally overdosed."

"Let's look at the video of the Keg parking lot," said the police officer.

The computer screen showed the area where Debbie had pulled in, highlighting the Toyota Corolla's headlights as it turned and parked under a flickering security light. The time stamp showed: 6:23 p.m. Only three other vehicles were present: a rusty pickup truck, a dented sedan, and Jack's Tesla. The video sped up, showing 10 other cars parking in the lot between 6:23 and 7:10, their brake lights flashing in quick succession. A red Ford 150 pickup truck pulled in next to the Toyota. A young couple emerged from the vehicle and walked toward the steakhouse, its windows buzzing with activity by this time.

Junkie

The restaurant doors swung open at 7:09, as Jack, Katherine, and Debbie walked into the cool night air. Debbie walked directly to her car and slid into the driver's seat while Jack and Katherine stood watching. At precisely 7:10, the explosion occurred.

"The most frequent reasons for car fires are fuel leaks, which are often easily overlooked," said the police officer, "and electrical faults that can sometimes be difficult to detect. Upon reviewing the video, it seems likely that is the root cause of what occurred," she added. "The Toyota, which appeared to be at least 15 years old, displayed significant wear and tear, and it was highly probable that it hadn't received any servicing for an extended period. The regulatory environment in the United States is considerably more lenient than its Canadian counterpart."

"Don't you think it is more than a coincidence that she thought Bill's death wasn't accidental?" suggested Jack. "And then she drives two hours to talk with us and dies in a car explosion a few minutes after?"

With a weary sigh, the police officer raised her gaze to meet the expectant eyes of both Jack and Katherine. "I know that this past week has been extremely difficult and traumatic for both of you. The process of fully recovering from the loss of someone close often requires a full year of grieving and emotional processing, allowing time for the healing to take place—"

Jack interrupted, "Yeah, I know all that. This is about a potential murder of my friend!"

Startled, the police officer looked up at Jack, her eyes wide, and mumbled, "I'm sorry about your friend. I know what I'm talking about. You will experience a process involving several emotional phases, starting with denial, progressing through anger and bargaining, then experiencing depression before finally reaching acceptance. Unfortunately, our work as police officers exposes us to the recurring patterns of death and crime."

Jack remained silent as the police officer went back to typing her report. They got up and headed back to Tesla. The drive back to Toronto was faster since rush hour traffic had subsided.

"I don't believe the police officer when she says it was likely a gas leak," said Jack. "An explosion happened initially, true, which was immediately followed by a fire that engulfed the car. But the sheer force and impact of that event were so intense that it felt like a bomb had gone off.

"And the force of the explosion pushed us back," said Katherine.

"Although I admit I'm not an expert, based on my understanding of how I would expect a gas leak to behave, we would have seen a more gradual ignition process for the fire, rather than the rapid combustion that occurred."

"You think someone planted a bomb?" said Katherine. "That's crazy. How? The video surveillance showed no visual evidence of anyone coming close to Debbie's Toyota. Maybe the depth of our grief over Bill's death is making us overreact to what was probably an everyday situation—the old car and all. The officer's explanation makes the most sense."

Throughout the rest of their journey home, Jack pondered the idea, quietly weighing its merits and remaining silent as they travelled. As a next step, he would reach out to Dr. Marcel Garner, who had previously served as Bill's mentor and preceptor during their collaborative work on magnetic robotic surgery. Their partnership had culminated in Bill delivering a presentation at the conference in Las Vegas several years prior. But since Debbie mentioned seeing his name on Bill's computer, they must have had some contact recently.

They arrived home emotionally spent. Katherine announced she was going to bed. Jack kissed her on the forehead and said he would join her soon. He sat down in the living room and opened his laptop. With a few quick keystrokes, Jack searched Google for "robotic magnetic surgery," the faint hum of his computer a backdrop to the quiet. A lecture by Dr. Marcel Garner appeared on YouTube. "The idea of performing surgery without incisions has become a reality," he explained in an engaging manner, captivating visuals displayed on a large screen behind him.

The animated video showed a simulation of magnets being swallowed and entering the stomach. "Using electromagnetic positioning, we can accurately place the magnets to anastomose the small intestine to the stomach, bypassing the intestine to effect weight loss in the obese patient," said Dr. Garner. "Eliminating the risk of anesthetic in these patients is the key to success. This can all be done with the patient awake and sent home in less than an hour."

Jack glanced at his watch. It was 11 p.m. He navigated the University of Toronto's staff directory. The screen filled with names. After a bit of scrolling, he finally located Marcel's email address. Jack drafted a message, the subject line URGENT, requesting a call with him about Bill. He pressed the Send button. All he could do now was wait. Jack stifled a yawn, the weight of exhaustion settling on his shoulders as he closed his laptop and got ready for bed.

A sudden chirp from his phone on the bathroom counter interrupted the rhythmic swish of his toothbrush. A name flashed on the caller ID: MARCEL GARNER. Jack spat the toothpaste into the sink and grabbed the phone.

"Marcel," answered Jack. "That was quick!"

"I'm shocked by Bill's death," said Marcel. "I hadn't heard. What happened to him?"

Jack spent 30 minutes meticulously outlining Bill's journey, starting with the quiet transition to Little Rock, then sharply contrasting it with the chaotic, almost surreal experience of a life in Iraq. He vividly detailed the propofol injection and the sombre atmosphere of Bill's funeral. He also shared Bill's unsettling email and mention his last conversation with Debbie, which ended with the description of her violent and unexpected death. After he finished speaking, a heavy silence hung in the air. "Marcel?" he asked, a nervous tremor in his voice. "Are you still with me?"

"Yeah, I'm here. I wondered what happened to him over the past year," said Marcel. "It was as if he disappeared off the planet. Knowing Bill as I do, and his cautious approach to adversity, his change of identity and hiding in Iraq makes sense to me."

"What do you mean?"

"Bill's mind operated on a plane far above ours. His thoughts and ideas were extraordinarily advanced. I always considered myself a smart, imaginative intellect, but Bill's brilliance far surpassed mine. This might seem like a tangent, but stick with me, Jack. Patent litigation, protracted and complex, has delayed promising research using robotic magnetic surgery, hindering progress. Bill had filed for patents long before we developed the process, resulting in a cease and desist legal ruling on our research."

"What? Does his death change anything for you? Are you able to proceed now that he's no longer alive?"

"I don't think so," Marcel replied, a hint of skepticism in his voice. "The patent law challenges are beyond my area of expertise. I'm the mastermind strategizing the research, but I don't do the hands-on legal work. The sheer financial power supporting this legal order is incomprehensible; it's a sum beyond my wildest imaginings, a mountain of money that dwarfs anything I've ever encountered. Introducing this technology could severely affect the United States surgical business by automating procedures and rendering many existing surgical practices obsolete, leading to job losses and market upheaval. The lucrative surgical business in the US, a multi-trillion dollar industry built on complex procedures and expensive equipment, would collapse if this technology was widely adopted. It has the potential to eliminate all surgery and close operating rooms, leaving surgeons and hospitals out of business and eliminating countless jobs."

A hush fell over Jack as Marcel spoke, his words so shocking. A chill travelled up his spine. *If Bill had been involved, the financial effort to suppress him would have been substantial, given his potential to expose this technology.* With the weight of life and death in his hands each day, even Jack, a seasoned surgeon, had no idea of the impact this new technology would have on him and his surgical practice.

Jack's voice dropped to a conspiratorial whisper. "It sounds like there would be plenty of reasons to make certain Bill kept quiet, wouldn't you agree?"

"Not sure about that," said Marcel. "The world is a big place, and the rest of the surgical community will inevitably share those concepts. There is no way to permanently shut it down. The process of getting regulatory bodies to accept change is slow and laborious, filled with bureaucratic hurdles and delays. Fifteen years—a period marked by countless meetings, revisions, and delays—is the average time it takes for new technology to clear these systems and finally be used in practice." Marcel paused for a moment before he continued. "But Bill was mostly interested in something else. He once told me he had the answer to longevity."

Chapter 19

"There is no way you are going to the Mustang Ranch without me," said Katherine, her eyes narrowed in suspicion. "Not that I don't trust you, but..."

"I tried to call and speak to the owner, Susan Austin," said Jack. "I couldn't get past leaving a message in the general mailbox for her to phone me back."

"It's pretty obvious why Bill went there," Katherine stated, her voice dripping with sarcasm. "Plus, the ranch is 10 miles away from Reno. The fantasy played out: massive gambling wins, followed by decadent nights at the ranch, filled with the intoxicating blend of lust and regret. Why do you think visiting will add any more information as to what might have happened to Bill? You saw him in action in Bermuda."

Jack laughed at Katherine's graphic assessment of Bill's motivation. "Yeah," he replied, "you're probably right. But something happened while in Little Rock."

"Have you thought about going to the VA hospital there instead? Compared to a visit to the planet's most notorious brothel, this option seems significantly more reasonable. You know, lacking the seedy smells and unsavoury characters. Have you considered how your CEO or chief of staff at the hospital would react if they found out you visited *a brothel*?"

Jack shook his head, a frustrated sigh escaping his lips as he thought about his lack of progress. "No one will speak to me about Bill," he said, his shoulders slumping in defeat. "Last night, I found myself on the phone for three hours. I reached out to the CEO of the VA hospital, his chief of staff, the head of surgery, and his office manager; the calls were all urgent. They put me on hold and I had to dial many times. The moment I uttered his name, the line went dead, or I was met with a sharp warning never to speak it again. Each response was immediate and hostile. The CEO had the audacity to inform me that should I come for a visit, security personnel would be available to see me out."

With a small sigh, Katherine took a sip of her coffee and then shrugged her lips in a straight line. "Why don't you just let it go," she whispered, the words hanging heavy in the air between them. "Let the devastating reality of Bill's death sink in as we process the loss of your best friend. Let's grieve like others, suffering in silence while the memory of his laughter is a reminder of what we've lost."

Jack's index finger brushed against Katherine's cheek. A shiver of warmth ran through him as he felt her smooth skin beneath his touch. He swallowed, the bitter taste of acceptance forming on his tongue as he realized she was probably right. He was becoming fixated on Bill's death, each unanswered question fuelling his obsession, convinced there was more to it than a simple overdose. The case felt suffocating. *Could it be that I'm clinging to this as a way to deal with his death? The memories, both happy and sad, flood back with painful intensity.*

"Look," said Katherine after a thoughtful silence, her voice barely a whisper, "if going to the Mustang Ranch, a place known to be a den of iniquity, will help put your mind at ease that he was visiting there like every other male client, then let's go. We need you to get your life back on track."

Jack's face lit up, a grin splitting his features as he felt the warmth of her changed heart. "I looked it up on the internet. There is a package deal. It includes a round trip flight with a free tour of the Mustang Ranch and the Wild Horse Saloon. A night at a local hotel is part of the package. The tour includes meeting some women who work there. All for $200 each! We can go this weekend."

Katherine laughed. "You are totally obsessed. Maybe it will be good for us to get away for a few days."

*****

The flight to Reno was a smooth four and a half hours, with views of fluffy clouds and distant mountains. A Mustang Ranch tour guide greeted them as they arrived at the airport, and escorted them to the luxurious Mustang Ranch limousine. The sun beat down as they shared the 10-minute desert ride with four other couples, the scent of hot sand and dry brush filling the air.

"Hello and welcome to the Mustang Ranch," said the attractive grey-haired, woman who met the limousine when they arrived. "I'm Susan Austin. We will give you an hour tour of the property and facility, and then treat you to our famous buffet for lunch, where you can meet some women who work here. Every month we get about 100 new applications from women who want to work here from across the US and Canada. I usually choose five of the most suitable applicants. The turnover is fairly brisk, so we always have fresh faces to greet our returning customers."

The tour included the main salon and a visit to the rooms. One had a king-sized bed and a large Jacuzzi. "The women will negotiate a price before coming in here with you, depending on what you are planning for, and how many of them you want to take part."

"This is like visiting a timeshare pitch," whispered Katherine. "I find this very creepy."

Jack nodded in agreement, while gently guiding Katherine toward the madame. "Ms. Austin," Jack said. "Could we have a word?"

"You can call me Susan," she said. "How can I help you?"

Jack looked around the room. The others milled about, checking out the Jacuzzi and other elements of the room. No one else seemed within earshot. "My close friend Bill recently died.

He had mentioned to someone that he'd spent some time at the ranch. I was hoping you could give us some information about his visits here. I hope I'm not asking too much, but am trying to come to terms with his death."

The madame, her face crinkling into a web of wrinkles, smiled warmly. "I remember Bill very well." She paused, running a veiny hand through her grey hair, before continuing. "We value the privacy of our clients, many of whom prefer to keep their visits confidential. Ensuring discretion is paramount. Unlike our usual clientele, Bill's focus was rather unconventional, piquing our curiosity. Yes, his email address is still in our system, so he's getting our marketing materials. Like our newsletter, showcasing our newest hires and program updates, which we send to our top-tier clients—a curated selection of our most loyal partners. Could we meet in my office, perhaps while the others are at lunch, avoiding the midday bustle and noise, for a more productive talk?"

Crimson velvet drapes and the scent of cheap perfume hung heavy in the air. The office décor was just as Jack expected in a brothel. A plush red leather couch and chairs, adorned with colourful, soft, fluffy cushions, invited you to sink in. In the glass cabinet, an array of objects related to sexuality were on display. The heavy oak desk that separated Jack and Katherine from the madame had a laptop opened.

"So what is it you wish to know?" Susan asked.

"Bill and I were both surgeons," said Jack. "He was also my best friend. Bill, according to his mentor, Dr. Marcel Garner, was onto something big, a groundbreaking discovery. He felt he had the key to longevity. Bill was involved with something here. Something that may have been responsible for his death."

"Look, I'm a businessperson. Men who frequent this place want one thing, and one thing only. What led you to think he was not the same as everyone else?"

"Bill possessed an extraordinary mind, capable of remarkable feats of intellect and creativity. Like a computer, it processed information quickly and efficiently. He sought something beyond the physical; a connection, an understanding, a solace that sexual satisfaction alone could not provide. His purpose was far more profound, a mission deeply ingrained into the very core of his being. He didn't need to come here to find women who wanted to have sex with him. There was another reason he frequented Mustang Ranch."

The madame, her eyes narrowed, silently observed Jack. His suspicion that she was a keen judge of character stemmed from her years of experience in the sex-work business, where she had learned to read people instantly. Jack desperately wanted to provide more details to prove to her the sincerity of his mission to uncover the truth about Bill's disappearance.

"Let's consider working together," he proposed. "If Bill discovered a lucrative opportunity, perhaps you, as a businesswoman, would consider getting involved, too?"

Susan continued to eye Jack suspiciously. Jack shrugged his shoulders, smiled, and said, "I'm desperate. If you could tell me what you know, I'll keep you informed if I find anything else."

Her gaze softened, a warmth spreading through her eyes. Jack felt a shift in her demeanour, a subtle relaxing of her shoulders, a sign that he was gaining her trust. He chose to remain silent, allowing the weight of the silence to dispel any lingering doubts about his honesty. The madame slipped on a pair of tortoise-shell glasses. She gazed at her laptop momentarily and then banged on the keys. Jack felt she had opened up a file where she kept notes.

"Bill first approached me with a business proposition," she explained, her voice low and hesitant as she fixed her eyes on the screen. "While I wasn't particularly interested in his proposal's specifics, the prospect of $10,000 per worker was incredibly tempting, a substantial sum that held significant appeal. His sole purpose was to gather bodily fluids produced during sexual activity, such as saliva and vaginal secretions. What he did with them, I do not know."

"That seems... unusual," said Jack. "Why would he want that?"

"He mentioned at some point something about particular proteins that are produced during intercourse. He also said that to get approval for this kind of study by research ethics boards would be impossible. The collection had to be done without the knowledge or consent of the participants; otherwise, it might contaminate the results. I told the women it was to check for viruses such as COVID-19 and others. I paid them each $2,000 to collect the specimens and kept the rest of the money for myself."

Lost in thought, Jack absentmindedly scratched his chin, a nervous gesture that often accompanied his concentration. "How many samples did he collect?"

The madame adjusted her glasses and peered down at her notes on the laptop, the clacking of the keyboard a counterpoint to the quiet hum of the room. She talked as she typed. "The government seized the ranch after the previous owner, a man known for his reckless spending and love for fast cars, skipped town for Mexico to avoid paying taxes. He left behind his beloved Mustang Ranch. I bought this place 20 years ago from the government for a bargain, with the promise to keep precise and detailed records. Ahh, I've been searching for this," she said as she finally located a file. "He paid me $10.3 million over two months, so you figure it out."

A low whistle escaped Jack's lips as his jaw dropped at the sheer amount of money.

Chapter 20

The lab at Quest Diagnostics on University Drive in Little Rock had accepted the fluid samples from the Mustang Ranch. Jack sat in the sterile, brightly lit reception area, flipping through a dog-eared magazine, waiting for his appointment with lab director, Jordan Lewis. Having flown from Toronto with a stop in Chicago, Jack felt the familiar chill of a Midwestern autumn. He was flying back in a few hours. Katherine had to work as it was a weekday, but Jack cancelled his day so he could meet with the lab director.

"You may be wasting your time, coming all the way to talk with me," Jordan had said to Jack when he'd called him. "I can't release any information without a written consent from Bill."

"But Bill has died," said Jack. "I'm his best friend and colleague. Can I at least sit down with you for 20 minutes and you can tell me whatever you feel comfortable telling me?"

With Jordan's agreement to meet, Jack had immediately booked a plane ticket. Now he was settled into a chair in the waiting room, checking his watch repeatedly as he waited for their 2 p.m. appointment. Jack stood up as a man in a white lab coat approached, the starched fabric rustling as he moved. The name, "Dr. Jordan Lewis," was embroidered in bold, crimson letters on the breast pocket. He had long, grey strands of thin and wispy hair hanging down, contrasting the smooth, bare skin on his balding crown. Jordan reached out his hand, engulfing Jack's in a firm grasp, a smile on his face.

"Let's go to my office," said Jordan, a hint of impatience in his tone. They walked into a small office, the metal desk gleaming under the fluorescent lights, a computer monitor glowing softly. He got straight to business. "I reviewed the contract with Bill, noting the specific clauses in red ink. Reviewing his emergency contacts, we found your name listed with his permission to share his test results with you. I'll answer any of your questions."

Jack breathed a heavy sigh of relief. "What was he looking for?"

"Bill instructed us to look for a particular protein and determine whether the levels were higher than expected. Using mass spectrometry, we analyzed over 3,000 proteins. We looked at 1,030 specimens labelled specimen 1 and specimen 2. He did not disclose to us the source of the samples. Here is the graph of what we found." Jordan spun the monitor around. "We eliminated all the proteins that fell within the normal levels, but the one protein that stood out in 879 samples labelled sample 1 and 922 samples labelled sample 2 was this one." Jordan pointed to the screen.

"What is the protein and what does it mean?" asked Jack.

"The elevated protein is brain-derived neurotrophic factor, or BDNF," replied Jordan. "Not sure what it means with these samples, as I do not know the clinical context of where the samples are from. The only experience we have with this protein in the lab is when we follow patients with intermittent fasting and weight loss. It is a reliable indicator if patients are compliant with their fasting program. We see the highest levels after a prolonged fast of two or three days."

Jack pulled out his phone and googled "brain-derived neurotrophic factor." He skimmed the results:

Brain-derived neurotrophic factor (BDNF) is a protein produced inside nerve cells that supports the survival of neurons and brain cells, promotes synaptic connections between neurons, and is essential for learning and long-term memory storage. BDNF activates the TrkB tyrosine kinase receptor. It essentially fertilizes brain cells to keep them functioning and growing, as well as propelling the growth of new neurons. For adults, BDNF also plays a vital role in neurogenesis, the creation of new neurons from stem cell.

Jack's face broke out in a confused expression. He glanced up at Jordan. "What does it all mean?" he asked.

A careless shrug of his shoulders and the subtle slump of his posture said more than words ever could. Jordan made it clear it wasn't his concern. Checking his watch, Jordan announced, "Your 20 minutes is up." His voice was sharp and impatient. "Should you have further questions, please don't hesitate to email me. I'll get back to you as soon as possible. Thanks for dropping by."

With a grunt, Jack stood. His muscles were still stiff from sitting on the plane for the four-hour flight. The meeting was clearly over. Jack shook Jordan's hand and walked out to the front of the lab, and flagged a taxi. Sitting in the lounge at the airport, Jack phoned Katherine, but the call went to voicemail. *She's still busy at work.*

Frustrated with his lack of understanding what Bill was up to, Jack did another Google search on intermittent fasting, the cursor blinking on his screen. An article that highlighted promising results from previous studies spurred research into caloric restriction in mice. Researchers were surprised that the rodents, whose daily food was reduced to 75 per cent of their normal intake, lived 50 per cent longer than mice with unlimited food intake.

Another more recent article suggested that in healthy volunteers, intermittent fasting would cause a five kilogram weight loss in three days. Upon examining the serum proteins, the researchers noted a significant increase in brain-derived neurotrophic factor, which led them to consider intermittent fasting as a potential factor for longevity besides the positive effect of weight loss.

A search on the physiologic effects of an active sex life suggested that sex five times a week reduced the incidence of breast and prostate cancer, reduced heart attacks, decreased the number of colds and flu-like symptoms, reduced blood pressure. In a YouTube interview with a leading researcher from Harvard about whether an active sex life leads to increased longevity, he simply shrugged his shoulders and quipped, "Who cares if you get to live longer with an active sex life? An active sex life is enough for a happier life."

The shrill announcement for Jack's flight jolted him back to reality. He settled into his seat on the plane, the gentle rocking motion a comfort as he closed his eyes for the trip back to Chicago. The jarring bump of the landing shook him awake. He fumbled to switch his phone off airplane mode. A missed call from Katherine. He called her, sharing what he learned from the laboratory.

"To me," said Katherine, "he seems to look for answers about what causes longevity. Ageing is inevitable. We learned that in medical school. Bill should know that, too. The longer lifespan of starved mice doesn't imply the same for humans. The metabolic rate of mice is such they have to eat all the time or they'll starve to death in just a few hours."

Jack laughed. "Maybe he hoped that if he had sex all day, he wouldn't get old."

Katherine sighed. "Ageing has little to do with sex. This limitation occurs because human cells have a finite number of replications before they become senescent. It's a process called the Hayflick limit. Telomeres are located at the ends of our DNA strands. With intricate mechanisms, they shielded the DNA from damage, ensuring its integrity. Every time a cell divides, a small part of the telomere is lost. When telomeres shorten enough, they cause DNA damage, triggering a cascade of cellular events that lead to cell death. When that happens on a large scale, the body's systems will start to shut down, leading to organ failure and death. Even if we could prevent the telomere for shortening, death would be inevitable."

"Why is that? I would think that would be the answer to a longer life."

"Nope. That's not the case. Each cell division causes minute breaks and alterations within the DNA molecule, a complex process involving numerous enzymes and proteins. An immortal cell, unchecked by natural limits, would undergo unregulated division, ultimately becoming a cancerous entity that overtakes the organism."

"Katherine, you're a woman full of surprises. How do you know so much about ageing?" asked Jack.

"I have to keep the mystery alive, Jack," she teased. Her voice sounded breathless. "Actually," she said, becoming serious again, "before my acceptance into medical school, I completed a master's degree on the molecular effects of ageing. But that was a long time ago, over 10 years, and I'm sure things have changed since I studied it. I lost interest when I started my psychotherapy practice, so I'm not up to date."

"How is it I didn't know this about you before now?"

"Honey, there are many things about me you have yet to discover."

"What's the story about brain-derived neurotrophic factor?" asked Jack. "This is the first I have heard about this related to longevity."

"I'm not sure what it means. I can try to find out from my former professor. Maybe give me a few days to track him down."

"Sounds good, honey. I gotta go. They just called my flight to Toronto. See you in two hours."

Junkie

As Jack was walking onto the plane, his phone buzzed. A new email had arrived. A slight chill ran down his spine, and a wave of icy dread washed over him. Bill's name jumped out of the subject line.

Hi Jack,

Sorry to freak you out with these emails coming from beyond the grave. You will only get a few more of them before they are all gone. I organized their delivery before my untimely demise.

No matter the obstacle, you always manage to do the right thing with your moral compass guiding your actions. By now, the weight of my discovery should be clear; you'll realize I was onto something truly significant. Surgeons may become obsolete with the introduction of magnetic robotic surgery. This groundbreaking advancement is set to transform the surgical process. The integration of machine learning is crucial for turning software programming into AI.

What is more significant is the development of cures for diabetes, hypertension, cancer, and strokes, each representing a critical medical challenge affecting millions, and the relief it would bring. This disruptive technology will revolutionize healthcare, leaving the multitrillion-dollar industry scrambling to adapt. You need to be very careful.

The email had no final salutation or "Best wishes," closing. *That's it? What the hell am I supposed to do next?* Jack's mind was reeling. Images of Bill looking down at him from above flashed before his eyes, sounds echoed in his ears, and a dizzying sense of confusion overwhelmed him. A shiver ran down his spine. This was far too peculiar for his comfort. Despite expecting devious tactics from Bill, the sheer complexity of this scheme still shocked him. It went beyond what he imagined. *Maybe someone else is sending me these emails?*

The quiet hum of the plane engine on the short flight back to Toronto provided a contemplative atmosphere for him to consider his next steps. The only logical explanation for the emails was that someone was tracking his every move, a chilling thought that sent an involuntary shudder through his body. Although it might be possible to trigger delayed emails to be sent after someone dies, which would be a rather morbid but a technically workable solution, Bill, in his self-assuredness, never considered his own mortality. Bill didn't dwell on death. The man was too confident in his ability to sidestep it, a conviction that radiated from his swagger and careless laugh. Jack decided to investigate the emails' origin and meticulously trace their digital footprints.

"Katherine," Jack said, his voice tight with frustration as he walked into the apartment, "I think someone else is sending me these emails. The writing style is completely different. The thought of death was so foreign to Bill that it would never cross his mind. He was sure he was immortal. To believe he'd planned this—expecting his own end—doesn't match his known temperament and behaviour."

Katherine, who was lying in bed reading a magazine, looked up with a startled expression. "Honey, you are getting far too wound up to think clearly. Come to bed. We'll talk about this in the morning."

Jack paced about the bedroom, clearly agitated. "I think I'm too wired to sleep right now. I'm going to sit in front of my laptop to see if I can figure out who is sending them."

"Jack," Katherine said, a hint of exasperation in her tone, "you're brilliant—but clueless when it comes to computer literacy. It would be a complete waste of your time. You'd gain nothing. Let me send the emails to my brother. He works as a computer programmer, creating and maintaining software systems for the Royal Bank of Canada.

A wide grin split Jack's face as he stopped his nervous pacing. The sound of his shoes on the floor ceased. "Really..."

"Yes, Jack. Constantly tracing emails and cyberattacks, he's become intimately familiar with the internet's intricate pathways and hidden corners. He's the only one with the aptitude to crack this conundrum. If anyone can do it, it would be him."

"You're right," Jack said, a smile playing on his lips. "I need to clear my head and think more rationally."

"First thing in the morning, I'll send you the emails so you can forward them to your brother."

Jack had a quick shower, brushed his teeth, and then snuggled into bed next to Katherine. With a solid plan forming in his mind, his restless energy subsided, and the silence lulled him into slumber within minutes.

Chapter 21

The aroma of freshly brewed coffee hung heavy in the air as they met Katherine's brother, Brian, amid the chatter and clatter of the Starbucks. With a sigh, Jack set his worn laptop down on the cluttered table, next to a stack of papers and a half-empty coffee cup. He quickly logged into his email, the *tap, tap, tap* of his fingers a counterpoint to Brian's droning explanation.

"Each email contains a unique code snippet that acts like a digital fingerprint, revealing its origin. At the bank, I'm frequently asked to verify emails aren't phishing scams, often checking for suspicious links or sender addresses."

With a smooth push, Jack slid his computer toward Brian. Brian immediately began to hammer at the keyboard. His eyes narrowed, focusing intently on the intricate details of his task, the muscles in his face tightening. Jack glanced at Katherine.

She shrugged her shoulders and whispered, "He's such a computer geek," her voice barely audible above the clatter. "Remember when we took him sailing a few months ago?"

Jack smiled as he recalled them drinking beer after the race night. "What you need is a computer whiz like me on your boat every night and you wouldn't come in last place," Brian had explained to Jack before the race started. "I can wirelessly feed the wind instrument data into the laptop and come up with a strategy to win based on machine learning from the computer, analyzing thousands of similar sailing conditions. Here, let me show you."

The laptop screen displayed a detailed map, the subtle one-knot wind current pushing them eastward highlighted with a gentle, flowing animation. Deviating sharply from Jack's preferred course, the plotted route would take them on the opposite tack—a change of plan visible on the nautical chart.

"But that would put us on a port tack," said Jack. "Forcing us to yield to every other boat as we round the first mark. The chaos of it all is too risky."

Brian countered, "It wouldn't matter because we would be the first ones to the mark and we would not have to yield to anyone. Give it a try. You need to get with this technology. It takes away the guesswork."

Jack, contemplating the complex interplay between the scientific principles and the artistic skill involved in sailing, responded with a thoughtful, "I don't know... Because of the many variables at play, from the wind to the currents, sailing is a highly unpredictable activity. Sometimes trusting your intuition is the best course of action... Tonight, my gut feeling is telling me to take a different path than the one you're proposing, leading me to the *opposite* side of the course."

Brian's jaw dropped slightly as he looked at Jack, his incredulous expression clear in his wide eyes. "Really?" he asked, his voice dripping with skepticism, indicating that he didn't quite believe what he'd just heard. "In the grand scheme of things, you are just one person. In its comprehensive analysis, this program has examined data encompassing thousands of sailors and thousands of nights mirroring the current conditions. Later tonight, you're going to be incredibly grateful that you decided to include me in your plans as we cross the finish line in first place."

With a sigh of resignation, Jack agreed to follow Brian's rather dubious suggestions, and they put them into practice. Real-time analysis on the computer had them constantly altering course, with numbers flashing and screens updating rapidly. Brian's voice boomed across the boat as he shouted the instructions to Jack. When the computer's calculations finalized with a sharp beep, he would roar, "Tack now!" the urgent command almost lost in the sounds of creaking masts and slapping sails.

They crossed the finish line in last place. The cheers from the winning boat gave a distant hum in the distance. Back at the dock, Brian sat in the boat's cockpit, shaking his head and sipping his Heineken. "I don't understand it," he said. "Despite real-time weather, wind, and instrument data streaming in, the computer model still made an inaccurate prediction. I think I'll stick with banking..."

Brian's animated voice brought Jack back to the present. "The email came from a computer in the Dominican Republic," he said. "It was a bit difficult to trace because I had to backtrack through a VPN." Brian slid the laptop back to Jack. A blue icon lit up on a spot near Los Haitises National Park in the Bay of Samana.

"It's a Mac laptop," said Brian. "I could probably hack into it, but I'll need to do it from my work computer. It has the specific encryption-breaking programs I need. The security would depend on the firewalls and whether their system is more advanced than a bank's—something I doubt."

"Is that even legal?" asked Katherine.

Brian smirked. "You wouldn't believe the hidden depths of the internet, the secret communities, the vast amount of information constantly being exchanged—it's a whole other world. As far as I'm concerned, using the information I gained for anything illegal would be the only way I'd be breaking the law; otherwise, it's a gray area. We're in a constant, high-stakes race against sophisticated criminals. Even when locked out, the urgency is felt as our team uses their combined knowledge to bypass security and access the computer that is threatening us. As computer geeks, we thrive on the mental stimulation and problem-solving inherent in a challenge. It's what we live for!"

Jack secretly hoped Brian, whose cyber-sleuthing skills were unmatched, could crack this mystery, unlike his recent disastrous attempts at computer sailing, which had ended in that humiliating last-place finish. With the discovery of the email origins, a wave of cautious optimism washed over Jack—*if the information was accurate*. Examining the Mac that sent the email might uncover crucial details, such as the user profile, browsing history, or even the culprit's keystrokes. Or maybe Bill had programmed the computer to deliver the email on a particular date following his death, the electronic message an apparition of his presence. Either way, it would be useful for Jack to find out if he was ever to understand what Bill was up to before he died.

"Why the Dominican Republic?" asked Katherine as they walked back to their apartment.

Jack's expression was one of deep contemplation. "Bill and I were there over 15 years ago with my dad. Our plan was to spend a week sailing the waters of the Bay of Samana, so we rented a sailboat. My father thought it would be a great learning opportunity to witness the annual whale migration. He wanted us to experience this phenomenon where these magnificent creatures travel to that specific location every winter. We went during our spring break."

"Did you learn anything?" asked Katherine.

"Not really," replied Jack. "The weather was quite rainy throughout our whale watching trip. The one we spotted was from a tour boat from about a mile away. Bill and I were teenagers; the only thing on our minds was meeting girls and drinking beer. We spent most of the week playing billiards at the hotel attached to the marina."

Jack's face broke into a smile. "We visited one cool place, though. Los Haitises National Park. It's home to many large caves containing significant pictograms made by the Indigenous population who lived in the area over 500 years ago. The coolest part of the whole experience was seeing all the bats flying in the twilight sky. Their approach seemed initially direct, aimed straight at us, yet with a sudden alteration in trajectory, they veered away just before impact. Thousands upon thousands of them were moving towards us all at once in a huge and overwhelming wave."

Katherine stopped in her tracks and stared at Jack. "Yuck! You thought that was cool? Are you sick? Bats are the major vector for rabies. A bat bite could have killed you. What about COVID? They could have transmitted a new virus and you would have been responsible for starting a new global pandemic." Katherine shook her head. "You'd never catch me in one of those caves."

Suddenly, overcome with amusement, Jack erupted in a fit of laughter. "During our teenage years, Bill and I both felt as though we were invincible, a feeling of invincibility that only teenagers can truly understand. We had the *best* times together."

He let out a heavy sigh, his shoulders slumping, thinking about his friend. "I guess I grew out of it. Bill didn't."

"Do you think that's a place Bill would have wanted to go back to later on in his life?"

"Bill loved it there, especially the bats; their leathery wings and eerie screeches made it unforgettable," said Jack, a shudder running down his spine at the memory of it. "The way most people recoiled at the sight of a bat, its shadowy form and unsettling squeaks fuelled their fear. That was something Bill found intriguing. He admired these misunderstood creatures and their unique existence. It wouldn't surprise me to find out he returned there at some point prior to his death."

"Bill was certainly full of surprises," whispered Katherine.

*****

Jack sat through the department meeting in the hospital's lecture hall under the hum of fluorescent lights and the inaudible murmur of voices. His phone chirped sharply, startling him in the quiet. It was Brian. He slipped out the back exit to take the call.

"I couldn't get into the Mac," Brian said, his voice tight with frustration. "To the best of our knowledge, the firewall we encountered was unlike anything we've ever experienced in recent memory at the bank. We have a strong track record of success, but this challenge had unique and unexpected layers of complexity that even our team couldn't break through."

"So, you don't know who sent the email?" asked Jack.

"Nope." There was silence on the phone before he continued. "There is something else. Whoever is using that computer knows we tried to hack into it."

"How?"

"They sent a coded message, telling us to back off or face severe consequences."

Chapter 22

The strong easterly wind, blowing at 20 knots, topped the waves in the Bay of Samana with whitecaps. The incredibly loud noise emanating from the twin 60 horsepower engines rendered conversation between Jack and Katherine impossible. It took 30 minutes to traverse the 15 miles that stretched across the expanse of the bay in the 20-foot inflatable boat.

"I can't believe," Katherine said once they had arrived at the other side of the bay, "that you actually managed to persuade me to join you on this utterly insane adventure! I had to cancel two days' worth of appointments—10 patients—to be here."

"But hey, just a five-hour flight from Toronto and here we are on the water, sunshine bathing us in its soothing warmth," he joked. "Besides, you know there is no other way to find out what this laptop business is all about." Jack sighed heavily. "My emotions are all over the place, and I need your level-headed advice to make sound decisions."

Katherine's laugh was tight, almost a nervous tremor in her throat, as if she questioned whether his words were meant to mock her. Jack's expression was serious, his brows furrowed in a deep, concerned line as he looked directly into her eyes.

"If Bill was truly murdered, then could this be a setup?" asked Katherine. "I wonder if there's someone out there trying to lure us into a trap, some sort of deceptive plan they've laid out for us."

"You are getting more paranoid than me," said Jack. "I still believe that Bill would never put us in any danger. Besides, our two bodyguards will keep us safe."

Jose, the boat driver and bodyguard, had expertly guided them to a safe landing on a pristine, sandy beach nestled within the breathtaking beauty of Los Haitises National Park. Alongside them, providing additional security, was another bodyguard named Luis. To guide himself to the laptop's last-known position, Jack consulted Google Maps on his phone, where a blue icon pinpointed where the email had originated.

Following the winding, overgrown pathway that cut through the dense jungle, they eventually arrived at a dilapidated hotel perched precariously on the steep slope of a majestic mountain. Abandonment of the property occurred long ago, and thick, heavy, overgrown jungle bush completely hid the stone steps leading up to the rooms.

"This is where we visited here with my dad 15 years ago. I remember them advertising it as an eco-lodge. Although the hotel was unoccupied, they offered us lunch here. Even back then, it was a mystery to us how they could have possibly kept that place running, given the conditions they were facing. We were the only guests for lunch. I guess they finally ran out of money."

On the property, there was a stream that flowed over a series of waterfalls that spilled into a crystal-clear pool. What had once been a perfectly manicured lawn had become overrun with mangrove brush encroaching on the edges of the natural pool. They made their way past the pool and up the stone steps to the first floor, occupied by three staterooms of varying sizes and styles. Flakes of paint, the color of faded rose, littered the floor beneath the chipped walls. The wooden doors, warped and bent, sagged in their frames, the wood worn smooth by time. The small, blinking blue icon on Google Maps showed the laptop was somewhere on this floor, likely in a nearby room. They tried the doors to the first and second rooms. They found both doors locked. As Jack reached for the handle of the third door, it responded with a loud creak as the heavy wooden door slowly opened.

"I'll wait here," said the guard as he positioned himself beside the door.

Darkness filled the room, where a thick layer of dust coated every surface. A bedframe without a mattress occupied one wall. A table, accompanied by a single chair, was situated close to the balcony, almost as if waiting for someone to use it. Resting on the table's surface was a sleek, silver MacBook, its smooth aluminum casing gleaming softly under the ambient light coming from the balcony's sliding door.

Jack glanced at Katherine as they walked to the laptop. "This is from where the email originated," whispered Jack. A thick layer of dust on the laptop casing strongly suggested the machine had remained unused and undisturbed for a considerable time. Extending from the interior to the exterior was a thin, black wire connected to a solar panel mounted securely on the south-facing balcony.

"I wonder if we could possibly open this thing?" Jack said inquisitively, suggesting they should try.

Gazing at the laptop with an expression of intense curiosity and wide-open eyes, Katherine appeared lost in thought, deeply pondering the meaning and significance of what she was viewing.

Jack flipped up the laptop. The screen came to life. An icon appeared. "Oh no," he said. "We need a password."

Katherine brushed the dust off the chair, then sat down. "Did you and Bill ever share a computer or a code to enter a building or something?"

"Hmm," Jack said. "Oh! Yes. We had a landline in our apartment." He leaned over Katherine and started typing on the dusty keyboard, whispering the numbers. "Four-one-six-four-eight-six..."

With a decisive click, Jack hit the Enter key, the sound in the stillness. He felt a knot of confusion in his stomach, his thoughts swirling like a chaotic storm. *Wait, the sequence was four-one-six, followed by four-eight-seven—I remember the distinct sound of each button.* The mistake he'd made was a sharp, stinging reminder of his failure to save his friend. With a decisive punch, he entered the correct number. A soft *click* sounded as the computer unlocked. Jack let out an enormous sigh of relief, the tension visibly leaving his body. They both leaned in, their breath misting slightly in the cool air as a message popped up on the screen.

Hi Jack,

I knew you would find this. If you want to find out what happened to me, click on the button marked VIDEO.

Jack looked up at Katherine with a confused look. "Should we do this?" Katherine shrugged her shoulders and nodded in affirmation.

Clicking on the button didn't initially result in a video playing, but rather a static image loaded, showing a picture of a rather small room. From the ceiling, the camera's lens seemed to be trained on a single bed. Then the video started when Bill entered the room. He walked to a small refrigerator, opened it, retrieved a can of Coca-Cola, swiftly pulled the tab with a decisive snap, and then consumed its contents in a few rapid swallows. Kneeling next to a cot, he located a small safe hidden beneath, carefully unlocked it, pulled out an item resembling a syringe, and filled it with a white liquid from an ampule. He then sat down on the edge of the bed. With a weary sigh, he kicked off his shoes. He took a yellow rubber tourniquet and placed it firmly around his left arm. With precision, he inserted the needle into his vein, methodically and carefully emptying half of its contents. His right hand moved quickly. He skillfully removed the tourniquet, and it dropped onto the floor beside the bed. As the effects of the drug began to take hold, a wide smile spread across his face. Euphoria.

With Katherine's and Jack's eyes glued to the screen, their faces became one of shock as they stared in disbelief at what they saw unfolding before them. A wave of nausea washed over Jack as he watched his friend's life slip away, a horrifying scene that left him profoundly sickened. Overcome with grief, he felt hot tears trace a path down his cheek as the painful memories returned.

Eyes still fixated on the screen, they barely registered the *click* of Bill's door opening a minute later, revealing a soldier wearing army fatigues. The man walked over to Bill and injected the remaining white liquid from the syringe into his vein. About to leave, the soldier slowly turned, his eyes suddenly locking onto the camera lens. A surprised expression twisted into a mask of fury; his eyes narrowed into slits, and the veins in his neck swelled, throbbing with rage. Jack watched as his muscular right arm jerked upwards before the screen abruptly went black.

With a shared gasp, Jack and Katherine looked at each other in disbelief. "No!" Jack shouted, frantically searching through the cluttered computer files, the cursor blinking mockingly as he tried to find the elusive video. "We need to bring this laptop home and have Brian find the video. I want to have a better look at the soldier who finished off Bill."

With a sharp tug, Jack detached the black wire from the solar panel, the plastic casing creaking slightly, then closed the laptop with a loud slap. The metal casing glowed a molten red, and acrid black smoke billowed from the gap between the lid and keyboard. A second later, with a whoosh and a roar, it burst into flames, sending sparks and smoke billowing into the air. Within a minute, the heat had reduced it to a smouldering heap, the acrid stench of burning plastic and metal filling the air as Jack and Katherine leapt backward in shock.

*****

"Both those emails from Bill came from that laptop," said Brian. "I wonder why he would rig it to explode if someone tampered with it?"

Katherine, Jack, and Brian were once again at the Starbucks discussing what they could do next. The flight from Samana to Toronto landed late last night, and Katherine and Jack were back at work for the day. Brian had agreed to meet with them that evening.

Jack shrugged. "He would have had his reasons, and they likely involved a complex web of motivations and circumstances. Some other files were on the laptop, but they looked like computer codes, which, of course, made no sense to me. While searching for the video, I spotted them. I wanted to get a better look at the soldier who injected the rest of the propofol into Bill."

"I tried to access iCloud for that laptop," said Brian with frustration, "but couldn't find it."

"So, there is no other way to retrieve the video?" asked Jack.

Brian shook his head. "The video disappeared with the laptop. I wonder why he didn't just send you the link to the video in the last email he sent. It would have saved you the trip to the Dominican Republic."

"At least now we know someone killed him," said Katherine. "I spoke to my old professor, Dr. Ramirez, about brain-derived neurotrophic factor, or BDNF, explaining my interest in its role in memory consolidation. In the central and peripheral nervous systems, BDNF supports the survival of existing neurons, stimulates the growth of new ones, and promotes the formation of synapses throughout its action on specific neurons. In the brain, it's active in the hippocampus, cortex, and basal forebrain—areas vital to learning, memory, and higher-level thought processes, influencing everything from forming new memories to complex problem-solving. BDNF plays a crucial role in the formation and retention of long-term memories, contributing to lasting cognitive function."

"Well, that flew over my head," said Brian. "In layperson's terms, please. What does that all mean? Did he know why sexual activity elevates it?"

"I don't think anyone knows what it means," Katherine said. "Dealing with the research related to the BDNF protein has presented significant difficulties. The protein seems unstable. Dr. Ramirez said that BDNF goes up with exercise, and it didn't surprise him that sex would do the same thing."

"Huh," said Jack. "Not sure what the next step is to get to the bottom of this. Without the video, I can't approach the base commander in Iraq. He wouldn't believe me if I told him what I saw in it. I'm not sure how this BDNF fits in with Bill's death, but there seems to be a connection."

A high-pitched *ping* sliced through the silence, announcing the arrival of a new email on Jack's phone. Everyone glanced at it. A jolt shot through him and trepidation filled his gaze as he looked up at Katherine and Brian. "It's from Bill."

"Don't open it yet!" Brian shouted. "Wait—let's go back to my office at the bank and see if we can trace where it came from. I can download the file directly onto our email tracer, the program we use to track criminals, and it might lead us to the computer it originated from. Us nerds have been creatively strategizing and devising plans to breach the firewall that previously stymied our efforts."

With a sense of urgency, the trio sprinted towards Brian's office tower three city blocks away. Breathless, no one spoke as the elevator ascended, carrying them to the 45th floor. Using his passkey, Brian smoothly opened the door that led into the office. Despite it being 8 p.m., four men were intensely focused on their laptops, their fingers furiously typing. They stopped what they were doing as Brian announced, "Alright, team, remember the challenge last time? Well, another email has come, so let's get to work on tracking down its origin and destination."

The four computer geeks, once engrossed in their individual tasks, huddled in the chairs around Brian's desk. He requested Jack use his credentials on Google to retrieve the email. Then Jack watched from a distance as Brian, comfortably seated in the computer chair, bashed away on the keyboard.

"Jason," said Brian to the tallest of the computer geeks, "I need your credentials to get in. You are the expert at this. Can you give me a hand?"

Jason slowly looked up at Brian and Jack, his gaze assessing them carefully. A perplexed expression settled on his face, his eyes wide and unfocused; it was as if he didn't understand what they wanted from him. Jack's expression turned quizzical, lifting his eyebrows slightly as he stared. It seemed to take forever for Jason to get up. A few crumbs from his bran muffin, clinging to his unkempt beard, fell onto the floor, joining the rumpled papers and dust motes under the desk, as he scratched his beard, sending more crumbs scattering. With a groan from the old chair, Jason pushed himself up, his long limbs unfolding as he swept his unruly red hair from his face.

As he sat in front of Brian's computer, he adjusted his greasy glasses, pushing them higher on his nose with a sigh. His fingers danced across the keyboard, a blur of motion as the screen flashed with each keystroke, the light bouncing off the plastic frames of his glasses.

"Got it," said Jason with a grunt. The screen continued to strobe, even though he'd stopped typing while the computer cycled through the program.

"You can read the email on your smart phone now," said Brian. "Jason has traced its origin, but it will take a few minutes to pin down the location."

Jack opened the Gmail account on his phone and read the message.

Hi Jack,

This will be the last email you'll get from me. I believe that by now, the evidence is so overwhelming that you will be completely convinced that I was murdered. It is important you know the reasons they targeted me. Although email tracing can offer some clues, acquiring a complete and accurate picture of what transpired may require considerably more effort and investigation. I'm sure you'll figure it out... eventually.

I love you.

Bill

A profound sense of sadness overcame Jack as a tear escaped and rolled down his cheek. He passed the phone to Katherine. Annoyed and perplexed at the message, she lifted her shoulder in a dismissive shrug. "Why can't he just *tell* us what's going on?"

"Bill always approached a problem differently," said Jack. "Maybe he is trying to protect us from whatever trouble he got into. None of this is making any sense to me right now." He shook his head.

"You won't believe this," said Brian, looking up from his computer. "The email originated from *your* personal laptop, which is sitting in your apartment. The tracer shows that someone sent it 30 minutes ago. This is getting a little spooky because whoever did that sent it from your apartment."

"What?!" shouted Jack. "That's crazy. We have the best security system..." He opened the app on his phone and looked at the apartment's security video from the last two hours. The footage showed Jack and Katherine exiting the apartment, their silhouettes framed in the doorway's dim light. A few minutes later, a loud creak announced the door opening, and a man's silhouette appeared in the doorway. The image was blurry, almost smeared, making it hard to discern the man's facial features. The intruder went to the alarm panel and punched a few buttons on the keypad. They observed him intently as he sat hunched over the computer, the rhythmic tapping of his fingers a steady beat against the backdrop of the whirring machine. In less than two minutes, he got up, reset the alarm, and exited the suite.

Katherine's face was aghast. "Let's take this to the police," she said. "We just witnessed a... a home invasion. Our home!"

"Hold on just..." Jack's voice trailed off, and a sudden silence filled the room. He replayed the grainy video, his eyes scanning the blurry image of the man, hoping to discern any recognizable features. He watched the man settle heavily into the chair before the computer. Jack's gaze darted from Katherine's worried look to the four computer geeks hunched over their keyboards before finally settling on Brian's thoughtful expression.

"We don't need to go to the police," said Jack. "I recognize that person. I know exactly who that was in our apartment." The room was silent as Jack smiled, his eyes twinkling, drinking in their captivated attention. He felt a thrill run through him.

"That was Bill."

Chapter 23

"Jason, one of the computer geeks from last night is in the emergency room," said the voice on the phone. Jack glanced at his smart watch, its dim screen glowing faintly in the pre-dawn darkness of his bedroom, charging on the night table: 3:43 a.m. The insistent chirping of his cell phone had jolted Jack awake. Disoriented, he recalled the late meeting with Brian's team, the blurry ride home in an Uber, and falling asleep with Katherine immediately after getting home.

Brian's voice cracked with panic as he continued. "Someone stabbed him in the stomach when he got home. Someone was waiting for him."

Jack was wide awake now. "What happened? Why...?" he whispered into the phone, his voice weakened with the shocked of the news.

"Not sure," said Brian. "He called me. I live just down the hall and I called 9-1-1. They took him to your hospital. Can you come see him? I'm here with him now and he's asking for you."

"Give me 20 minutes," Jack said, his voice tight with urgency as he started grabbing clothes with one hand. In the car, his mind raced and a frantic drum beat against his ribs as he sped to the hospital, ignoring red lights and weaving through slower cars, narrowly avoiding collisions in the oncoming traffic lane.

The frantic energy of the emergency room spilled into the resuscitation room, where they had placed Jason on a gurney, a plastic oxygen mask pressed against his skin, as he struggled to breathe. Intravenous lines, filled with clear fluids, dripped rapidly from the tall metal stand. A look of terror filled Jason's eyes as he spotted Jack, his gaze darting around the brightly lit room, searching for a sign of danger. Every creak and whisper seemed to heighten his fear.

"It hurts," Jason said, his face contorted in a grimace, eyes squeezed shut.

Jack glanced at the vital signs monitor, scanning the fluctuating numbers and the rhythmic beep of the heart rate monitor. Jason's heart was beating rapidly at a rate of 120 beats per minute, while his blood pressure measured 100/62 and his oxygen saturation was at 100 per cent. Jack lifted the heavy, starched bedsheet, the crisp cotton cool against his fingertips. The knife had plunged deep, its hilt buried up to the guard in the right side of the abdomen, just below the ribs. Someone wrapped a length of gauze around the knife to soak up the dark blood slowly seeping out.

With a click, Jack opened the CAT scan and studied the images displayed on the monitor next to the gurney. He identified a moderate amount of fluid in the abdomen; it appeared blood-like in density. The knife sliced deep into the right lobe of the liver.

Determining the extent of the damage to the adjacent duodenum or biliary tracts from the CAT scan images proved challenging.

"The OR just called," the nurse said to Jack, her voice laced with urgency. "If you're prepared to take him, they are waiting for him. Cross-matched blood is being sent to the OR by the blood bank."

With a soft thud, the porters carefully loaded the IV bags, heart monitors, and other medical equipment onto the gurney as Jack hurried to the waiting room to find Brian. The sound of Jack's hasty entrance startled Brian. He shot up from his seat, eyes wide. "Is he... is he okay?" Brian asked, his voice trembling with worry.

"So far, he is stable," replied Jack. "I'm taking him to the operating room. He's on his way there now. What happened?"

Brian shook his head, a frustrated sigh escaping his lips. "This is all my fault," he cried, the tears hot on his cheeks. "In retrospect, I realize involving these guys was a grave error of judgment with serious repercussions. They love a challenge, so I wanted to include them. Now look what happened..."

Jack put his hand on Brian's shoulder. "You're not to blame. Look, I have to run up to the OR. I'll track you down when I'm done."

When Jack arrived in the OR in his scrubs, the anesthesiologist had already put Jason asleep, and the circulating nurse had prepped the abdomen with chlorhexidine. His partner, Dr. Larry Klapman, was already putting on the drapes as Jack got gowned.

"Should we put in a laparoscope or go right for a laparotomy?" asked Larry.

"A considerable amount of blood in the abdomen is visible on the CAT scan," replied Jack. "I'm concerned about the possibility of a significant vascular injury when we remove the knife, so it would be wise to proceed directly to a laparotomy for better management."

"Good idea," said Larry.

After a brief "time out" to ensure they were operating on the correct patient for the correct procedure, Jack made a large upper-abdominal incision, slicing through skin and midline fascia. Upon entering the abdomen, a sudden gush of blood erupted, yet Larry managed to swiftly suction up the majority. Jack's eyes focused on the exact spot where the knife had penetrated the liver. Thankfully, the path of the knife seemed to be contained within the liver. A thorough examination of the duodenum and gallbladder showed no signs of trauma.

"Let's pull the knife out and see what happens," said Jack.

Larry reached over, carefully extracting the blood-stained weapon from the deep wound, and handed it to the waiting scrub nurse. Jack waited with bated breath, every nerve ending alert, to see if anything would happen. There wasn't much blood, only a faint crimson seeping through the laceration in the liver capsule caused by the knife. He breathed a huge sigh of relief, the tension visibly leaving his shoulders.

Suddenly, the liver laceration seemed to split in just a few seconds, transforming from a small two-centimetre cut to a gaping 10-centimetre gash, releasing a torrent into the abdomen. The warm gush of blood and bile under pressure spurted from the split liver. It forced Jack to recoil sharply from the operating table, desperate to avoid being soaked in the crimson torrent.

Larry reached over to the back table, grabbed a handful of rough, damp sponges, and frantically stuffed them into the split liver, pressing hard to stop the bleeding. He used his large hands to apply steady pressure to the blood-soaked sponges, successfully stopping the hemorrhage.

Jack looked over the drapes to the head of the bed at the anesthesiologist. "We've got some major bleeding from the liver. Is he okay?"

The monitors showed that Jason's blood pressure had plummeted to a dangerously low 70/40, while his pulse rate had soared to a frantic 140 beats per minute, the rhythmic beeping a stark counterpoint to the silent alarm in the room.

A barely audible "Oh shit!" escaped the anesthesiologist's lips as he frantically pumped two units of blood into the large-bore veins in a chaos of sounds the rhythmic whoosh of the blood, the hiss of the IV tubing, and the frantic beeping of the monitors. While the anesthesiologist worked on resuscitating the patient, Larry maintained steady pressure on the sponges in the liver.

After 10 minutes, the pressure was 110/70, and the pulse had come down to 110. Jack looked over at Larry and asked, "Should we have a look to see if we can stop the bleeding? He seems to be stable now."

Giving a noncommittal shrug, Larry seemed to say, "Why not?" With a slow sigh of relief, he released the pressure on the sponges, carefully peeling them away. A torrent of blood, warm and viscous, once more filled the abdomen. Larry hastily stuffed a fresh set of sponges into the torn liver.

"I'll contact our hepatobiliary surgeon," Jack said, removing his gown and heading to the phone on the wall. He continued to talk with Larry as he dialled the number. "The previous and only other time I encountered this amount of bleeding from the liver was during what should have been a straightforward and routine gallbladder surgical procedure. We packed the liver with sponges and came back in 48 hours to remove the sponges. The bleeding had stopped. The patient did fine. Just keep pressure on the sponges."

Jack scrubbed again after the phone call and surveyed Jason's liver. "The surgeon agreed that might be the best approach, to leave the sponges in the liver. The compression applied by the abdominal wall will act to staunch the flow of blood, preventing any additional loss. We'll take another look at this in approximately 48 hours."

Following the closure of the abdomen, the surgical team carefully transported Jason to the intensive care unit, where he would receive ventilator support and continuous monitoring, while awaiting the next scheduled operation in 48 hours. Jack looked for Brian in the waiting room; Katherine was with him. The two looked up at Jack, their faces filled with hopeful anticipation.

"We just transported him to the ICU," Jack said, his face conveying worry. "He's stable... for now." With a grim expression, Jack detailed the critical liver hemorrhage, outlining the 48-hour plan to rush Jason back to the operating room. "I just don't understand," Jack added. "Why would anyone stab him?"

Brian, stealing a glance, looked over at Katherine. She nodded. "You can tell him," she said, reassuring her brother.

"Jason stayed at the office and traced a few more of Bill's emails," said Brian. "He discovered someone had illegally accessed Bill's email a few months ago, tracing the digital footprint to the culprit's location, an Atlanta computer. Jason swiftly downloaded several files from the computer and emailed them to me. My thought was that they put a trace on Jason and found out where he lived. Here's the video from his security system."

The shaky, almost silent footage on Brian's phone showed a man in a black balaclava slipping into Jason's apartment. A minute later, Jason stepped inside the dimly lit living room. With a sudden brutal movement, the intruder plunged the knife into Jason, the sound somehow muffled. A loud thump swiftly followed it as Jason's body fell to the hardwood floor. The intruder sneered, "I doubt that will kill you. This was to warn you and your friends to back off." His voice was a low rasp that sent a shiver down Jack's spine. The intruder was gone, his presence fading like a whisper in the empty room. The video showed Jason's hand reaching for his cell phone. Jack could see his fingers brushed against the smooth glass surface.

Brian closed his own the cell phone and said, "That's when he called me."

The video of Jason's brutal attack had left Jack reeling, his heart pounding, as he processed the senseless harm inflicted upon him. "What was in the download Jason sent you?" he asked Brian.

"I forwarded it to Katherine," he said. "I didn't really understand the medical jargon."

Katherine frowned as she opened the attachment and read the document, summarizing it for them as she skimmed. "A shadowy internet security firm, hired to stifle innovation, appeared to be behind the suppression of some groundbreaking medical technology. As far as I can tell, this technology will prevent common diseases, eliminating high blood pressure, high blood sugar, wheezing lungs, clogged arteries, obesity, and cancerous tumours. The major health care companies, drug companies, and for-profit hospitals have come together to suppress this technology until they have a plan to prevent themselves from going bankrupt."

"And somehow, Bill is connected?" said Jack. He thought back to the video of Bill in his apartment when he attempted to email from beyond the grave. Despite the grainy quality of the video, Jack instantly recognized the familiar slope of Bill's shoulders and the way he held his head. His unique physique was memorable, yet the constant, irritating sight of him wiping his nose with his sleeve whenever he felt anxious was distracting; the damp stain spreading on the fabric was a testament to his nervous habit. Jack also recognized Bill's distinctive gait—that rolling, almost swaggering walk. What really gave him away, though, was the familiar sight of the crack of his buttocks exposed because his pants fell partway down from his protuberant potbelly.

"Brian," said Jack after a few moments of silence. "I need your help to find Bill."

Chapter 24

"Our advantage is that Bill is completely unaware that we are actively searching for him," said Jack. "He's certain we believe him to be dead, a notion that fuels his secretive actions."

"We track people at the bank in several ways," Brian explained. "It is currently not allowed by law, but we must be ahead of the criminals to protect ourselves. As bank employees, the weight of our clients' secrets rests heavily on our shoulders. As cybersecurity experts, employing this technology is a necessity in our line of work to effectively prevent fraud. Investigators used security camera footage, transaction records, and other data to piece together what happened."

The fluorescent lights in the Royal Bank flickered overhead as Katherine and Jack huddled around Brian's computer, the air thick with the smell of old paper and stale coffee. "To achieve the best results, we plan to use the city's current video camera system and implement our specialized facial recognition software. By keeping the device running constantly, we can monitor his every move."

"Is that... legal?" asked Jack. "Wouldn't that be a breach of privacy laws?"

Brian scoffed, the sound sharp and dismissive. "The idea of privacy is becoming obsolete in our increasingly transparent society. Every action, every click, is tracked and stored. Did you know every cell phone conversation in North America is filtered, with algorithms constantly scanning for words associated with terrorism, creating a massive and ever-growing database? Your Google timeline silently tracks your movements, displaying a map of your day's journey, even without your explicit consent. China's video camera's production assembly lines are a blur of activity, producing the vast majority of the world's video cameras. The Chinese government can secretly review videos from every camera they produce using embedded microchips. This allows them to monitor footage without the owners' knowledge. The technology is unsettlingly invasive. These are the programs we've hacked to get identical data as they can get in China."

Jack laughed at his own naivety. "During a busy workday, I distinctly remember a conversation about Tesla's autopilot capabilities with a colleague. My cell phone was in my pocket. When I finished the conversation, the insistent buzzing of several text message alerts pulled my attention to my phone. I'd received a series of notifications about the dealership's latest Tesla deals, the subject lines promising exceptional savings. An icy dread of violation of my personal space washed over me as I discovered my phone had been monitoring my conversation."

"That is the least of it," said Brian. "When a customer walks into a bank seeking a loan, even before taking a seat, we have a comprehensive profile. This could even include recorded conversations with his parents about past loans. The bank, despite their denials, uses facial recognition technology from strategically placed security cameras to quietly evaluate his credit, collecting data surreptitiously. With a barely perceptible delay, the information appears on the computer screen, a clean, crisp display."

Katherine said, "So, as soon as Bill appears on a camera, we'll know about it?"

"Well," said Brian, stretching and yawning, "we'll start with that. I can also look for financial transactions, including bank statements and credit card records, analyze phone conversations using voice-recognition software to identify key phrases, and employ other investigative methods. I suspect his carefulness stems from the widespread belief in his demise. Everyone thinks he's dead, so he moves like a ghost. I doubt those hunting him have the same level of technological resources and bandwidth at their disposal."

Jack and Katherine returned to their apartment, its familiar comfort wrapping around them like a warm blanket. Exhausted from a long day, they ordered Mexican food from UberEATS, the late hour only heightened by the rumbling of their stomachs. Twenty minutes later, a delivery person appeared at their door with steaming plates of tacos and guacamole. The aroma of cilantro and lime filled the air as they sat down to eat.

"How's Jason doing?" Katherine asked, a hint of concern in her eyes.

Jack swallowed his mouthful of tacos and took a swig of beer before answering. "Surprisingly well," he said. "Yesterday, Larry and I brought him to the operating room to remove the packing from the liver. No bleeding occurred, which was a tremendous relief. The liver laceration looked clean and showed no signs of reopening. We left drains and closed the abdomen. The ICU team transferred him to the surgical ward this morning. Jason is drinking protein shakes, and this afternoon he was up and walking. He's going to be fine. His breathing is steady, and his pulse is strong."

"Phew," said Katherine, "That's a relief. I hope..."

A *ping* interrupted the conversation. Jack opened his cell phone. It was a text message from Brian:

Our software analysis of security footage revealed an individual bearing a resemblance to Bill entering an apartment building on Lakeshore Drive. The video shows the man entering the elevator, going to the 24th floor and into suite 2402. Look out for an email from me in the morning. I'll send you the video then.

"Huh," said Katherine when Jack showed her the message. "How are we going to see if it is him? If we knock at his door, we'll just spook him, and he'll cover his tracks. We'd likely never find him again."

Jack nodded his head and said, "We would have to trick him somehow into coming out of the apartment. Let's think about this and come up with a plan."

*****

Jack and Katherine sat in Einstein's Bar and Grill in Toronto on King Street, near Bill's apartment. The restaurant was nearly empty and quiet, with only the clatter of dishes in a constant background hum. As they sipped tea, Jack's doubts grew about their plan and the reason they were here today. When they'd reviewed the videos from Brian, Jack scrutinized the man's face in the footage, but the angle and resolution made identification difficult. However, Bill's unmistakable cocky swagger as he walked left Jack with no doubt it was him.

A nagging worry, something Jack had been trying to ignore, surfaced again. He remembered the sly smile of Susan Austin, the madame at the Mustang Ranch who had confirmed that Bill remained on their exclusive newsletter list. It seemed peculiar—actually a jarring thought—because Jack felt, with unsettling certainty, that Bill was already dead.

He'd asked Brian, "Is there a way to find out if Bill was still receiving the emails from the Mustang Ranch and if he was even bothering to open them?"

"Let's find out. Give me a minute," said Brian, opening his computer and tapping at the keys. "I hacked into Bill's mailbox. He's definitely getting the emails, and he's definitely opening them."

Sipping their tea at Einstein's, Jack realized that they'd jumped to conclusions about Bill, picturing him in shadowy dealings based on little more than gut feelings and whispers. The research on brain-derived neurotrophic factor, interwoven with the high-stakes financial world of medicine, and Bill's intense focus on extending lifespan, formed a complex and intricate network.

"Looks like we were wrong," said Katherine. "It doesn't look like he's turning up."

Jack's gaze swept across the quiet, dimly lit room, and he realized Katherine was probably right. It had seemed farfetched thinking that they could entice Bill with Jessica, a fulsome brunette in her twenties from Mustang with unusually high BDNF levels, as indicated by Bill's lab tests. But the idea itself was well executed. Through a complex series of commands, Brian had bypassed Mustang's defenses, sending an email to Bill, which appeared to originate from Jessica. In her email, "Jessica" asserted her understanding of his BDNF research, highlighting her own remarkably high protein levels as a reason she believed she could help him. She suggested they meet in person at the Einstein's Bar and Grill in Toronto.

Jack and Katherine sat in a quiet corner booth for a full hour, the air thick with anticipation, the restaurant waiting for the after-work rush to begin. "Let's just go," said Katherine.

"Wait. I..."

A man walked in, light from the street seeping inside, almost as if announcing his arrival. He had dark hair and glasses, with a prominent nose and chin.

"Nah. False alarm." Jack was quite certain he had never seen him before when the man paused and looked around the bar. As he walked past the partially hidden booth where Katherine and Jack sat, Jack said in a loud voice, "Hi Bill."

The man stopped in his tracks, turned around, and looked at Jack and Katherine. He smiled. "I was hoping you would find me," he said as he sat down and gave them both a hug.

Chapter 25

"You are such an asshole, Bill," Katherine seethed, her face burning with rage, her hands clenched into fists. "During your funeral, we cried, our vision blurred by tears as we said our last goodbyes. We consoled your grieving mom, who still holds onto the belief that you are no longer alive. We witnessed the horrifying scene of Debbie's car bursting into flames after our meeting. How do you reconcile your existence with your own moral compass?" she ranted loudly now that they were no longer in a public place.

A sharp intake of breath escaped Bill's lips as Katherine's admonishment hit him, a visible wince betraying his discomfort. In his Lakeshore apartment, the plush carpet muffled their footsteps as they moved through the spacious living room overlooking Lake Ontario from the 24th floor. Dozens of computer screens lined the walls, their faint blue glow illuminating the room. The hum of the six separate computers created a low, constant drone. "You're right, Katherine, but it was the only way," he said in a breathy voice. "Let me show you something."

Bill pulled up at the table with the keyboard. He banged at the keys and an image of a video appeared. "You've already seen this," he said. It was the video of him self-administering the propofol and the soldier entering the room and topping it off.

"Well," said Bill, "obviously he didn't kill me. I had at least five more cameras in my room. Here's some more footage."

The image flipped to another view, which time lapsed to 20 minutes later. The video showed Bill stirring at first and waking up. He sat on the edge of the bed. Slightly unsteady, Bill trudged to the chair in front of his computer and turned it on. Jack and Katherine could see him review the video of the soldier coming into his room. "This was it, I realized—my chance to disappear, to reinvent myself, by faking my own death."

Debbie appeared in the next video, quietly slipping into his room, her nervous smile caught by the camera. Her eyes darted around the room, a silent assessment, before she cautiously checked the bathroom. Debbie searched the room, completely unaware of Bill, who pressed himself flat against the floorboards beneath the bed. The silence in the empty room was heavy as she left and closed the door.

The soldier responsible for the extra propofol burst into the room less than 10 minutes later, his frantic breathing and wide eyes betraying his anxiety. This time, Bill was there to greet him. He was hiding behind the door and plunged a syringe into the right jugular vein. The soldier collapsed.

"It was an accident," Bill insisted, his eyes wide with regret. "He fell and hit his head. That's what killed him, I'm certain of it. My 3D printer, a marvel of technology, can duplicate almost anything. I've used it to make several hyper-realistic masks of my own face."

The next video image showed Bill pulling the body onto the bed and slipping a mask that looked identical to Bill over the soldier's head. He placed the IV into the man's left antecubital vein and attached a syringe with some propofol. To all appearances, it looked like Bill had died from an accidental overdose.

"What about the autopsy that said you'd ODd? asked Jack.

"Ha!" Bill laughed, the sound echoing through the living room of the apartment. "The pathologist at the base once confided to me that despite a decade of army service, he'd never actually performed an autopsy. As an alcoholic, with the dull ache of a hangover and the desperate need for another drink, he consumed his days in a haze of cheap Scotch. I knew he wouldn't do one on me, either. He would perfunctorily complete the forms as if he had already conducted an autopsy. Then he would report the results he predicted, as if he had performed a post-mortem examination before going back to his drink."

"So why was this all so necessary?" asked Katherine, shaking her head in disbelief.

A deep sigh escaped Bill's lips, heavy with frustration. "This is going to take a while," he muttered, running a hand through his already dishevelled hair. "It's already after midnight. I think it would be best if you two went home now, and then we could all get together again this coming Saturday. I can show you a few things."

With wide eyes, Katherine and Jack remained rigidly seated, speechless, and motionless. Bill looked at them, and it must have dawned on him they were at an impasse, and he had to explain his recent actions to move forward. He leaned over his keyboard and began typing. The largest monitor on the wall sprang to life and what appeared to be a large molecule rotated on the screen. "This is the protein brain-derived neurotrophic factor or BDTF," he said.

They watched as the molecule on the screen split in half and a smaller entity labelled mRNA appeared. "While I was undergoing surgical residency, I developed a mRNA that has the ability to replicate BDTF, and subsequently administered it to myself. Compared to normal levels, the mRNA can produce proteins at levels that are hundreds of times higher. The average person doesn't use even close to their full brain capacity, only about 10 per cent. Even the smartest people. Did you know that?" He didn't wait for an answer. "Well, now I use significantly more. My memory is truly exceptional, allowing me to recall details with stunning accuracy. My problem-solving skills are so advanced that they outshine those of the most intelligent individuals on the planet."

A shocking sensation, a powerful surge that ran from his head to his toes and left him breathless, suddenly overcame Jack's body as he parsed what Bill was saying. The injection of an experimental substance, one that had not undergone the rigorous oversight of a randomized, double-blind, controlled study, represented a clear and unacceptable breach of established ethical boundaries. If discovered, those involved faced mandatory prison sentences. The research demanded a rigorous methodology, necessitating the careful and consistent following of established parameters and guidelines.

"I know, I know... it was risky," said Bill as he watched Jack's reaction. "But I'm glad I did it. This protein causes growth of neurons in the brain, especially in the hippocampus, and not only increases memory, but improves cognition and other higher brain functions." Bill's arm swept around the room. "All this is possible because of my improved cognition and memory. I can write computer programs that no one else can dream about and leave it to AI to amplify the result."

"Is that how you can beat the odds at the blackjack table?" asked Jack.

Bill smiled. "One thing about having increased brain capacity is the ability to think in ways no one could ever imagine."

Bill pulled out a deck of cards, still with the wrapping on it. He handed the pack to Katherine. "I'll turn around and you open the deck and choose a card. I'll tell you what it is."

Bill faced the wall while Katherine took out a card.

"That's the five of clubs," said Bill.

Katherine split the pack in half and chose another one.

"Queen of spades. Oh, you just put it back in the pack and the one you are holding now is the four of diamonds."

"What the fuck?" cried Jack. "How do you do that?"

Bill turned to face them. "Micro chips send a signal to my cell phone. This relays a voice message to a micro receptor I've implanted in both of my ear canals that tells me which card you are holding."

Jack could feel his jaw open. He shook his head. "That's fine with these cards, but how about the cards in the casinos? There is no way you can tamper with them," said Jack.

"You're right," replied Bill. "The three primary manufacturers of playing cards globally are the United States Playing Card Company (USPCC), based in the United States; Cartamundi, a Belgian company; and Legends Playing Cards, an Asian manufacturer. Although many companies manufacture playing cards, these three alone handle the production of tens of millions of decks annually. A plastic enamel covers each paper card. All the companies get the plastic coating from a company in China. I hacked into the computer that controls what goes into the plastic and I programmed microchips to be mixed in."

"Oh my God," whispered Katherine. "You have created a monster within yourself."

In a gesture of dejection and surrender, Jack buried his face in his hands, his elbows resting heavily on the table. "Who else have you injected with this mRNA?" said Jack, his voice noticeably rising as he looked up directly at Bill. "Jessica from the Mustang Ranch? Her blood BDTF concentration was dramatically higher than that of the rest of the participants, reaching levels hundreds of times greater. Is she experiencing a notable enhancement in her cognitive abilities and functions? Did she consent to this Frankenstein-like witchcraft?" As Jack's anger intensified, his voice grew louder and louder, swelling and booming until it filled the apartment.

Bill smiled. "No. I'm the only one who received the mRNA injection. Jessica had the amazing good fortune of spending an unforgettable night with me, a night that she will always cherish and remember fondly. It was my, um, overachievement with her that led to the high levels attained. I was looking forward to the possibility of her seeking me out for another session. That would have been nice..." Letting out a heavy sigh, a dreamy expression washed over Bill's face, replacing any previous emotion with a look of blissful contentment.

"So why are people trying to kill you?" asked Katherine.

With a hopeful expression in his eyes, Bill looked up at Katherine and Jack, a glimmer of anticipation in his gaze. He looked like he desperately craved their approval, his guilt palpable after subjecting them to such hardship, his heart heavy with the weight of his actions. A film seemed to cover his eyes, dimming their light as his shoulders slumped, the weight of the world pressing down on him.

"I possess the key to unlocking the secrets of living a long life. It is my sole intention to rid the world of all medical diseases."

Chapter 26

With utter fascination, Jack intently watched Bill's skilful and precise movements as he remotely performed the complex surgical procedure. Earlier that morning, the patient, a migrant farmer from Guatemala who now lay on a gurney covered with a crisp white hospital sheet, had arrived at the private clinic in St. John's, Antigua. Bill had already taken care of the cost of his airfare, ensuring his upcoming trip from Huehuetenango, a city in northern Guatemala, to Antigua was a sure thing. That evening, the patient had a flight scheduled to take him back to his home in the farming community. While seated at Bill's computer terminal in suite 2402 in Toronto, Jack watched as Bill remotely manipulated the nano-robots with his specialized cursor.

"I met this poor fella when I was on a medical mission to Guatemala eight months ago, while I was still in Little Rock, before my sudden departure," Bill explained, speaking to Jack as he sat there in the chair next to him drinking coffee. "They would organize a team every year to go into the remote mountains of Guatemala to help those most in need of medical care," explained Bill. "He has a massive colon cancer that is metastatic to his lungs and liver. Were he to find himself in Canada, his treatment plan would entail a six-month course of chemotherapy, to be followed by a series of three extensive operations targeting the colon, then the liver, and finally the lungs, with the ultimate goal of eradicating the cancerous growth. The financial burden on

Canadian taxpayers would be a substantial and shocking $200,000. Truly a staggering amount."

While Bill carefully positioned the minuscule nano robots, Jack fixated his gaze on the sophisticated overlay of the CAT scan's digital images that were superimposed onto the live video feed of the patient undergoing the procedure. The tumour was of considerable size, a truly massive growth. Considering its proximity to major blood vessels, the pancreas, and the bile ducts, Jack deemed it inoperable. Surgical resection presented significant risks, making the attempt a considerable gamble with potentially serious consequences. Jack, a highly skilled surgeon, utterly convinced himself that he would never undertake such a complex and challenging case of advanced-stage cancer.

"In the coming month, the nano robots will systematically eliminate the cancerous cells, allowing the healthy tissue sufficient time to recover from the damage caused by the tumour's removal," said Bill. "I've also given him a retrovirus that will replace any of his native genetic coding that would cause diabetes, atherosclerosis, hypertension, renal disease, and any other common medical condition you can think of. This fella's going to live a long time."

From his vantage point, Jack observed the patient steadily drinking a whole litre of clear liquid from a commonplace plastic water bottle. Abandoning the gurney, he sprang to his feet and began his journey towards the exit. A nurse, her crisp white outfit and hat neatly arranged in her curly hair, gave him a six-pack of bottled water. "His instructions are to provide a bottle to his wife and five children, intending to ensure that they do not suffer from the medical conditions prevalent in our society."

The video depicted the patient's departure as he vanished into a waiting taxi, presumably to be transported back to the airport. "The total cost for the cancer curing treatment was $849.00 for the flight," said Bill proudly.

With a sudden movement, Jack stood up and took a walk through the room, pacing the expansive space. A tumultuous sea of emotions overcame him, a swirling mix of feelings, both positive and negative, as the full impact of what he had just seen sunk in. Throughout the entirety of his surgical career, he had diligently adhered to and followed all established practices and professional guidelines within the field. The lack of usual checks and balances in the experimental treatment violated every ethical principle he held dear, causing him great distress. The action of exploiting a trusting, naïve Indigenous man from a remote Guatemalan village within a developing nation in such a manner was truly reprehensible and morally wrong. A rising anger built inside Jack, making him feel increasingly agitated. It was crucial for him to calm down and have a serious conversation with Bill to make his friend see reason.

Bill remained hunched over his computer. "I know what you are thinking," he said. "What I'm doing has violated every principle when caring for a patient. You would want to see peer reviewed scientific studies comparing those patients with conventional treatment to those having nano biotic therapy. Am I right?"

Jack halted his restless movements and fixed Bill with a fierce, angry glare. "Bill, the crux of the matter lies in securing each patient's informed consent and actively involving them as collaborators in the development and implementation of their personalized treatment plans. In all honesty, you can't accurately claim that this application fully aligns with established medical science principles and practices, as it lacks the necessary testing and validation."

Bill scratched his chin and said, "Have a look at this."

Jack walked over to the computer screen that Bill was working on. A series of code appeared, and the computer whirred as it spun out some numbers.

"Using AI has completely changed the scientific principles and practices," explained Bill. "Common practice has made medical treatments acceptable if it meets a threshold of ninety-five per cent probability of being correct. That means that five per cent of the time, the information about the medical treatment is blatantly wrong. Think of all the harm we have caused as doctors giving incorrect treatment at least one in 20 times." Bill let that sink in with silence.

After a moment, Jack said, "Sure, that is a limitation, but think of all the good we have done for the other 19 in 20 patients by following rigorous scientific principles."

The computer screen they were watching had some numbers pop up. "There is no need for randomized controlled studies when using AI probability projections," said Bill. "When applied to the treatment I just administered to the Guatemalan patient, the chance of a successful cure to his cancer is..." Bill punched the enter key with his index finger to emphasize the point. The number 99.999999999 per cent appeared on the screen.

Bill continued. "Compare that to an anastomotic leak rate of five per cent and the chance of pneumonia or significant respiratory complication of 12 per cent. The death rate is at least two per cent. The overall morbidity following any major colon operation is 43 per cent. Yet we just witnessed this man hopping off the gurney and head to the airport to take a flight home."

Jack found himself speechless, unable to give any counter arguments, having witnessed those complications in many of his own patients and wishing there was a better way of treating them. When Bill described treatment failures with modern-day medicine, Jack knew it was an underestimate. He had always believed a better way needed to be found. *Could Bill be on to something here?*

"Wait just one minute," Jack insisted, his tone suggesting a need for immediate pause and consideration. "While technology offers many advantages, it's become clear that complete dependence on it is not as advantageous as initially believed." Jack described the last place finish when using computer models to predict the best course during a sailing race when he followed Brian's advice.

Bill burst out laughing. "Ultimately, a program's effectiveness and quality depend on the capabilities of its designers. Next time, take me and the sailing program I design. I'm certain and can guarantee to you, without a single doubt, that you are going to finish in first place... but I would never do that to you. For you, the essence of sailing lies in the constant struggle against the forces of nature, where the skilful use of experience and intelligence are crucial for success."

Jack was only now beginning to see the wisdom of Bill's vision. He would need more time to process everything. "What are some next steps you would consider to further your goal of eliminating all medical diseases?" he asked.

Bill didn't answer immediately, as he seemed keen to choose his words carefully. "I would want to add the nano robot-linked reverse transcription retrovirus to the drinking water of all inhabitants in the world. This would wipe out the need for doctors, nurses, and many hospitals, as no one would ever get sick. Unfortunately, death is not preventable, but the average human would live to be between 120 to 150 years old."

Jack said, "The nano robot technology is in its infancy. Investors have spent billions of dollars into the technology. It will probably be at least twenty-five years before clinical applications are possible."

Bill smiled while shaking his head. "My work has culminated in a folding-DNA nanobot, each between one to 100 nanometers. I designed this microscopic machine to precisely detect and image tumour-related biomarkers within living cells, offering a new level of detail in cellular analysis. This nano robot, a minuscule machine built from two nanoparticles, uses a DNA aptamer as a bio-recognition element, linking the two components with its precise molecular architecture. Linked to reverse transcriptase retrovirus, it can enter cells, replicate, and correct DNA code responsible for every medical condition, including any cancer you can think of."

Jack looked at Bill with a confused expression. "Your words were like a jumble of incomprehensible sounds to me. I understood nothing. How is it possible for you to accomplish the task you claimed you did?"

"Ninety-five per cent of the work is done with AI using machine learning. I have the ability to design computer codes to create these complex processes. Linking nano robots to the reverse transcriptase virus was the most troublesome part. It is only possible to do this because of computer programming. I'm 50 years ahead of the nearest competitor. The AI can analyze all available data on the internet related to the field. With my computer programming, AI can accurately predict how to accomplish the task you want to perform, even when it has never been done before. In my case, I want to eliminate all medical diseases. I now know how to do this."

Jack thought about that. "And you would do this without anyone's consent. Just assume that is what they wished? Don't you think that is a little paternalistic? Everyone should have control over their own life. Don't you think?"

"Look," said Bill. "Seventy years ago, public health added fluoride to the public drinking water supply. This decision has since been credited with significantly reducing dental cavities, particularly among children. There is now very little doubt, and perhaps no doubt at all, about the extremely wise decision to proceed in this manner. Our ancestors made this moral decision after carefully considering the ethical implications and principles. I would make the same choice. My actions would be no different. The only difference is that no one would know it was me who cured them of future and current medical problems."

Jack shook his head and thought about that. "I would like to know if I someone was infecting me with a virus even if it was to cure me of future medical conditions."

Bill gave Jack a quizzical look. A look that Jack knew well from past experience. One that always made him feel slightly uneasy. When caught doing something he desperately wanted to keep secret, Bill had a tell: he looked sheepish.

"Bill," Jack shouted, "You *need* to tell me!"

Bill went quiet for a moment. "It was in the stuffed red peppers I cooked for you last year on the boat in St. Martin. Katherine ate them, too."

Chapter 27

Outside the clinic in St. John's, Antigua, Jack sat in his rented truck, the tropical air thick and humid around him. The process of producing the nano robot-linked reverse transcriptase retrovirus was intricate and involved multiple complex steps. Bill, using his expertise in computer technology, boasted he successfully implemented a fully automated system for the entire process.

Exiting the truck, Jack made his way toward the clinic and entered the building. Driven by a desire for firsthand knowledge, he felt compelled to observe the process to fully grasp its complexities and requirements. After he completed a series of security checks that included enduring retinal scans, facial-recognition cameras, and fingerprint scans, he entered an elevator. It was strangely devoid of any buttons whatsoever, rendering it unusable without help. From a speaker inside the elevator, a woman's voice announced that a scan was going to happen and that he shouldn't worry. A soft humming filled the elevator car, a constant background drone that was suddenly and briefly punctuated by a bright flash of light before the soft sound disappeared. It made sense to Jack. *This system scans and detects dangerous viruses, potentially harmful bacteria, and explosive devices.* The elevator doors closed.

The elevator began its descent, taking 15 seconds to reach the designated floor, at which point its doors smoothly opened.

Bright LED lights created a vibrant and energized atmosphere. The room, expansive as a football field, was unoccupied except for Jack. It appeared as though there was an endless supply of benches filled with glass tubing and an array of glass containers. As Jack walked down the facility's central pathway, the impressive and intricate workings of the production line filled him with wonder. From the gentle flow of liquid through the filters and quiet pumps came the soft, soothing sound of water flowing. In the far corner of the room, dozens of plastic bottles were gradually accumulating a transparent liquid. Moving along the production line were more plastic bottles, each filled to the brim with the virus. After capping the bottles, the automation loaded them onto grids, then grouped them into six-packs.

An intricate and complex array of computers and monitors lined one wall of the room, their flashing lights and constant digital hum filling the air with a sense of technological intensity. Bill provided a detailed explanation of the process he'd developed, which leveraged both machine learning and artificial intelligence. He'd explained: "Once the computers have learned your objectives, they possess the capacity to significantly enhance production within mere seconds, a task that would demand a human lifetime to accomplish."

Returning to the elevator, Jack's presence once again started the scanning process before ascending to the ground floor. Despite his inability to know the specifics of the production facility's operations, he reassured himself that a significant amount of digital effort and work had been dedicated to its development and upkeep. With the aid of computers, quality-control processes underwent comprehensive management and oversight, guaranteeing a superior end product and adherence to stringent standards. At the clinic, a small, dedicated staff of three maintained both security and a consistently clean and sterile environment, encompassing all their various duties.

Jack reflected on Bill's explanation of how the viruses behaved in the environment. His programming activated the viruses' self-replication capabilities upon entering a human host. The viruses exhibited a remarkable resilience to both high and low temperatures, proving capable of surviving even in aquatic environments. If these viruses infected another species, they would remain stable, but no adverse effects would result: their reverse transcriptase was only compatible with human DNA and thus unable to affect other species' genomes. Birds and fish, if they consumed the virus, would pass it through their systems and release it in their waste, enabling its continued flow through the ecosystem. The consumption of the bird or fish by a human would trigger the virus to repair their DNA, consequently protecting that person from developing common medical conditions. With the dissemination of the retrovirus into every corner of the world, every human being would eventually be affected. The sophisticated computer models forecast that every person across the globe would receive protection within a period of less than six months.

Walking back to the truck, Jack sat in the driver's seat next to Katherine. "I'm still mad at Bill for administering the virus to us without our consent," she fumed. "Although delicious, I'll never eat any of his stuffed peppers again. I don't trust him."

Jack held Katherine's hand. "I wholeheartedly agree with what you've said. He ought to have consulted with us in advance. A prior discussion would have been much more appropriate. His claim was so unbelievable that I would never have believed him, a fact that he was surely aware of. Bill wanted only the best for us. He understood our likely objections. His idea was never formally brought up to us. He believed that seeking forgiveness after the fact would prove to be a simpler and less problematic approach than the alternative of first getting our permission."

Katherine pouted quietly before she said. "Although I must confess, throughout the entire past year that we've spent together, I haven't experienced a single common cold. Last winter, during the peak of the flu season, it seemed as though everyone I knew, except for you and me, became afflicted with the influenza virus."

There was a brief break in the conversation as Katherine stopped to reflect. A single tear welled up and formed in the corner of her eye, threatening to spill down her cheek. Her shoulders slumped, as if the weight of the world was pressing down on her. A defeated sigh escaped her lips. She trembled, her hands shaking so violently that she could barely hold her breath.

Jack looked at her, a sudden shiver of fear running up his spine. "Katherine, is—"

"There's something else that I have never shared with you before, something I've kept secret until now. I discovered a lump in my breast some time before I embarked on the sailing trip. Upon my return, my intention was to visit my family doctor for a check-up. However, I found that the concerning lump had disappeared. With a significant family history of breast cancer, I had an unshakeable belief that I would unfortunately also develop the condition. My grandmother and mother both had it in their early thirties."

Jack looked at Katherine incredulously. "Why didn't you tell me?"

Katherine looked over at Jack with her eyes now filling with tears. "That sailing trip was such a magical experience for me. Time seemed to move slowly. I cherished every moment. You brought me a happiness I'd never experienced before. I was certain I was going to die from breast cancer when I returned to Toronto. My grandmother died at age 32. I wanted to enjoy the remaining time I had on the planet alone with you. That the lump had disappeared when I got back, I attributed to the magical power of love, and the strength I felt being with you. Now I know the truth. It was all because of Bill's nano robot-linked reverse transcriptase retrovirus, which corrected the damaged heredity DNA responsible for the cancer."

A tidal wave of emotion crashed over Jack as he reflected on the news of Katherine's miraculous escape from breast cancer. Jack, too, felt tears welling up. Unable to control the emotions washing over him, he sobbed. He reached over and held Katherine in a tight embrace. "I don't know what I would do without you. You coming into my life is the best thing that's ever happened to me. I feel I can manage any adversity that comes my way with you by my side."

Flooded by his deep emotional connection to Katherine, he was prepared to agree to any request, anything at all, to ensure they could remain together for eternity. If Bill's reverse-transcriptase viral infection would bring him a step closer to achieving that, he felt happy Bill had administered it to him and Katherine. Overwhelmed by the magnitude of Bill's actions, he felt a wave of gratitude and appreciation for his friend suddenly wash over him, contributing to the overload of emotions he was already feeling.

"I'm grateful Bill did this to us," he said to Katherine after the wave of emotion passed and he could talk without getting choked up. "I want to keep you with me forever."

Katherine smiled at Jack. "Although I hate to admit it, Bill did me a huge favour. I'm surprised he didn't try to inoculate us with the mRNA for the BDNF protein and increase our cognitive power like him," she mused.

"Bill explained to me that the effects are less predictable," explained Jack. "To illustrate, the heightened concentrations of BDNF could potentially amplify or worsen any pre-existing psychiatric characteristics or tendencies an individual might possess. Bill's struggles with risk-taking behaviours and addiction have intensified to where he finds it increasingly challenging to manage them effectively. The computer modelling of a successful outcome is currently only at around 25 per cent. Bill has told me he expects this will dramatically shorten his life unless he finds a solution."

Katherine and Jack sat in a comfortable silence, the weight of Bill's ambitious, selfless plans settling upon them like a warm blanket. With the truck fully loaded, the engine roared to life as Jack began his 45-minute drive back across the island to Jolly Harbour. Pulling into the bustling marina, Katherine helped him load the heavy crates of plastic bottles onto a rusty trolley. Their destination: the *Ileana*, their sleek sailboat tied to the dock, bobbing gently, the salty air and sounds of gulls surrounding them. Jack's mother and father were sitting in the cockpit, each engrossed in a magazine. Upon seeing the two of them together, a smile spread across their faces.

"Here, Mom and Dad," said Jack. "I have something for you."

Jack opened a six-pack and handed his mother and father each a bottle of the clear liquid.

Chapter 28

On the stern of the sailboat, Jack and Katherine leaned closely together, their heads bent over the map displayed on the chart monitor situated directly in front of the starboard steering wheel. They had sent Jack's parents back to the condo in Toronto, where they would stay in the spare bedroom. Given the multitude of events unfolding, Jack decided against exposing them to any undue or preventable hazards. In early September, the height of hurricane season, the time-honoured advice for sailors was to steer clear of the Atlantic Ocean, a practice born from years of experience navigating its unpredictable storms. Bill, however, was primarily concerned about the individuals who had become aware of the potential financial ruin of the medical system that would result from the release of the virus.

The possibility of this as a cure for common medical conditions was the subject of a *New York Times* article, which also speculated on the significant ramifications for the healthcare industry should this claim prove accurate. It is highly probable that they learned about this technology through Guatemalan doctors, who may have been the source of their information. Doctors in Guatemala raised a red flag when a cluster of patients had travelled to Antigua for an experimental cancer treatment and returned home to find their cancers had vanished, prompting further investigation into the efficacy and safety of the procedure.

Jack came to realize it was a stroke of luck they got the precious liquid to their sailboat in time. Having completed his initial task of packing the first load containing the bottles of virus into the sail locker, Jack made a return trip to the clinic to collect an additional shipment. He would have parked his rented truck in front of the clinic, but another pickup truck with a cover over the back occupied the only space, so he had to park further down the street. With a click, he turned off the engine. The vehicle instantly fell silent.

As Jack left the truck and slammed the door shut, a low rumble vibrated through the ground, a tremor that sent a shiver up his spine. A sudden blast of wind ripped the front door of the clinic from its hinges, sending the parked pickup truck careening across the road. With a ferocious roar, flames burst from the front door. The ensuing explosion, a deafening clap of thunder, sent the roof soaring into the sky in a chaotic shower of shingles and sparks.

Jack reeled away backwards in shock as he witnessed the carnage. Coming at him from down the street were two men running at full speed, both carrying guns. "There he is!" shouted one as he began firing.

Jack immediately ducked into a narrow side street. The sounds of pursuing footsteps echoed behind him. He ran for his life. The bullets ricocheted off the buildings lining the narrow street. Their sharp, metallic pings bouncing off the walls in the alley with loud cracks. Jack was in great shape, the result of daily gym sessions with Katherine in their Toronto apartment complex. His muscles felt toned and strong. While in Antigua, he ran 10 kilometres daily, feeling the warm sun on his skin and the gentle sea breeze in his hair as he pounded the pavement. Now he easily outran the men, weaving through the narrow side streets, the sounds of their pursuit fading behind him as he doubled back. He was sweating heavily, the smell of smoke thick in the air, as he hid behind parked cars, watching fire crews battle the clinic fire with powerful water streams.

Leaving the rented truck where he'd parked it, Jack called Keanu, his usual Antiguan taxi driver, the familiar jingle of his phone cutting through the morning quiet. In under 20 minutes, Jack was on his way back to the marina. He paid Keanu $50 at the marina office. The gentle rocking of the boats tied at the docks created a soothing rhythm, contrasting with the panic that filled Jack's body. His feet pounded the weathered wood of the dock as he sprinted toward *Ileana*, the salty air filling his lungs.

"We need to get out of here!" Jack's yell cracked across the water's surface, a desperate sound, as he scrambled towards the bobbing boat. Katherine was sunbathing on the foredeck when he appeared and leaped up with a start. He quickly explained what had happened to the clinic.

They had prepared themselves... for something, anything. Crammed into the boat's hold were barrels of preserved food, crates of fruits and vegetables, rice, pasta, and frozen fish, enough to last three weeks if they had to leave suddenly. The docking lines came loose with a splash as Katherine and Jack quickly disconnected the shore power, feeling the boat's gentle rocking as it began to drift. In less than 10 minutes, the boat motored down the harbour, the salty spray cooling their faces as they headed into the vast open ocean.

The easterly trade winds were a constant force at this time of year... unless interrupted by a hurricane. Jack called his weather guru, Chris Perkins, the most dependable sailing meteorologist in the Caribbean.

"Chris," said Jack when he answered the phone after three long rings, "I'm heading back to Toronto via New York City. How's the weather looking for the next 10 days?"

"Give me a minute to pull up the predictions on my computer," he answered. "It's not the best time of year to be out on the open Atlantic Ocean, you know. We are expecting an active hurricane season this year."

"I would normally want to wait until November, or better yet, May, but we ran into a little trouble and have to get back home quickly,"

Jack could hear Chris pecking away at the keyboard. "Well, you might be in luck," he said after a minute. "At least initially. There is no active weather in your vicinity right now. There is a pocket of energy over Cape Verde that could develop into something, and another less threatening system in the Gulf of Mexico we'll need to keep an eye on. But for now, you should have smooth sailing for at least the next five days."

"Okay, thanks," said Jack. "Can you send me an update by email in a few days? I expect it will take 10 days to get to New York City, so I'll want to stay on top of the weather."

After hanging up, Jack told Katherine, who was at the helm, about the weather prediction. "It is not the smartest thing we've done, heading out in the middle of hurricane season," he said.

"Perhaps," answered Katherine. "But we could always duck into the Bahamas, or even Bermuda again if we run into bad weather."

As the sun dipped below the horizon, painting the sky in fiery oranges and reds, Jack put a second reef in the mainsail. The boat sliced through the waves at 8.5 knots on a broad reach, the gentle rocking a soothing rhythm. With Katherine at the helm for the next three hours, Jack prepared dinner, the rhythmic creak of the boat a steady background to his work. He thawed the firm, white filets of tilapia and carefully wrapped them in parchment paper with sweet onions, pungent garlic, juicy tomatoes, and a bright lemon, adding a dash of fiery hot pepper flakes and fragrant dill. Next he prepared rice on the stovetop, then blanched green beans just until they turned vibrant. The aroma of their roasted dinner filled the cockpit as he served it. He and Katherine ate ravenously in silence, the gentle hum of the autohelm background to the quiet evening.

After clearing away the dishes, Jack said, "I'll catch a few hours' sleep up here in the cockpit. Could you wake me up in two hours to relieve you?"

Katherine sat beside Jack as he made himself comfortable on the cushions. "I turned off the AIS," she said. "I don't want anyone to track us as we head north. In the morning, maybe you can email Chris our GPS coordinates, and he can give us a weather update. He won't be able to track us, either." Jack turned towards Katherine and reached his head towards hers to give her a kiss. "One more thing I should tell you," she said with a mischievous look.

"I dumped two litres of the clear liquid into Jolly Harbour when we left. Those Antiguans are going to live a long time, thanks to Bill."

Chapter 29

Jack woke up to the sound of his watch alarm. It was just past midnight. He glanced up at Katherine behind the wheel. Her face illuminated by the light of the chart plotter as she scrutinized something. Bill got up and put his arms around her, and kissed her neck. "What are you looking at, honey?"

She pointed to an icon of a boat that was about five miles behind them and a few miles to the east. "I can only see this on the radar," said Katherine. "They must have turned off their AIS."

"Sometimes fishing boats turn off their AIS when they don't want other fishermen to poach on their catches," suggested Jack.

"It is almost as if they are following us," Katherine whispered, her voice barely audible above the sound of the wind through the rigging. "I first noticed them when you drifted off to sleep two hours ago. I switched on the radar, hoping to see if any squalls were headed our way, and a blip appeared on the screen. From the moment I first observed the boat, it has remained at a consistent distance from our current position. If we can see them on the radar, they can see us on theirs." Katherine tilted her head back, her eyes meeting Jack's. A deep worry had outlined itself in her face. "I'm terrified," she whispered, her voice barely audible.

With a frown, Jack peered at the chart plotter, the numbers and lines blurring slightly through his tired eyes. The sea was empty, stretching out in all directions; not another boat was visible for 20 miles. St. Martin lay 50 miles to their north, and to their west was St. Kitts, a distance of 30 miles. *Assuming the boat is a hostile entity plotting an attack, it would most likely occur in the morning hours, taking advantage of the early light.*

"Why don't you catch some sleep in the main cabin, and I'll keep watch up here," said Jack. "If I'm worried about that target you identified on the radar, I'll call for a mayday on Channel 16."

Katherine sighed and went to the cabin. Jack watched her trundle down the companionway and close the door. He thought back a few nights before at the Antigua Yacht Club.

"So, who did you piss off?" Tommy, the dockmaster, asked. "Some of the roughest characters I've seen in my life were asking about you this afternoon."

He and Jack sat at the bar, nursing their beers, while they talked. As the sun sank below the horizon, the sky was ablaze with the fiery hues of twilight. Katherine was busy purchasing some last-minute food items to ensure they had enough supplies for the journey back to Toronto. As Jack waited patiently for her, Tommy's offer of a beer, accompanied by the joyful clinking of glasses from the nearby bar, was a welcome distraction.

Jack looked around and saw no obvious threats. "I can't tell you, Tommy. But what I can say is that I need to transport something back to Toronto on my sailboat, and some others are trying to stop me."

Tommy took a swig of beer before he continued. "Look," he said, his voice low and urgent, "these islands are crawling with unsavoury characters—cutthroats and thieves who would happily toss you overboard for your cell phone. You need to protect yourself and Katherine if you encounter any dangerous individuals while at sea. Keep a lookout and be prepared to defend yourselves."

"I'm a surgeon with no experience in defending myself," replied Jack. "I plan to sail fast and turn off my AIS."

"That's not going to help if someone really wants to find you," said Tommy. "I've been the dockmaster at the marina for the last 40 years. I know a thing or two about these criminals and how to protect yourself. I'll tell you what. Tomorrow morning, I'm going to drop around your sailboat and show you some simple things you can do to defend yourself in case you get attacked. I'll be there at 9 a.m."

The next morning when he'd arrived, Tommy recounted his experiences in the Gulf of Oman to Jack. "The constant threat of pirate attacks made it a challenging but effective training ground for us sailors. I'm going to show you how to integrate a few of those key principles into your daily sailing life, so when you experience an attack, you will emerge unscathed."

Suddenly, a stark white icon on the chart plotter screen flashing against the surrounding darkness jolted Jack back to the present. The vessel's approach was unmistakable. The radar showed a CPA, closest point of approach, of 10 metres... collision at 6 a.m. painted in stark, dreadful detail against the brightening dawn. To face what lay ahead, Jack knew he'd need to be prepared, both physically and mentally.

With a grunt, he threw open the starboard locker, revealing a canvas bag crammed with the jumble of equipment and devices Tommy had offloaded onto him. The smell of old canvas filled the air. Jack kicked himself for not familiarizing himself with the tools sooner. It was a harsh reminder of his negligence and the now-looming attack he'd foolishly hoped to avoid. Jack carefully laid out what he felt he would need on the cockpit cushions. He would ask Katherine to take control of the helm while he did what he could to thwart the attackers... if they were to actually get attacked.

The galley was warm and inviting as he filled his Thermos with coffee. He would need to stay alert through the long night, the cold air raising goosebumps on his skin as he scanned his surroundings. He made his way back to the chart plotter, the gentle rocking of the boat a counterpoint to the ever-decreasing distance between them visible on the glowing screen. The CPA had the boats within 20 metres of each other at 6:10 a.m.

Katherine emerged from the companionway at five. "Hey, love. How's the radar target looking?" she said, momentarily startling Jack, who jumped when she spoke. He'd been fixated on the chart plotter, its faint glow illuminating his face.

Jack looked up with a worried look as she yawned, her facial expression quickly turning serious. "Jack... is everything okay?"

"Sorry, honey, I'm a little tense. The vessel is within a mile of us now. I'm certain they are after us."

With a frown, Katherine peered at the complex nautical chart plotter, her finger tracing a plotted course. "Oh Jack, I can't believe it. What are we going to do?" Panic filled her voice, and her eyes darted to the ocean where the vessel was approaching. "I'm certain they switched off their running lights to avoid being seen."

"I didn't discuss this with you before. To avoid burdening you with needless worry, I... I wanted to spare you the anxiety. Tommy gave me some equipment which we can use to protect ourselves. While I grab a few things, I'll need you at the helm to keep us on course. We can't be sure they are after us, but the hairs on the back of my neck are standing on end. Maybe it's the coastguard monitoring us," he said, a question in his voice.

With a raised eyebrow, Katherine's quizzical look clearly communicated, "Tell me another one."

They watched the chart plotter as the boat was within 200 metres. The early morning light suggested it was a 40-foot trawler, likely a fishing boat. The boat pulled up along the port side of the boat about 50 metres away from their sailboat. Jack could see two men, one with binoculars, and the other man looking through what appeared to be a rangefinder of a rifle.

"Keep the boat on autohelm and keep down," shouted Jack.

Jack held a small, metal laser pointer, complete with a built-in rangefinder. Looking through it, the man with the binoculars appeared 10 times larger, his features magnified, just like the man with the rifle. Jack fired a pulse of laser at each of them. He watched, mesmerized, as the beam of crimson light snaked its way up the rifle's rangefinder and into the right lens of the binoculars, a silent, pulsing connection. Following a simultaneous shriek, the binoculars and rifle crashed to the wooden deck, the sound jarring and sharp.

Three other men emerged onto the deck, pointing at Jack with expressions of anger and betrayal. One man dashed to the trawler's stern and launched the 10-foot RIB inflatable, its small engine already humming. Once in the water, the other two jumped in, and the man at the back revved the powerful engine, the sound echoing across the water. He aimed right at the sailboat. Jack pulled out a small, white egg-shaped object, smooth and cool to the touch.

He hurled it at the oncoming inflatable, hearing the satisfying crack as it hit the fibreglass hull of the inflatable dinghy. Jack peered across the cockpit, crouching down and bracing himself. Nothing happened. Then suddenly, a loud bang ripped through the air as the dinghy burst into bright, furious flames.

With a desperate scramble, the three men launched themselves from the burning dinghy, flames licking at their heels, and began their arduous swim back to the trawler, each stroke fighting against the waves and the encroaching smoke.

"Katherine," yelled Jack. "Get me closer to the trawler."

She turned off the autohelm, the wheel responding immediately to her touch as she guided their sailboat toward the boat, its fishing nets hanging heavy on deck. Once close enough, Jack could see the first two men on the trawler's floor, their whimpers echoing in the enclosed space as they thrashed around in pain. Jack launched another one of the egg-like objects, the impact bouncing on the trawler's metal deck as it cracked. A deafening boom shattered the morning calm, and the trawler erupted in a fiery explosion, sending a plume of black smoke into the sky. Crackling flames quickly engulfed the wheelhouse, burning the ship's steering mechanism. *This should effectively stop them in their tracks!*

With a determined grip on the wheel, Katherine steered the boat away, her nose wrinkled at the acrid smoke, setting a course for the distant lights of New York City, a nine-day journey across the choppy waves.

Chapter 30

Jack's mind raced, a whirlwind of thoughts preventing him from even thinking of sleep, although he was exhausted. The near miss with the pirates, the sounds of clashing steel, and their desperate cries still echoing in his ears, was all too recent. Despite his certainty of their murderous intent toward him and Katherine, a profound unease settled upon him. Despite their evil intentions, he hoped the wounded men would live. Even now, from two miles away, they could still see the thick, black smoke billowing from the burning trawler, a grim sight. Jack flipped the switch on the VHF radio, the static crackle filling the cockpit.

"Mayday, mayday, mayday," shouted Jack into the radio. "A vessel is on fire. The GPS coordinates are 17°43'29.0 N 62°50'30.9 W. Any vessel nearby, assistance is requested." Jack repeated the message a few more times before turning off the radio.

A fleeting sense of relief washed over him, momentarily easing his guilt, before he turned to Katherine, who still stared at the thick smoke billowing from the burning vessel, a blank expression on her face.

"Honey," he breathed, his voice barely above a whisper, "they would have killed us if we hadn't disabled them. I can still feel the cold sweat on my skin. Almost certainly, someone will rescue them. I can feel it in my bones. By the time anyone finds them, we will be in the middle of the vast, empty Atlantic, our AIS and Starlink systems deliberately disabled, leaving no digital trace for anyone to track us."

Katherine burst into tears, her shoulders shaking with sobs. Jack wrapped his arms around her, holding her close. She buried her face in his shoulder, her tears dripping onto his bare skin as her sobbing intensified, each breath hitching and ragged. The sound was of utter despair. "I'm so scared," she whispered, her voice trembling. "How could we have been so foolish as to let Bill lead us into this disastrous situation?"

Knowing any words would be inadequate, Jack let Katherine cry, the silence punctuated only by her quiet sobs. With a gentle rocking motion, the sailboat continued its steady 8.5-knot pace toward New York City, the morning sun on their faces as they cut through the calm, blue waters. The steady easterly trade winds, warm and comforting on his skin, were a stark contrast to the chaos Bill had caused.

As Jack thought back, it was Katherine who, after a moment of thoughtful consideration, advised that they comply with Bill's instructions, a suggestion that felt both sensible and slightly unsettling. It surprised Jack that Katherine, a vocal advocate for personal autonomy in her work as a psychotherapist, would agree to something that seemed to contradict her principles.

Upon discovering Bill's treachery when Jack revealed the contents of his proudly displayed stuffed peppers — his "poisoning," as she described it—she seethed. A furious red flush rose in her cheeks. "On top of all the awful, self-absorbed, paternalistic, and power-hungry things Bill has done, this is the most disgusting!" she shrieked with fury. "How dare a self indulgent, sex-crazed, drug addict assume we would be in favour of this!"

After the tearful confession, when she realized the virus Bill had administered without her consent and knowledge had eradicated her breast cancer, her hardened stance softened. Jack stayed quiet, the weight of Bill's kindness settling on him, letting her puzzle it out, privately agreeing that Bill had done them both a considerable favour. Comprehending the far-reaching positive consequences, they wholeheartedly embraced Bill's strategy. Two months ago, a quiet, almost sombre conversation with Bill marked the last time they spoke with him. Bill, with his characteristic vanishing act, now was nowhere to be found. Messages on his phone, emails, and texts remained unanswered, the silence amplifying his absence. Jack and Katherine were on their own.

Katherine seemed to have calmed down now they had sailed further away from the burning vessel. As they gazed at the horizon, the faintest wisps of smoke from the distant trawler were gone, leaving only the vast expanse of sea and sky. The lack of sleep weighed heavily on Jack. His body ached with fatigue. "Are you okay if I hit the sack for a few hours?" he asked, yawning widely as he rubbed his tired eyes.

Katherine nodded. "Tell me something before you go. What do you think Bill is up to?"

Jack smiled. "Not sure, but he is certainly secretive. What? It's been two months since we've heard from him. I called him again before we left Antigua to let him know there were some people after us. The call went right to his voice mail, but the voice mailbox was full."

"Do you think that was him we saw with Elon Musk on CNN?" asked Katherine.

Jack's mind drifted back to the news clip, the flashing images still seared into his memory. A hush fell over the audience as Elon Musk announced a groundbreaking project poised to reshape humanity, his eyes gleaming with barely contained excitement, yet offering no specifics. Next to him stood a man wearing a white shirt and white pants, which matched his white headscarf. He declared himself a Saudi with a confident air. They vaguely mentioned some kind of joint venture. It was only when the man walked away, his shoulders rolling with a cocky gait, that Jack recognized the swagger. Bill's pants sagged low, revealing more than he intended. His butt crack was visible for the world to see.

"No matter how cleverly he disguises himself, I would recognize Bill anywhere," said Jack.

He crawled into the cabin and fell asleep in less than 10 seconds. Before long, a sudden shift in the boat's motion awoke him. They were heeling more than when he went to bed. Still very tired, he felt he should get up to investigate. He put on his clothes and made his way to the cockpit, glancing at his watch. The time 12:05 flashed on the screen. Katherine was sitting on the bench behind the wheel, looking at the instruments. She smiled when she saw Jack.

"The wind has picked up to 25 knots," she said. "Let's put in the second reef." Jack nodded in affirmation. Katherine lowered the mainsail to the predetermined mark on the halyard, while Jack tightened the second reefing line. The heeling of the boat settled while the speed remained at 8.5 knots.

"I'll check the weather app," said Jack. He turned on the Starlink and waited until he was online, then loaded the offshore weather app and entered his location and his destination: New York City. He waited while the information downloaded. There seemed to be a lot of red and black areas in the direction they were heading, and his heart skipped a beat. He immediately dialled Chris Perkins, the weather guru.

"Chris," said Jack. "It looks like we are heading into a heap of trouble. Can you give us some advice about what we should do?"

Jack could hear the furious pace of Chris's typing, a staccato rhythm against the background of his voice. "I tried to contact you this morning, but it seems your phone was unreachable... Yes, a major storm with 50-knot winds is heading your way. Prepare for the worst. The storm arose in the Gulf of Mexico, its swirling clouds were visible from satellite images, and it's predicted to slam into Miami in two days. From there, the prediction shows it tracking up the eastern seaboard as a downgraded category-one hurricane, with sustained winds expected to be around 74 miles per hour. To ride out the storm, you can hunker down in the British Virgin Islands. You might experience the full force of the storm there still, or you can head further east, facing heavy winds and perhaps torrential rain."

"Not sure I want to go to the BVI. I feel safer on the water, given the circumstances we are facing. To avoid the worst of the approaching storm, could you please provide us with some GPS coordinates that would direct us further east?"

"Will do," said Chris, whose voice carried a worried tone. "And Jack, good luck."

Jack went up to the cockpit and told Katherine about the bad weather heading their way. "Chris thinks we can avoid the worst of it by heading east. He also suggested a stop in the BVI as an option."

Katherine shook her head. "No way I want to be anywhere we could get attacked again. Let's try to outrun the storm. I would much rather take our chances on the open ocean."

Jack's phone pinged, indicating a new email. As expected, it was from Chris who supplied the easterly GPS coordinates he'd requested. Jack carefully entered the numbers into the chart plotter's designated input field. As the sailboat turned towards the east, maintaining a close reach, it heeled over significantly from the wind. The force was too much for the boat to handle, so to reduce the sail area, Jack put in the third reef, causing the boat to flatten significantly.

"Honey," he said, "we are going to hit the worst of this in two days from now. We will need to be rested. Why don't you get some sleep before it gets too rough?"

Katherine had a worried look in her eyes. "I'm too wired to sleep now, thinking about the storm. Why don't you go."

Jack nodded and went below to the cabin. He placed cushions along the side of the bed to avoid rolling off as the boat heeled over. Once again, he fell asleep within 10 minutes.

Chapter 31

Jack had never before encountered such exceedingly harsh and unforgiving conditions while at sea. It was after midnight on a cloud-covered night. The sky was pitch black and the powerful winds, which were blowing at a constant 55 knots, were further intensified by gusts that reached speeds of up to 70 knots. Having lowered their sails several hours earlier, they had lost the ability to steer the boat and were now laying "ahull," helplessly riding the waves. Although Jack was familiar with the concept from his prior readings, he had yet to put his knowledge into practice by personally trying it out.

Despite being completely at the mercy of the turbulent sea outside, the main salon offered a surprising tranquillity, allowing them to converse in hushed tones for once without having to raise their voices. With waves crashing over the cockpit and the dangerous conditions, Jack deemed it unsafe to remain outside. To prevent the powerful, erratic movements of the waves from breaking the rudder, he'd secured the steering wheels to the winches with lashings. The boat's interior was violently tossed around, much like the chaotic swirling action one observes inside a washing machine during its spin cycle.

Katherine seemed unconcerned about the violence of the storm and remained surprisingly calm. "The crazy part is that we are heading directly for New York City at six knots! The GPS says we'll be there in 10 days!"

Despite his calm exterior, Jack's inner turmoil was escalating rapidly as he felt an overwhelming panic. The ocean's waves outside were steadily increasing in size and intensity, foreshadowing a potentially dangerous situation. If a wave were to strike them from the side, the boat would inevitably capsize, resulting in the mast snapping. A broken mast could easily punch holes in the ship's hull, which would cause them to sink. Jack possessed a sizable drogue, a parachute-like device intended to function as a sea anchor. However, deploying it necessitated his venturing onto the deck of the vessel. Horrific images of being swept away by the unforgiving waves haunted his mind, bringing back the terror of his previous experience. He sighed. The moment when the drogue should have been deployed was long gone anyway, lost in the passage of time. Considering the circumstances, remaining inside the boat was the safest option, while also remaining hopeful for a favourable outcome.

"You look stressed, Jack," said Katherine.

He stared at her with a look of disbelief and incredulity washing over his features. "How can you remain so calm?" he laughed. "I remember you saying those very words to me during our trip to Antigua. Specifically, after I had a terrifying near-drowning experience, when a gigantic wave threatened to pull me overboard. Remember?"

"Well, we are in a situation where there is nothing more we can do," said Katherine. "We may as well enjoy the ride. This boat will carry us through it all, I'm sure. Besides, it seems so calm down here inside compared to the screaming wind outside."

"I checked the weather app," said Jack. "The predictions on the course of the hurricane were a little off. It is going right over Bermuda now, not up the eastern seaboard, which would have taken the system hundreds of miles away from us. That is why the winds are so strong. The good news is the winds are going to settle down by morning and, with any luck, we will be able to put up the sails."

"It's a little too wild to sleep," said Katherine. "Should we—"

A loud crash interrupted her. With a sudden jolt, Jack immediately sprang to his feet. As a scraping sound echoed through the main salon, he frantically pulled on his foul-weather gear and life jacket, his movements fuelled by a sense of urgency.

"I need to go out to see what happened," he shouted. Jack climbed the companionway, moving deliberately. Upon reaching the top, he carefully opened the hatch. An enormous wave crashed over the side of the boat, surging into the cockpit, where it drenched him and filled the boat with water. He heard the bilge pump kick in to empty the water. In a hurry, he slammed the companionway door closed.

"It's not safe to go out there," shouted Katherine. "You need to stay inside."

Jack shook his head. "I think the topping lift broke. That's what keeps the boom from falling onto the deck. The boom needs to get secured. Otherwise, it could make a hole in the boat, or we could lose our mainsail. I'm going to tie a rope around my waist and you hang onto me. I'll also use the tether to tie me to the jacklines."

Jack thought about what he needed to do. The main halyard could hold up the boom, replacing the broken line... if he could get to it. The waves were crashing into the cockpit every 30 seconds. He needed to crawl onto the deck, release the shackle of the main halyard that was tied to a fixture near the mast, and then get back before the next wave hit the boat.

In preparation to fetch the main halyard, the first manoeuvre was to free the line so he would have enough slack to reach the cockpit. Jack leaned with his body out the door and released the jam cleat in front of the power winch that kept the main halyard taut. He scampered back into the safety of the companionway in less than 10 seconds and closed the door. The wave arrived a few seconds later and washed harmlessly on the door.

Jack cautiously opened the companionway door and attached his tether to the jackline. He closed the door before the next wave hit with a large splash. After the wave subsided, he opened the door again and in a mad dash raced to the deck and crawled to where he had attached the mainsail halyard. The shackle was one that had a bolt at the pin, which he had to unscrew, wasting several valuable seconds. Jack looked up and saw a massive wave approaching the boat. The top of it was curling, ready to break directly on him. Grabbing the halyard, he raced back to the cockpit and dove into the companionway with the enormous wave sweeping him inside, along with gallons of seawater. The wave forced him onto the floor, and the impact momentarily winded him. With the bilge pump whirring, it pumped 10 gallons of water a minute out through the hose at the stern of the boat.

Extreme heeling threw Katherine against the starboard side of the main salon. The wave hit with a terrifying roar, sending Jack sprawling across the wet, unstable floor. Seawater sprayed everywhere, the salt stinging his face. Jack closed the door with a forceful push to keep the water out, then gave Katherine a quick wave, a silent "I'm okay."

"That was a close one," Jack croaked, his voice raspy from the seawater that still clung to his throat, the taste of brine thick on his tongue. "I'm going to attach this halyard to the back of the boom, then crank the winch to raise the boom and clear the dodger. I can feel the familiar strain on the line." Jack proudly held up the shackled end of the main halyard, the cold metal biting into his palm.

"That is not a good idea," whispered Katherine. "You almost didn't make it back."

Jack shook his head and smiled. "I'm always up for a challenge. Besides, the hard part is done. The rest I can do from the relative safety of the cockpit." Another enormous wave crashed into the companionway door. "I'll go after the next one."

As the wave crashed and receded, Jack reacted quickly. With a creak, he opened the companionway door, the sound of waves echoing around him, the smell of brine sharp and clean. If it wasn't so dangerous, he'd be exhilarated by it all. The halyard snapped neatly into place on the boom as he secured it—a practised movement honed over years, with took less than 10 seconds. The 600-pound boom, heavy and cold, rested on the aluminum frame of the dodger, the metal groaning under its immense weight. Jack crouched before the powerful electric winch, the metallic sound in the air, and raised the heavy boom. With the boom secured, Jack dove into the boat, slamming the door shut just as a monstrous wave crashed over the deck, washing his face with brute force.

"We did it," said Jack, gasping. "Let's keep our fingers crossed. The worst is over."

The boat pitched and rolled wildly, making sleep impossible in the main cabin. By wedging themselves between the plush velvet bench and the sturdy oak table in the main salon, using pillows as buffers, they minimized the jarring effect of each monstrous wave that tossed the boat about. Despite the discomfort and the unsettling sounds of the night, they somehow drifted off to sleep.

Hours later, Jack woke up disoriented. He'd fallen between the plush sofa pillows and onto the cool wooden floor of the main salon. Trapped, his shoulders and head were wedged between the rough-hewn centre support beam of the heavy oak table and Katherine, her limp body sprawled on the same cold, hard floor. The boat, now floating steadily, no longer pitched and rolled erratically; the waves had calmed. Sunlight streamed inside. He pushed himself up onto the bench and opened the creaking companionway door, the sound of the ocean around him. A 22-knot wind howled from the east, whistling through the wind instruments.

Jack raised the mainsail, unfurled the jib, and set the course for New York City. Somehow, they had come out of the other side of the hurricane unscathed.

Chapter 32

Nine days later, the Statue of Liberty came into view as they entered New York Harbour, a breathtaking sight against the morning sky. Only a few distant cargo ships, their hulls barely visible on the horizon, came within 10 miles. The vast ocean otherwise remained empty. Jack frantically searched the internet, refreshing pages repeatedly, hoping to find any news about the missing boat and the five attackers, but the search yielded nothing.

The three-hours-on, three-hours-off night shift, with its predictable rhythm, worked well. Nightly, a comfortable routine settled in. Jack, nestled in the cockpit, slept soundly, ever-ready to aid Katherine with the ship's systems should anything arise during her shift. During the daytime hours, he would sleep in the cabin.

While travelling up the Hudson River by motor, Jack experienced his typical anxiety while he watched the rapid pace of the New York City ferries speeding across the water from Manhattan to New Jersey. As Jack piloted his boat north on the Hudson River, Katherine, seeking to recover some lost sleep, had already made her way to the cabin. To successfully avoid collisions with the speeding vessels, it was necessary to accurately predict both their intended paths and their speeds. The chart plotter's helpful icons, which flashed to indicate potentially colliding boats, allowed Jack to take evasive action.

While Katherine slept, he spent considerable time contemplating New York City, the modern centre of civilization and the significant transformations that were imminent. In the American economy, healthcare accounted for approximately 18 per cent of the GDP, with a dollar figure twice as high as Canada's, where healthcare is a government-funded universal system. The loss of revenue from healthcare institutions, once the virus began its work repairing damaged DNA and preventing diseases, could potentially trigger a significant economic downturn and push the economy into a severe recession. Jack firmly believed that any economic system that profited from the suffering and misfortune of others, such as American healthcare, was inherently unstable and destined to ultimately collapse.

Following a journey of a few hours, Jack and Katherine successfully docked at Newport's Riverfront Marina, on the Hudson River, a picturesque waterfront location. They had an adequate amount of time to complete the task at hand. They booked an Uber and embarked on a journey to the Shawangunks, also known as the Gunks, a stunning hilly range near the charming town of New Paltz. Making their way along the trail, Katherine and Jack spent the afternoon hiking in the woods. It was a gorgeous day; the sun shone brilliantly in the sky, and a light, refreshing wind blew gently. They sat beside a small stream and marvelled at the surrounding beauty. Each opened a plastic bottle and dumped the clear contents into the bubbling water.

Upon returning to the sailboat, Jack immediately powered up his laptop and logged into his tracking software. The radioactively labelled tracer, which Bill had carefully attached to the virus particles, had successfully navigated its way through the complex network of the Catskill Aqueduct and finally reached its destination in New York City. Through the use of complex computer modelling, Bill predicted that a week from then there would be a noticeable decline in the number of people visiting the emergency room and, therefore, a decrease in hospital admissions.

Continuing their journey motoring up the Hudson River, Jack and Katherine navigated the Erie Canal system, eventually reaching the Hudson River's headwaters, Lake Oneida, where they disposed of two more bottles of the clear liquid. Several days later, they arrived at Lake Ontario, the vast expanse stretching out before them, a cool breeze carrying the scent of the distant woods. Once they reached the centre of the lake, the still water reflecting the morning sky, they emptied all but two bottles of the clear liquid overboard.

As they arrived at their home yacht club in Port Credit, Ontario, they dumped the contents of the final two bottles of clear liquid into the lake; the splash barely disturbed the calm water. Three weeks had passed since their frantic escape from Antigua, the memory of howling winds and lashing rain still fresh in their minds. Emotionally and physically drained, they knew it would take a few days of rest and recovery to get back on track. With the sailboat securely fastened to the dock, Jack and Katherine snuggled together in their cozy cabin, the gentle rocking of the boat lulling them into a deep sleep.

Chapter 33

An extensive search yielded no results. Bill remained elusive, and his disappearance was a mystery. In the vacant suite 2402, Katherine and Jack stood silently in the stillness. The walls were completely barren, devoid of any decoration or adornment whatsoever, creating a stark and empty atmosphere. Someone had removed all the computer screens that had previously lined every wall. Workers made and smoothed the plaster repairs, concealing the screw holes where the monitors had been mounted. They freshly painted the wall surfaces white. With the computers gone, the office felt strangely empty. The silence amplified the missing hum of hard drives and whirring fans. The removal of all the furniture left only faint impressions—indentations in the white carpet where a computer table had stood. Someone thoroughly cleaned the carpet at some point, leaving it spotless, the room filled with the delightful and fragrant scent of freshly picked lilacs.

"We left Bill to his own devices for a few months," Katherine said, shaking her head in disbelief, "and then, incredibly, he vanished again."

"Despite employing their sophisticated facial-recognition and body-movement software, Jason and Brian have been unsuccessful in locating Bill. Their prevailing theory is that he has sought refuge in a place where there are no security cameras. Maybe a secluded, uninhabited island in a far off tropical location would be the perfect getaway."

"The Mustang Ranch," Katherine said, her brow furrowed. "That's the last place anyone saw him go, right? The video footage showed Bill entering a room at the ranch. This is one room we saw when we were at the ranch. He was with a woman who Brian and Jason identified as Jessica via the website picture of her."

Katherine continued. "Brian said they remained in the room together for 24 hours before they emerged, with smiles on their faces and a palpable sense of affection between them. He said they were hugging each other and holding hands. When Jack bid Jessica farewell, she burst into tears. Bill then hopped into the waiting Uber, which brought him to the airport. He took a direct flight to Houston, Texas, arriving at 16:45 a week ago last Tuesday. That is where they lost any further contact with him."

"Bill is going to surprise us," said Jack. "He has a good heart and seems driven to *do good*. It's hard to understand how this is all going to work out, but his parting words—that humanity would benefit in unimaginable ways—keeps running through my mind."

Lost in thought, trying to decipher Bill's plan, a heavy silence fell between them as they walked out of suite 2402. They remained quiet as they headed home, gears still turning in their minds.

When they reached their apartment, Jack immediately went to the fridge, pulling out two bottles of Heineken. The familiar clink of glass bottles was a welcome sound. Katherine turned on the television, its screen glowing brightly in the room, only illuminated by a small table lamp. The murmur of the early evening news, a low hum of voices and static, filled Jack's ears as he popped the beer caps.

"Jack!" Katherine cried, the urgency clear in her voice. "Come over here and see this!"

A video of an empty, eerily silent emergency room, with only the faint hum of machinery audible, filled the screen. A reporter, seated behind a massive, mahogany desk in the studio, announced, "Emergency room visits across the province are down by an astounding 50 per cent," his voice calm despite the surprising statistic. The next video showcased several emergency rooms from across the province. Rows of empty stretchers lined the sterile, quiet rooms. "We have a comment from the Ministry of Health."

A man in a crisp business suit stood outside the imposing legislature, a microphone clutched in his hand, the sounds of the city almost muted around him. "Our preventive medicine programs, including mandatory vaccinations, routine mammograms, and colonoscopies, are showing positive results, with a noticeable decrease in community illness and disease. We're seeing fewer cases of preventable diseases, and a healthier community overall. This is precisely what we have been predicting for years, and the data finally confirms it. We expected this, and you can expect additional gains from the upcoming programs we're launching."

The video cut to a busy downtown university hospital. Doctors in starched white coats and nurses sat chatting on the sun-drenched grass outside. With a slight click, the reporter extended the microphone towards the doctor. The indistinct murmur of the crowd was background noise to their conversation. "This is nothing more than a lull before the typical seasonal illness, with the usual sniffles and coughs. We're enjoying the warm sunshine and light breeze before the sick patients return. Health officials are predicting a particularly nasty flu season, with more infections and hospitalizations than average. This is just the calm before the storm."

The news reports from New York City were more thorough, painting vivid pictures of the city's bustling streets and frantic atmosphere. "A representative from the Sloan Kettering Cancer Hospital, his face lined with disbelief, reported he'd never seen anything like it," said the reporter, with his microphone held close to the iconic hospital's entrance. "With an astonishing number of cancers disappearing mid-treatment, half the hospital is now strangely quiet, the absence of their suffering palpable in the empty wards. Experts put all cancer surgery on hold while they search for answers."

The video next depicted bored ambulance drivers, their faces lined with weariness, sipping coffee in a hospital parking lot. Ten empty ambulances stood in a stark, straight line. A circle of paramedics sat in lawn chairs, their hushed conversation punctuated by the chirping of crickets. "For seven days straight, this is what it's been like," the African American ambulance driver told the reporter, his voice weary from exhaustion. "If this continues, the hospital administrator warned, they will lay off some of us." He shook his head, muttering in disbelief, his jaw clenched tight.

Jack and Katherine stared at each other. "This must be what Bill was talking about," she said. "In less than two weeks since we dumped the bottled liquid from Bill's lab into the New York City water supply, there's already an effect." Katherine's face crunched up. "Jack, have you thought about how this could affect your ability to make a living as a surgeon?"

Jack stared off into space, his mind racing through the possibilities before forming a conclusion. "Unfortunately... yes, my current employment as a surgeon will change dramatically, and it will eventually end. Right now, with the complexities of the human body, the need for precision of surgeons will probably always be necessary. Remember that emergency rooms also frequently treat patients suffering from injuries sustained in car accidents and gun violence. A significant portion of my medical practice focuses on treating conditions like painful symptomatic hernias and gallstones, conditions largely unaffected by the nano robot-linked virus. In the long run, it's likely that these conditions, along with the overall health of the population, will improve and eventually disappear. I'll need to search for alternative employment opportunities soon." He shrugged thoughtfully. "Considering the reduction in global pain and suffering, that is a comparatively small price to pay."

Chapter 34

The packed emergency medical staff meeting was thick with tension and all was silent except for the occasional cough as the hospital CEO addressed them. From the back of the room, Jack observed the stunned staff listen wordlessly as Nancy's voice boomed. She had called for the meeting to address the rapidly deteriorating situation—the lack of patients to treat. The air crackled with tension as frightened staff, their faces pale and drawn, listened intently. Jack, in his quest to remain anonymous, sat in the dimly lit back row, ready to make a quick, quiet exit, his heart pounding in his chest.

"The emergency room has averaged 400 patients a day for the last 10 years," said Nancy. "We saw fewer than 10 today. The low numbers of emergency room patients is something we have never witnessed. This morning, the city's hospital CEOs convened urgently. A critical, identical pattern was emerging across all the facilities in Toronto. Emergency calls have plummeted and the ERs are empty, creating a noticeable decrease in the usual hectic atmosphere. In a press conference, the Minister of Health announced the immediate cancellation of all elective surgeries."

Jerry Hoffman, an orthopedic surgeon, rose to his feet, the squeak of his shoes audible in the tense silence, and demanded attention. In the middle of the packed hall, even the faint murmur of the rare conversations between shell-shocked staff fell silent as he yelled, "Nancy, you have no right to cancel orthopedic surgery!" his voice echoing in the tense atmosphere. "Six months—that's how long some of my patients have waited for hip-replacement surgery, their pain evident in their every movement. I absolutely refuse to cancel the surgery. The need is too great." His last words hung in the air as he turned abruptly, the door creaking loudly behind him as he left. A hush fell over the room, as if someone had sucked all the air out of it.

Nancy cleared her throat, then addressed the crowd who were getting restless, chatting among themselves, many rising from their seats. "Jerry, I think, has perfectly captured our collective exasperation at the events that have unfolded," she said. "Just a few patients remain in our hospital. I recognize how disturbing it is. The silence in the hallways is a stark contrast to the usual sounds of medical equipment and hurried footsteps. A drastic reduction in nursing staff—50 per cent sent home—has left us with just one operating room for emergency surgeries. All part-time staff have been let go. Regarding patients in line for hip-replacement surgery, the experts researching this cohort concur that... whatever has happened means they may no longer need the surgery. Their pain and immobility have disappeared."

A cacophony of shouts and clatter erupted as the medical staff, a whirlwind of white coats and anxious faces, surged forward, their urgent questions a torrent of sound. Still hunched in the back of the room, Jack felt a knot of conflict tightening in his stomach. The loud shouts of the other doctors around him felt like needles in his ears. His colleagues, the ones he'd spent countless hours with and depended upon, could not accept that their livelihood and their commitment to helping those in need were on the brink of collapse. He thought about the satisfaction he had enjoyed as a surgeon. He loved the precision and challenge of his job. His career was soon coming to an end, much more quickly than he had first anticipated.

The din of urgent questions and anxious whispers from the medical personnel drowned out Nancy's voice, silencing her further words. Jack slipped out the door at the back of the room. His role in the economic destruction of the lives of his friends and colleagues weighed heavily on him. Although the cause of the remarkable medical breakthrough remained a mystery, shrouded in secrecy and speculation, its discovery was inevitable. When that happened, he could be in big trouble. The consequences could be severe and far-reaching. There would be those out to possibly kill him, in revenge for ruining their lives. *The road to hell is paved with good intentions,* he thought.

As he was walking out of the room, he ran into his friend and colleague, Larry Klapman. "Jack, there's little to do here," said Larry. "Why don't we go down the road for a beer? You can tell me about your adventures down south."

Jack stopped in his tracks. His goal was to remain inconspicuous, to lie low and weather the disease-free storm until normalcy returned. As a colleague, Larry was not only dependable but also a genuinely pleasant person to be around. His easygoing nature and willingness to help made it easy to be friends.

Jack would sanitize the action-packed trip, glossing over the terrifying boat attack and the explosion that rocked St. John's, avoiding details of the chaotic scenes of fire and lives lost. "Sure," Jack said, a smile playing on his lips. "We are completely free, with nothing to do."

They walked the half block to Finnegans, the evening air crisp and cool on their faces. At 5 p.m., the bar was surprisingly empty except for the faint murmur of conversation and the clinking of glasses from the bartender. Seeking a secluded spot after getting each a draught beer, they settled into a corner table, the dim light casting long, mysterious shadows around them.

"I think we could both use a break from surgery anyway," said Larry. "This could be a time to catch up on other things. Don't you think?"

"What were you thinking about?" asked Jack

"Well," replied Larry, his voice strained, "I was thinking about getting out of surgery altogether. The hours are ridiculously long, the pressure is immense, and the weight of someone's life in your hands is a crushing burden." Larry took a long swallow of his beer.

"Wow, you of all surgeons, facing a burnout. Never would I have expected that."

"I feel I have to live a little more, and lately I'm overwhelmed with the need to feel alive. On a deserted beach, I long to feel the warmth of the sun, the wind in my hair, and the sand between my toes. You have been living the life of an adventurer on the high seas. Tell me what really happened on your trip."

Jack recounted the uneventful parts of their voyage, omitting the pirate attacks and the how he and Katherine poured the liquid virus from plastic bottles of Bill's invention into the drinking water of Toronto and New York. The salty tang of the sea air filled his memory, even as he glossed over those dangerous moments. Jack watched Larry's eyes widen. The hurricane's relentless waves and howling wind were palpable as he described battling the broken topping lift to save their boat. Larry remained quiet during the story, the suspense hanging heavy in the air. Jack sensed a touch of envy coming from his friend as he dramatically recounted the wave that crashed over him, tossing him into the main salon. He described the boat filling with water, the deluge mercifully ending when the companionway door slammed shut, and how the bilge pump then cleared out the remaining water, its rhythmic whirring a welcome sound.

"That's quite the story," said Larry. He went quiet for a moment, as if thinking about what he wanted to say. "Tell me about Bill. We operated on him together all those years ago. He wouldn't tell me what happened—why someone shot him in the stomach—although he said he would never visit Las Vegas again." Larry chuckled lightly. "I would never want to trade places with Bill, but he certainly knew how to live a good life." He quickly became sombre. "I heard he died, though. What happened?"

"He died while on active duty as a surgeon during a tour in Iraq."

"That's not what I heard," said Larry. "I'm good friends with Marcel Garner, the surgeon who worked with Jack on the disruptive magnetic surgery technique. He said Bills died from a propofol overdose."

Jack looked down at his beer, unsure how much to tell Larry. After a moment, he said, "That's what the medical report said. I was there at the funeral and spoke with the MPs who found him."

"That's not all," Larry said. "Marcel also believes he is alive. He doesn't think Bill would be careless enough for that to happen to him. What do you think?"

Jack shrugged his shoulders. "I said a few words at his funeral. I saw him lying in his coffin. There was even a Coke can stuffed into his pocket."

"According to Marcel, Bill had discovered the key to living a long life and was deeply involved in developing a groundbreaking solution designed to eliminate every human disease. Do you know anything about that, Jack? Could you perhaps share any insights or details you may have regarding that issue?"

Jack again shrugged his shoulders. "Bill, a master of the unexpected, spun tales of surprising adventures and cunning plans, but these were just talk, a captivating performance rather than reality. His desire to eradicate disease, a relentless pursuit fuelled by compassion, is entirely in line with his character."

Larry took a swig of beer. He took a deep breath and looked directly at Jack. "I know what really happened in Antigua," whispered Larry. "I know also that your life is currently in grave danger, and I want you to know that. I need to hear directly from you a complete and explicit account of what transpired and the extent of your participation in the entirety of these events. Your life depends on it."

Chapter 35

"We need to disappear," Jack said to Katherine, urgency in his voice palpable, a stark contrast to the quiet and calm of the apartment. A worried frown creased Katherine's brow, her eyes wide with apprehension. "Larry knows everything what we did," he said, his voice tight with fear. "That our lives were in imminent danger. He fears for our safety and wants to prevent any misfortune."

"What did you tell Larry?" asked Katherine. "We had agreed not to tell anyone."

"Larry was intimately familiar with the St. John's lab, its clandestine projects, and what it produced. He knew about the explosion and the destruction of the facility. He pressed for details about our defence against the pirates and the explosions, wanting to know how we'd survived their bloodthirsty assault on our small sailboat. I started by offering only the barest details, but it was clear he possessed a wealth of unspoken information. He knows Bill is still alive. He wants us to find him. I made it clear to him it was something that simply could not be done. Despite the vast number of video cameras—millions upon millions manufactured in China—not one has captured any visual evidence of him. He has vanished without a trace."

Jack's gaze moved slowly and methodically around the apartment, meticulously observing and absorbing every detail in the room. There were only a scant few items within the confines of the home that resonated with him on an emotional level, leaving him feeling rather unmoved by his surroundings. He felt little to no attachment to his sparse belongings. "Some of Larry's investments in the medical equipment sector are facing an imminent collapse, resulting in significant financial losses. Aware of the impending global recession, he made the strategic decision to liquidate a significant portion of his stock holdings. In a shrewd financial move, he purchased gold, adding to his portfolio of precious metals." Jack looked at Katherine firmly. "I took Larry's advice and called David when driving home. I gave David the same instructions."

"What? You gave *our* financial advisor instructions on selling *our* assets without consulting me?"

"I know, I know. I was in a panic. We currently possess approximately $500,000 in gold reserves. We can anticipate a substantial increase in value—a doubling or even tripling—as the complete ramifications of our actions become fully apparent to the market."

"Does Larry have a plan?! Or is he going to throw us to the wolves?" shouted Katherine. "How do we know we can trust him?"

"Larry wants to disappear as well," said Jack. "His wife left him a few years ago. His children are all grown up. According to him, this offers a welcome chance to branch out from his career, pursuing activities that differ from his usual routine of medicine and surgery. He has a detailed plan of action that he's eager to implement."

"I can't just walk away," Katherine said, her voice barely audible, a statement of her inability to comprehend the situation. "It has required years of dedication and hard work to cultivate and grow my psychotherapy practice to where it is today." Jack watched, heartbroken, as her eyes became glassy, then tears welled up, falling as she blinked.

"Both our lives are in danger. They will kill us if we stay," he murmured, wiping her tears away. "We need to leave tonight."

"Jack, this is crazy. I need some time to think about things. Let's sleep on it and come to a decision later. I can't think straight right now." Hot tears continued to stream down Katherine's face, her shoulders shaking with silent sobs.

"Honey," said Jack, "we have to get a move on. We need to get out of here tonight." Jack was pleading with Katherine now. The longer they delayed, the greater the risk. Larry had made that clear. Those that were tracking him were following their cell phone signal and monitoring their calls. All indications pointed to an attack during their sleep tonight.

"Okay. You win, Jack," she sobbed. "Let me grab a few things."

"There's no time," he yelled, his voice tight with urgency. "Let's go!" With a tug, Jack helped Katherine to her feet. With nothing but the clothes on their backs and their wallets and their passports, they left their cell phones behind on the counter as they departed. They hurried towards the door, and just as Jack was about to grab the brass handle, he heard several pairs of heavy footsteps thundering down the hallway, a sound that made his heart pound in his chest.

"We are too late," he whispered. "Let's go to the balcony."

As Jack contemplated their situation, a cold sweat slicked his palms as he peered over the edge and saw the dizzying drop to the twenty-third floor directly below. They would need to climb over the ornate, slightly decaying railing and swing across the considerable gap to reach the empty balcony in the apartment below them. Looking down, they saw it extended two feet beyond their own, a subtle but noticeable difference. Terrified, Jack helped Katherine onto the railing, the cold metal biting into his palms as he held her, and she safely dropped to the balcony below.

Jack could hear banging at the door as someone was trying to force it open. He glanced over the railing. Immediately, a wave of vertigo washed over him as he thought what would happen if he missed the balcony. Jack glanced at the door and noticed that one hinge had flown off from the force of someone pounding on it. Only a minute or two before they were in the apartment and his life was over. *At least Katherine was safe.* Jack took a deep swallow. He crawled over the railing and lowered himself slowly, holding the bars until he ran out of the railing. Closing his eyes, with his head spinning from dizziness, thinking of the possibilities of what could happen if he had miscalculated, he let go. Landing on the balcony, he lay for a second before Katherine helped him up.

They opened the sliding door, the sound of it whooshing against the frame barely audible above the city noise, and slipped into the empty apartment. With a sickening certainty, Jack knew whoever was after them had the fire exits and elevators locked down tight, making escape impossible. But Jack and Katherine had planned for that. The apartment featured a compact service dumbwaiter that went into the basement. They'd rehearsed using the oddly shaped vessel many times, folding themselves into tight positions to fit.

With a low whirring of its electric motor, the dumbwaiter inched downwards at three feet per second, the journey to the basement taking over 90 seconds. With a jolt, the dumbwaiter came to a stop. The door swung outward, revealing a dark and cluttered corner of the garage, the air thick with the smell of oil and dust. Jack and Katherine hopped out, the sudden stillness almost unsettling compared to the previous clanking. They glanced around, seeing no one. Next to the door, a silver Ford-150 pickup truck sat waiting. Katherine hopped into the driver's seat, then quickly slipped on a baseball cap, a hoodie and glasses, her features swallowed by the disguise. Jack crawled into the back of the truck, pulling a heavy canvas drop cloth over his body, and wedged himself between two bulky five-gallon cans of paint. A baseball bat lay at his feet. The truck's engine roared to life as Katherine started it and drove up the incline to the garage door, which opened automatically as she approached.

Jack could see them through a slit in the drop cloth as he looked through the window from the back of the cab. At the top of the incline stood two men. One waved his arms, pantomiming that he wanted her to stop. Jack grabbed the baseball bat. He watched as the second man walked to the driver's side. The man glanced at a picture displayed on the phone he held in his hand. Through the heavily tinted glass, he gestured to Katherine to roll down the window. Katherine shook her head. Once again, he looked at his phone. This time he waved her through, perhaps realizing she was not the one he was looking for. Katherine stepped on the accelerator and sped away.

As planned, she pulled into an all-night McDonald's parking lot and backed into a spot in the corner. Jack hopped out and got in the passenger seat. "That was a close one," he said.

Katherine pulled off her hat and glasses. "What now?"

"Leaving the country is our only option," Jack declared firmly. "According to Larry, the multi-corporation conglomerate believes we are planning to dump more samples into the water supply. That's why they have hired men to stop us. Unfortunately, they remain ignorant that it is now too late. At this very moment, the virus is actively spreading through the global food supply, posing a serious threat to the economies of the entire world, but curing all medical conditions. For the next six months, we must remain concealed, avoiding any contact or detection, until the full extent of the damage is completely apparent. Only then it would be clear to everyone that further pursuit would be pointless."

"We knew we would get ourselves into a heap of trouble," sighed Katherine. "I would have hoped we would do the world a favour, but it seems to have had the opposite effect."

With a soft, almost imperceptible "Ahhh," Jack released a sigh that carried the weight of his emotions. "You know that isn't the case. As medical professionals, the core purpose of our existence, the very reason we dedicate our lives to this profession, is the alleviation of pain and suffering for those in need of our help. Let's take a moment to reflect on all the lives that we have saved. It is quite remarkable. While there will undoubtedly be some short-term economic downsides, the long-term benefits are immense. Consider the influx of highly intelligent and trustworthy medical professionals entering the workforce in other fields. They bring with them exceptional problem-solving skills and the ability to build rapport with people. They foster trust and compassion. The world will be a better place, filled with more empathy and understanding."

"We've got our passports," said Katherine. "Where are we headed?"

"I suspect they're using every trick Brian used to find Bill to monitor us," Jack said, his voice tight with suspicion. "Video cameras are being used for facial and body recognition technology. Our credit cards, bank transactions, cell phone locations, and flight details are all potentially accessible for monitoring, giving them an incredibly detailed view of our lives. With the AIS turned off for safety and secrecy, our sailboat provides the only safe passage. This is our best chance of escape— a narrow window of opportunity amidst the chaos."

Katherine placed her head in her hands, her fingers tangled in her hair as she thought about this. "Let's go," she mumbled, her voice barely a whisper.

Now behind the wheel of the truck, Jack drove to the yacht club. It was a blustery autumn night, and the winds whipped in powerfully from the lake, creating a chilly and somewhat turbulent atmosphere. As he pulled into the club's parking lot, he had a feeling that it would only be a matter of time before the vehicle was towed away.

Accused of drug-related crimes, the tenant who had lived below them had hastily escaped. He abandoned the truck Jack was now driving. When the police arrived to execute an arrest warrant, just like Katherine and Jack, he'd used the dumbwaiter to escape from his precarious situation. Knowing Jack was a surgeon, he'd found his contact details on the hospital website and sent Jack an email message. The contents were mysterious. He asked if Jack might take care of his truck while he was away. If Jack and Katherine successfully escaped from their pursuers, he knew a return to Toronto for them within six months would be highly unlikely.

With a gentle tugging motion, the sailboat, firmly attached to the dock by its mooring lines, strained as the wind and waves pushed and pulled it. Small waves churned up by the strong wind rocked the boat, their rhythmic slap against the hull a constant sound. Jack fiddled with the padlock with cold fingers until he heard a stiff metallic click as it released. He and Katherine hurried through the companionway door. They donned their oilskins and sou'westers, bracing themselves for the brutal Lake Ontario crossing. A bitter wind whipped across the water's surface. Jack turned the key, and the sailboat's engine coughed and sputtered to life. Katherine untied the mooring lines. Within 10 minutes of arriving, they were off.

It was after midnight when they began their journey east down the length of the lake.

Chapter 36

Safe on the sailboat, Jack breathed in deeply, taking the fresh Lake Ontario air into his lungs, the gentle lapping of waves against the hull a soothing balm after the violent rocking and salty spray of the hurricane. The wind was 30 knots with gusts to 35, but they were running with the wind, using their headsail only. They sailed at 10 knots. Despite the torrential rain and fierce winds lashing against the canvas awnings, the ride was surprisingly smooth. Although the plan was still in development, Jack aimed for the Azores. With no way anyone could identify him, it would burn up a month of time to reach the Portuguese islands. The escape plan, conceived as a contingency during the return voyage from Antigua months ago, occupied Jack's thoughts.

Their trip would take them through the St. Lawrence Seaway locks, catching glimpses of the old-world charm of Montreal, and Quebec City—plus a quick stop in Rivière-du-Loup to stock up on food supplies at the quaint local market—then on to the Gulf of St. Lawrence, and finally, out to the vast expanse of the North Atlantic. The typical ocean currents, a powerful eastward flow, would carry them past Greenland and Iceland, finally reaching the port of Horta in the Azores, about 2,000 nautical miles away and a trip of 30 days from leaving Toronto. More than a thousand sailboats, each with its own story, visited the marina annually, making it easy for them to blend in.

With €10,000 and $10,000 securely stashed in the boat's safe, Jack felt confident they could survive at least six months at sea, provided he and Katherine were frugal. He meticulously avoided digital traces, relying solely on Starlink with a VPN connected in Tokyo. Jack only needed to know what was in store for the weather and he could plot false routes as a further layer to conceal his use of the internet. It felt great to be on the water again.

The sun peeked over the eastern horizon, painting the sky with vibrant oranges and purple. The biting wind slice through the waves, the remnants of the Atlantic hurricanes bringing a taste of winter in October. Katherine slept in the dark and spacious forward cabin, the rhythmic creak of the ship her only companion. Sleep had evaded Jack, leaving him at the helm, the wind rattling through the rigging, his only companion. The past 24 hours were a nonstop rush. Adrenaline still coursed through his veins. His mind was a whirlwind of chaotic thoughts and racing emotions. Too many things had happened, leaving him in a state of stunned confusion.

With the chilly winds of late October, few boats dared venture onto the lake, save for Jack. He avoided a few close calls with the enormous cargo ships that seemed to loom large against the darkening sky. A steady beep from the radar, which was constantly active, alerted him to their approaching presence. When Katherine awoke, she came to the cockpit with a steaming cup of coffee.

"I can take over for a while," she said. "We can get back to our usual routine. It actually feels comforting to be on the boat where no one can find us."

A wide grin spread across Jack's face as he savoured the incredible fortune of having such a supportive and understanding partner. Katherine, with a quiet strength, seemed to effortlessly navigate the turbulent waters of the past six months. He felt a deep sense of comfort knowing he could always depend on her, no matter the situation. Her unwavering support was a constant. He crawled into his bed in the forward cabin and quickly fell asleep.

*****

"We should arrive in Horta within the next 24 hours," Jack said, a hint of excitement in his voice as he gazed at the approaching coastline. It was late November, and the seas were calm. Aside from a brief stop in Rivière-du-Loup, they'd been at sea for 34 days. At one point, the remnants of Hurricane Roxy forced them to veer 200 miles north of their intended route, battling strong winds and torrential rain. For the last 100 miles, though, a stillness had fallen over the sea, and the ship motored on in quiet solitude without wind to fill the sails.

Katherine turned on the internet to catch up with any news. She tuned into CNN. "The stock markets have plunged to more than half, a situation never seen before since the Great

Depression. The cause of this is now clear. America's economy depended on human sickness to continue."

The video image flipped over to the closed emergency rooms and hospitals. A reporter stood in the front of the hospital. "This scene has been played throughout the country. Private hospitals and institutions have filed for bankruptcy. Massive amounts of money have left the stock market in a panic, leaving all trading suspended. Traders have transferred much of their wealth to gold, which has reached an all-time high of $6,000 per ounce."

The video cut to a man wearing a white coat. Underneath his image was the name Dr. Jacob Mercer, Infectious Disease Specialist. "We now know what has happened," said Dr. Mercer. "A reverse transcriptase retrovirus was released into the drinking water of New York and Toronto. This virus has now infected most of the population in North America, and is spreading to Europe. It is not a natural virus and the current theory is that someone created it in a lab."

The next image was the FBI office, the J. Edgar Hoover Building in Washington, DC. A sombre appearing man in a blue suit with the name Christopher Wrigley, Director of the FBI underneath, spoke. "This was a criminal act, the dumping of an unregulated substance into the drinking water of New York, infecting the entire nation. This illegal act is responsible for the economic collapse you witnessed in the stock market over the past few weeks. We have issued warrants for the arrest of this man."

Bill's picture appeared with his name and position: thoracic surgeon, Little Rock, Arkansas.

The footage showed him operating in Little Rock. "...at first, they thought he had passed away peacefully in his sleep while serving in Iraq, but a thorough investigation revealed that he may still be alive."

The reporter shared details about Bill's research in Canada before talking about his move to the US to work as a thoracic surgeon. He described how he fulfilled his duties as a civilian surgeon in Iraq until his unexpected death in his sleep six months ago. The reporter displayed a video showing the charred remains of the facility in St. John's. "Here is the facility where we believe they produced the virus. An explosion destroyed the plant, but not before the virus was released into the ecosystem."

The reporter continued. "It is our belief that other misguided doctors may have had some involvement. Anyone with information is to contact this number." A toll-free number appeared on the screen, along with two faces. "These are two people wanted by authorities for questioning. They may be witnesses..."

Jack's mind went numb as he and Katherine stared at the computer screen. Everyone around the planet had received this news. Their faces pasted over every news report. "Oh my God, Jack. What should we do now?" Katherine barely choked out the words.

"The engine is running on fumes, so we need to refill out diesel tanks," said Jack, as calmly as he could muster. "I think we should stop in Horta and stock up on supplies. We need some fresh vegetables and fruits. We can get a sense if anyone recognizes us."

"Is that a good idea?" asked Katherine. "In a week, we could be in the Mediterranean. We could hide out in Corsica. The hundreds of secret coves and bays could shelter us for a long while until everything settles."

Jack glanced over at the horizon, where the silhouette of distant mountains stood against the fading light. "We'll never make it without stopping for food and fuel. I think we have to go to Horta. It'll be okay. You'll see."

*****

The next morning at dawn, Jack and Katherine sailed into Horta Marina. Jack smiled as they passed its signature walls covered in murals. There were no empty spaces. Yachtsmen had completely covered the concrete walls with paintings so that luck would smile on them on their sea voyage. Tradition had made the busy port an open-air gallery. Jack motored to his assigned dock. Some sailors and marina staff appeared and helped with the docking.

Someone placed a wooden board on the sailboat's stern, which Jack and Katherine then used to exit the cockpit with their heads down, trying to remain inconspicuous. They turned to walk down the dock on the way to the supermarket to get supplies when Jack heard a familiar voice.

"Hi, Jack. You and Katherine need to come with us."

It was Jack's partner, Larry Klapman.

John Hagen

Epilogue

A smile stretched Bill's lips as his gaze fell upon the extensive economic damage Jack had so carelessly wrought. Even though the odds were against them, he knew he could count on Jack to succeed, whatever happened. It was a definitive goodbye this time for Bill, a departure that ensured he would never again return.

Accessing the high-resolution feeds from the satellites orbiting the Earth, he reviewed the video when Jack and Katherine returned to the yacht club in Port Credit over two months ago to dock their boat at the harbour community near Toronto. They were on the foredeck of the sailboat, clasping each other tightly. They enveloped themselves in a mutual embrace, a silent acknowledgment that their difficult struggle had finally come to an end. He remembered feeling that with any luck, they could return to their normal lives and, hopefully, live happily ever after, free from the troubles that had plagued them. The thought passing through Bill's mind that he would never see them again was not something he felt he could live with.

The complex computer program on the spacecraft had Bill heading for Gliese 12b, the closest habitable planet 40 light years away. Although he would have been an old man had he stayed alert for the next 40 years on the spaceship, once he was far enough away from planet Earth, he would enter himself into a state of suspended animation. The system he had designed with

Elon Musk's backing was similar to what bears do when they hibernate. He would age, but at about 0.1 per cent of the normal rate while in animation. His heart rate would be one beat per minute. His body temperature would cool down. To maintain only vital structures like his brain, it would slow his metabolism.

In his possession, Bill had 100 frozen human embryos, which he intended to bring to life using advanced technology once he successfully arrived at Gliese 12b. He aimed to create a superior human race, genetically engineered to overcome the diseases that had long afflicted humanity on Earth, initiating a new era for humankind. The exceptional cognitive powers resulting from his mRNA-driven production of elevated BDNF protein levels needed ongoing maintenance on his part. Bill realized that surviving on the new planet in four decades from now would require the full extent of his expanded mental capabilities to navigate the inevitable challenges and difficulties that were certain to arise.

Bill's mind wandered back to his last visit to the Mustang Ranch two days prior, where he had spent a full 24 hours with Jessica. When he tested her production of the BDNF protein after their marathon session had finished, it was completely off the scale... but his own level was even higher by a factor of 10. A slow smile spread across his lips as he remembered the exquisite details of the encounter, each moment vividly clear in his mind—the feel of her hand in his, the sound of her laughter, the scent of her perfume.

Bill, now weightless, floated into the sterile, humming animation chamber, the low thrum of the machinery a constant background to the 40 years he would spend suspended there while the spacecraft hurtled through space at light speed. With no earthbound gravity to hold him, he hauled himself along the handrails effortlessly. He lay on the plush bed, its silken sheets cool against his skin, and stared up at the ornate, gold-leaf ceiling of the grand chamber. He rolled over and glanced at the computer pad beside the bed.

Bill logged into the animation system, the low buzz of the servers in the background, and programmed his suspended animation to begin in 60 seconds. A rapid series of sharp, electronic beeps punctuated the silence, beginning the timer's countdown. Bill needed the timing to be perfect; his future 40 years from now hinged on this precise moment, a weight settling heavily on his shoulders. The ticking hands were a stark reminder of the dwindling time. Fifty seconds flashed on the screen in a blur of motion and sound. He knew he had better get moving; the urgency pressing down on him like a physical weight.

Bill quickly glanced over at the other bay of suspended animation, noting the rhythmic hiss of the life support systems and the faint glow of the containment fields. Larry Klapman lay in suspended animation, the hum of the spaceship a low vibration against his body, probably dreaming of governing the new planet that had been promised when they arrive. To escape the nauseating effects of G-force, a common ailment for astronauts, Larry secured himself in the animation chamber's cool, padded embrace before liftoff.

He glanced over at the next chamber. Katherine and Jack embraced, their bodies trembling slightly, and remained locked in each other's arms until they reached their destination 40 light-years away. Bill noted how peaceful they looked, their breaths soft and even and slow. Both had shut their eyes, their faces covered with serene smiles, a sense of contentment radiating from them. The happiness emanating from the couple was unlike the artificial highs Bill was accustomed to. It was real, palpable, and deeply affecting. They had achieved this on their own with each other. Bill sighed, a deep breath that spoke of years of frustration, wishing he could one day achieve what they had been able to do naturally.

Bill secured himself tightly to the bed, the soft cushions lining the bed frame pressing against his skin, and then pulled out his tourniquet, tightly wrapping the rubber elastic around the smooth skin of his left arm. Plunging the 50cc syringe filled with propofol into his left antecubital vein, Bill felt a burning sensation spreading through his arm. Before loosening the tourniquet, he relived the most passionate moments with Jessica, the memory vivid and intense, a flood of sensations that he knew would continue to resonate within him, fuelling his cognitive functions for the next four decades and bathing his brain with excessive levels of BDNF protein production to expand his already impressive cognitive function.

His right hand, steady despite the tremor in his arm, worked to undo the tourniquet. The last thing Bill's mind registered was an image of Jessica, a mischievous gleam in her eye, sitting astride him. As the propofol took effect, the release of dopamine, serotonin, and other pleasure hormones from the hypothalamus flooded his body with a wave of intense euphoria, leaving him with a heightened sense of ecstasy that he knew would last for the next 40 years.

And then blackness.

About The Author

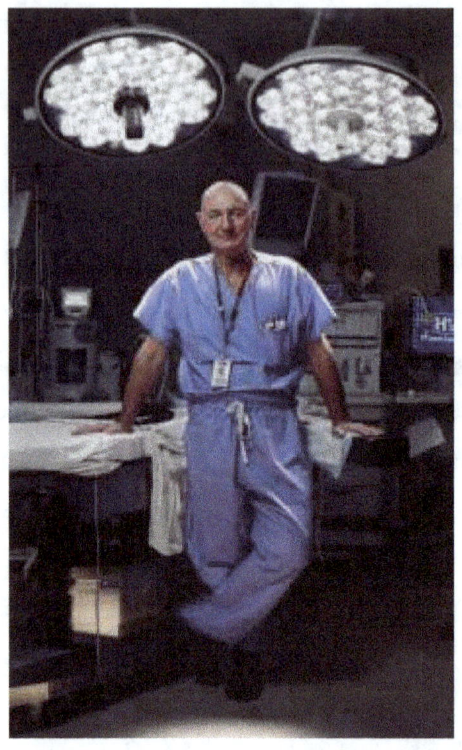

Dr. John Hagen completed his doctor of medicine (honours) degree from the University of Alberta in 1979, later attaining general surgery specialty training at the University of Toronto. He's spent much of his practice in Toronto-area hospitals in roles such as attending surgeon, division head of general surgery, surgical director of bariatrics, and chief of surgery, chief of staff, among others. Now retired from practice, Hagen has taken on several instructor responsibilities: in roles as supervising surgeon and instructor at the University of Toronto Surgery

Training Program. He has won several teaching awards for his work. Since 2005, Hagen has lectured widely and delivered myriad courses and live demonstrations, particularly in laparoscopic and bariatric surgery, in Canada, the US, UK, Europe, Mexico, Nepal, Colombia and China.

The Junkie is Hagen's eighth novel, following seven other medical thrillers, *The Downfall, 2025, The Heir*, 2024, *The Clinic*, 2024, *The Embryo* (2023), *The Mission* (2024), *The Complication* (2024) and *The Sailor* (2023). Along with being a dedicated lecturer and volunteer at medical missions in Guatemala with his wife, Ileana, the couple are avid travellers and sailors. They live in King City, Ontario, and spend time taking excursions on their 51-foot sailboat, *Ileana,* having sailed to the Caribbean and the Bahamas for the winter months. Read about his sailing adventures on www.dreamingofileana.com

www.ingramcontent.com/pod-product-compliance
Lightning Source LLC
Chambersburg PA
CBHW071239300726

48975CB00002B/487